A FATAL GILDED
High Note

CECELIA TICHI

A Fatal Gilded High Note

Copyright © 2021 by Cecelia Tichi

All rights reserved. No part of this book may be reproduced or transmitted in any form or by any means without written permission of the author.

ISBN 979-8-9851216-2-9

In the Val and Roddy DeVere "Gilded" Series

A Gilded Death
Murder, Murder, Murder in Gilded Central Park

Chapter One

MY HUSBAND FOLLOWED OPERA the way some men tracked racehorses. The celestial voices, he said, gave reason to endure New York winters. When the curtain rose at the Metropolitan Opera, our private box—Box 17—found us seated while the orchestra tuned and we waited for the asbestos curtain to rise. Mozart's *Don Giovanni* would open tonight, January 2, 1899, starring two famed sopranos and a "matinee idol" baritone.

The singing was a bonus because the Metropolitan Opera House stole the show, from the sweeping stairway to the "Diamond Horseshoe" of private boxes with full views of the stage (and twinkling jeweled bosoms in surrounding boxes). An American *palazzo*, I dubbed the hall, as if King Midas ran riot to gild the plaster and coat every beam and board in gold. At times, the voices lost out to the glitter.

Operatic murder and mayhem had been a private joke between my husband and me in the three-plus years of marriage. My husband, Roddy (Roderick Windham DeVere), pointed out that bloodshed had long been a big part of grand opera. Knives and swords drew blood in *Macbeth* and *Faust*, he said, and audiences always gasped when the blade of a jealous lover (a tenor) fatally stabbed the Gypsy cigarette factory girl, Carmen.

"Roddy, my love, does *Don Giovanni* include murder?" I asked this evening in the closed carriage as we rode down Fifth Avenue and Broadway to the opera house entrance on 40th Street. Our coachman, Noland, drove the high-stepping midnight-black Hackneys, Apollo and Atlas, that pulled our brougham over city streets freshened by a light snowfall. The gas streetlamps glowed, and the soft thud of the horses' feet gave the feeling of a snow globe. Ready to spend a few minutes with the program before the curtain rose, I had not yet read the plot of the Mozart opera.

"Any murders tonight?" I had asked Roddy in the carriage, more a quip than a question.

He held up a gloved forefinger and winked.

"Just one? One measly murder?"

We shared a little laugh and held kid-gloved hands across the tufted seats.

In my western hometown, Virginia City, Nevada, where Roddy and I had met, the operatic drama took place in the streets, not in the opera house. Virginia City was often mistaken for Silver City because Big Bonanza silver mines enriched a very few beyond most mortals' wildest dreams. The promise of silver, however, lured the violently desperate along with the well-intentioned, such as my late papa, Patrick Mackle, who had emigrated from County Donegal, Ireland, to seek his fortune in the West. When Papa struck his Big Lode and became a "Silver King," he moved the two of us to Virginia City and built a Queen Anne Revival house on "B" Street and enrolled me in the Fourth Ward School. He also hired a prudish widow to teach me ladylike manners for the boomtown that boasted new-found sophistication. In this, Papa had meant well.

Tempers flared, nonetheless, into knifings and shoot-outs in public. Undertakers rivaled doctors for business. Papa spared me the specifics, but *The Territorial Enterprise* daily newspaper reported every gory detail. We had no need for onstage grand opera in Virginia City. Our blood was shed in the streets.

In this first month of the New Year, my past and present were to meet in the versatile word, "opera." As the bride of a fifth-generation New Yorker, I had entered Society with entrée to exclusive balls, parties, and whatnot. To this day, however, I got frosty "welcomes" from Gilded Age New Yorkers offended that I tarnished their posh doings. My name and birthdate prompted snickers behind their china teacups—Valentine Louise Mackle, born on the fourteenth of February, St. Valentine's Day in the wastelands of the West.

Roddy urged patience when I wondered aloud why Virginia City should be laughable or "Valentine" sillier than "Isabel" or "Gertrude" or "Hermione."

No matter, I would forever embrace girlhood in the West, including Piper's Opera House in Virginia City, where I thrilled to melodramas by touring companies from the East, and to banjo recitals, variety shows, Irish orators, Shakespeare, songs by a San Francisco contralto, and a demonstration of wrestling with half-nelsons, headlocks, and hip-heists. Come rain or shine or snow, come sleet or hail or ankle-deep muddy streets, my late papa and I took front row seats at Piper's.

It all seemed innocent, two opera houses—Nevada and New York—both safe spaces for entertainment. So it was, until tonight, the first Met performance of 1899, when murder burst its bounds to reach the Diamond Horseshoe in the box beside our own—inside the ill-fated Box 18—and brought a black cloud of suspicion down on me.

The fact was: if my Roddy had not touched the wet stain darkening the carpet of our box during the second act of *Don Giovanni*, we would never have known anything was amiss. Over the next months, our lives would have taken a very different turn.

Thinking back, I wish I had insisted on a quiet evening by the fire—like a western campfire—with Roddy and our French bulldog, Velvet. The opera had loomed like a chore after the New Year's Day ritual that tested New York ladies' stamina to the hilt. In Colorado and Nevada, it was said "there was nothing Western Folk admired so much as pluck in a woman."

Western "pluck" often meant taming a fractious horse, shot gunning coyotes, or roping an ornery calf. In New York, my New Year's Day "pluck" meant sitting in a chair from morning to night, as if hogtied in a drawing room of our French Gothic chateau at 620 Fifth Avenue, where I received rounds of gentlemen callers who bid me a Happy New Year.

Origins of the custom were lost, but Wall Street shut down on the first day in January, and idled businessmen were pressed into annual New Year's Day social duty, as were all adult men in Society, including my law school-trained husband.

In small groups, the gentlemen sojourned from house to house—rather, from mansion to mansion on Fifth and Madison Avenues and to residences in the upper East 60s, 70s, and 80s. They handed calling cards to the butlers, gave servants their coats and top hats, and entered each household drawing room, in turn, to wish the compliments of the season to the lady of the house. Then they streaked to the refreshment table, where liveried footmen ladled "spiked" eggnog from silver punchbowls that reminded me, in size, of horse troughs in the West. (The later in the day, the higher the spirits.)

We ladies, feeling roped to our chairs, sipped pale fruit punch from crystal cups and smiled till our jaws ached. Those with marriageable daughters seized opportunities when wealthy young bachelors called. The rest of us endured the hours. My close friend, Cassie Forster, confided that on New Year's Day, she felt like a figure in Madame Tussaud's Wax Museum. She also advised me to cope with the annual New Year's sit-down-and-smile without fuss.

"You mean, pick my fights?" I had said to her. "My papa always said, '"pick your fights."'"

My friend said, "Trust your late father's wisdom."

I often did just that, also trusting this one close woman friend, Cassie, a full-fledged member of New York Society. Cassandra Van Schylar Fox Forster did not need to explain herself to anyone, anywhere. "Blue-blooded Cassie," I once teased her, asking if her "sixth sense" came with the social pedigree.

She had cringed, and I perspired, afraid this new friendship would come to a flat-out dead end. I would never again joke about Cassie's "peculiarity," which my husband explained as her lifelong superstition. Friends in Roddy's social circle remembered Cassandra's "dreaminess" from childhood. At times, she "saw" future events that actually did happen, including accidents. She explained that her beloved nanny, Saffira, had cuddled her in early childhood with chants and fragrant oils and had whispered that she, Saffira, would open secret worlds to Cassie. My friend loved Saffira, whose devotion meant everything to the child whose mother was icy-cold and always angry. In time, rumors spread that Saffira's influence had warped little Cassie, and the nanny was let go and never heard from again. The children told nasty tales about their playmate's "weird" predictions, Roddy said, and Cassandra quieted down, only voicing "predictions" on rarest occasions.

If only I had listened on this rare occasion. Cassie "foresaw" something ugly in the first few January days and advised Roddy and me to stay close to home.

Too vague a warning, my husband said, and I let it pass. My maid, Calista, selected a gown for the "Diamond Horseshoe" of private *parterre* boxes. For tonight's *Don Giovanni*, it would be *ciel*-blue satin bordered with black fur, designed for me by the House of Worth, one of several gowns in my wardrobe. (I joked with Roddy that Worth prepared me for social rodeos.)

Fortunately, clever Calista knew secrets that let me dress without feeling strait-jacketed. She had fashioned a "ladies combination garment" that allowed deep breathing.

"And your jewelry, ma'am?" Calista asked. "Perhaps something from the rosewood casket?"

My maid's tact spared me reminders of the 'DeVere jewels,' meaning gems from my mother-in-law, who bestowed ancestral baubles on Christmas and birthdays, though the only "jewel" I wanted was Roddy. I smiled when Calista dangled the star-cluster diamond necklace that Roddy called my Pleiades, the one necklace that I cherished. The name reminded me of our first get-together, when he and I viewed the night sky together. The Pleiades, Roddy had pointed out, were seven stars in the constellation, Taurus, and called the "Seven Sisters."

At that time, peering skyward, I knew only about weather fronts that hampered papa's work. Silver mining left us too tired for star gazing, I confessed, then heard Roddy DeVere say his interest in stars came from a tedious year in Arizona where his parents took him to "dry out" from addiction to alcohol. They had found a book, *How to Mix Drinks, or, The Bon-Vivant's Companion* among his things and jumped to the conclusion that their son-and-heir was enslaved to cocktails. He had laughed at their mistake and tried to explain his interest in new drinks to sip and savor, but his horrified parents whisked him off to the desert on doctor's orders. So, he took up astronomy but never lost interest in the new beverages that were sweeping the country, including our Virginia City, where Roddy and I met. The strapping, broad-shouldered Roddy DeVere first courted me by demonstrating a theatrical, flaming cocktail that shocked his parents, amused my papa, and dazzled me when the DeVeres and the Mackles met, of all places, in the Silver Queen Hotel & Saloon in Virginia City, Nevada.

Cassie declared our match was a destined Decree of the Universe, but the earthly fact was Rufus DeVere's desperate effort to recoup his family's cascading fortune. I would not have been dressing for the Metropolitan Opera tonight—much less a resident of New York and soon to be drawn into a strange homicide case with my husband—had Roddy's father, Rufus, not been a catastrophic investor who fled to Virginia City like a lamb sacrificed to the Wall Street slaughter.

The Arizona winter in a village hacienda had left Rufus at loose ends, and he convinced himself that a notorious

Wall Street wolf, Jay Gould, had launched a railroad stock scheme. Rufus wired his broker, invested heavily (against the broker's advice), and spent tense days in a village telegraph office before learning that a Wall Street crash that nearly devoured the DeVere fortune.

Undaunted, Rufus grew certain that a Nevada silver mine would replenish every vanquished dollar. With his wife and son, he hastened to Virginia City on the Virginia and Truckee Railroad ("Queen of the Short Lines"), expecting that vaults of silver bars awaited his arrival. Against my papa's best advice, Rufus bet hard on a played-out mine that failed.

Roddy and I, however, had "bet" on one another, and when Papa died, the Mackle millions came to me.

Eleanor and Rufus DeVere have kept mum on the hard fact that their fortune was saved by the improbable romance of their beloved only son and the daughter of an immigrant "Silver King." Bless him, papa lived long enough to see us wed, but the senior DeVeres hadn't a clue about my papa's hard work sleuthing silver ore in the rocky terrain of the West. My in-laws thought him an Irish peasant who got rich by dumb luck. They also suspected that my late mother, Kathleen Louise Mackle, had been a Gaelic floozy operating in mining camps.

In fact, my mother, Kathleen Louise O'Hara Mackle, fled her native country during the potato famine and survived steerage passage in a hellish "coffin ship." So did my papa. Both had escaped starvation before they met in Brooklyn, where papa was a shipyard worker and mama a housemaid. They married and went West to seek a better life. My mama survived the Irish potato blight and steerage in the coffin ship, but she did not outlast the couple's hard years in Colorado mining camps. She was gone before I knew her but lived in Papa's loving descriptions and in my middle name, Louise. Born on February fourteenth, I was named Valentine Louise Mackle.

Roddy's parents had their pride, but Mackle money saved them from "genteel" poverty. At risk: their Fifth Avenue chateau (built in 1887) and the twenty-two room Newport "cottage" named Drumcliffe. Also, the private railroad car, the paintings, the stables, blooded horses, club memberships, servants, and on and on, including the family jewels and the opera box. Every Metropolitan private box, a snooty critic had written, "perfumes the air with the odor of crisp greenbacks." For a fact, the late Patrick Mackle's years of hard toil now scented the air of Box 17. I never took that fact for granted. Neither did my husband.

Roddy and I arrived for *Don Giovanni* a good twenty minutes before curtain time. Thinking back over this evening, as we would do in countless "brainstorms" over the next weeks, nothing seemed out of the ordinary. Our arrival was routine.

In the corridor, a swarthy young man in livery had stood ready to unlock the door with our name engraved on a brass plate—*DeVere*—the box owner. The adjacent box—Box 18—with its nameplate, *Wendell*, reminded me of the DeVeres' family friends who were abroad this winter.

Roddy had promised to keep an eye on their box, which was rented to a "Coal King" for the season. As we were to recall, the *Wendell* box had not yet been unlocked, which was not unusual, but the tarnished nameplate prompted Roddy to have a word with the attendant, which he did.

With the door unlocked and opened, the swarthy young man stood aside for me (lady first) to enter our saloon, a sort of private coat room for wraps and overshoes. Separated from the box by a closed curtain, our saloon featured a cushioned bench and dun colored walls that my mother-in-law called "muted gold." ("Saloon décor, Valentine, will be your challenge one day," she had intoned in a hint of competitive saloon décor.)

A maid appeared promptly to help me out of the hooded black satin opera cloak and fur overshoes. Then Roddy entered from the corridor, as usual, and he doffed his hat, coat, and slipped his rubber "overs" from his opera slippers. He stood before me, nearly six feet in height and resplendent in his tailcoat, white waistcoat, white tie and white gloves. The maid had stepped out. The attendant closed the door.

My husband took my hand and gazed into my eyes. "Beautiful, my dearest Val…"

To look into his deep blue eyes…time stopped. "My love…"

Orchestral tuning thrust us into the moment, and Roddy pulled back the curtain to usher us into our box, where six Victorian chairs, three and three, rested on light beige carpeting. We sat side by side, alone in the box—and alone in the Diamond Horseshoe, which was not surprising. Left or right, not one soul in sight of us.

Fashion dictated that Society must arrive in the boxes once a performance was well underway—about an hour "late" because it was "not the thing" to arrive on time. It was understood that one's box served fashion, not the music. Ralph Pulitzer, the newspaperman's grown son, had written that "the box parties go because the opera is fashionable, and the opera is fashionable because the box parties go." Recently, Mr. Edison had installed five thousand electrical lights in the opera house, every watt showing off the ladies' pendants, chokers, rings, tiaras, stomachers, aigrettes, and ropes of perfectly matched lustrous pearls.

Strictly speaking, the gemstone display posed no problem for us, nor did others' tardiness. Roddy's devotion to the music had made us an "odd couple" who defied fashion by arriving on time. For that reason, few social friends accepted invitations to join us.

Soon enough, we regretted that a close friend had not come along tonight, since another witness to "the most unfortunate event" might have helped us sort through the sordid, fatal tangle and cleared me of suspicion. At the moment, we simply awaited the evening's performance. For me, this meant stunning scenery, fabulous costumes, and the heart-wrenching arias. For Roddy, it meant voices trained to sing for the Angels in Heaven.

Promptly at eight p.m., the curtain rose, and a thunderous opening turned into a lighthearted violin tune. In the days ahead, I would study the plot summary of *Don Giovanni*, but the opening scene needed no explanation. A servant in a pretty garden grumbled in a bass voice about his master when, suddenly, a masked man came running into the garden, chased by a furious young woman, a famous soprano (and Roddy's favorite), who sang while ripping at his mask. The audience on the ground floor stirred because the man was Don Giovanni, the current baritone "heart throb." (Roddy had told me the character was patterned after the womanizer, Don Juan, and I guessed that he had tried to assault the furious young woman.)

A deadly duel erupted when the young woman's father arrived, confronted the fleeing Don Giovanni in the garden, blocked his escape, and drew his sword. As I suspected, the opera's one-and-only murder was about to take place. Yes, the villainous Don Giovanni plunged his own sword into the older man's breast and fled. The audience, including Roddy and myself, held our breath as we watched the paternal *Commendatore*'s death throes. His sword had dropped, and he staggered, bleeding, clutching at his heart as he fell to his knees and collapsed in a widening pool of blood.

To think, I had joked about operatic murder this evening in our carriage. The mirth I had felt vanished at this scene of death, the vigorous man felled, and the blood...so much blood.

The next onstage events could be foretold—the daughter's horror at discovering her slain father, the vow of revenge, the episodes proving Don Giovanni to be a flagrant libertine, then seduction, confusion, disguises, and betrayal. The bloody image of the murdered man lingered in mind as the scenes unfolded, but predictably, new distractions came midway in the third scene, when noise erupted on either side of us in the adjacent boxes.

Society did not quietly ease into its boxes. It *arrived*. The saloon curtains rattled, and Society swept into each box with rustling, bustling, and audible murmurs. Seat selection stirred whispers that sounded worthy of the theatrical stage until, at last, opera glasses were raised, and the Diamond Horseshoe inspected its glittering self.

The noise drove Roddy mad, especially this season because the Wendells' rented box sounded more like a dance hall, with giggles and guffaws that could not be ignored. Charles Wendell had boasted that he scored a coup leasing the box for a princely sum. The DeVere family friendship with the Wendells had cemented Roddy's promise to keep an eye on the box.

"Otherwise, Val, I would gladly give it up and sit downstairs with the music lovers, where we belong. I know you don't love the opera as I do," he had said, "but we both deserve an evening free of distraction. Every performance this season, the same commotion from the Wendells' box."

It was true, the hubbub had started in early December when Charles and Anne Wendell set sail for warmer waters and the "Coal King" took over their box. Somehow, the party sounded especially raucous this evening, with loud male voices, a female, and clinking of glassware? Drinking in an opera box? No one dared drink at Piper's Opera House. As for tippling at the Met in Gotham? Out of the question, so I thought.

Roddy folded his arms tight across his chest, and I watched for my favorite soprano, the renowned diva known as Nordica. She had begun life as Lillian Norton from Farmington, Maine, a backwoods start that appealed to me. Playing one of Don Giovanni's jilted lovers, Nordica appeared briefly in the fourth scene in the garden outside Don Giovanni's palace, but the story had become hopelessly snarled, and, by Scene Five, with no sign of the diva, I was eager for the *entr'acte* interlude.

So was the entire Diamond Horseshoe.

The curtain dropped, applause crackled, the house lights brightened, and the boxes buzzed like hives come to life. The space between the acts— *entr'acte*—permitted precious box-to-box visits when gentlemen opened the box doors, and foot traffic flowed into the corridor. The Horseshoe stirred with chatter and light laughter.

We both stood up, but Roddy did not open our box door. "Aren't we 'receiving' this evening?" I asked.

"Val," he said, "I'm going next door to have a stern word with the 'Coal King.' The opera box is no place for revels. It's outrageous." My husband's white kid gloves pulled tight across his knuckles. "If you'll excuse me...."

Roddy stepped out, and I tried to eavesdrop. Every detail about this evening would need detailed recollection in the weeks ahead. First, I pressed an ear against the box wall from raw curiosity. It would have been easy, instead, to lean forward and peer around the half-wall to see the scene about to unfold in the next box. In the weeks ahead, I regretted not doing exactly that. This much I did hear: the bawling laughter in the box subsided with Roddy's entrance. His tenor voice mixed with deeper male tones and a woman's high chirping. It sounded like introductions, then pauses, perhaps for handshakes and a bow to the lady.

I slipped off one diamond hoop earring to press my ear tight against the partition that felt as thin as a tent flap in a mining camp. Roddy would keep his fury in check, I felt sure, but my husband would make his point. Roddy's work in New York civic affairs and his courtroom defense of taverns harassed by Temperance crusaders had honed his skill in what westerners called "jawing." The voices rose and fell, combined and halted. One burst of laughter, and the voices sank to mumbles. The chirp became a birdcall.

Roddy came back just as the bell rang to announce the second act. Seated beside me, he murmured, "Taken care of... they're leaving soon." He added, "Val, have you lost an earring?"

This prompted my last smile of the evening. The diamond hoop was put back in my left ear with a flick of my fingers—fastened snugly, so I thought—as the curtain rose outside Nordica's house. She appeared at her window, and a trio sang. At that moment, the bustle in Box 18 meant the Coal King and his guests were departing. We recalled a silence, then a few more sounds, as if one of them came back to retrieve a hat or cane. Then total silence. Roddy gave me a "good riddance" glance, and we turned attention to the stage.

I recalled Roddy glancing down at the left side of his chair just as Don Giovanni strummed a mandolin and sang to the maid. My husband reached down and seemed to pat the carpet. Twice, he bent to touch the carpet, a movement I'd never seen by this man who goes in for opera, as Papa would say, "whole hog."

My husband raised the gloved fingers of his left hand, and I saw dark smears on the white kidskin.

The next moments were predictable and bizarre. The opera ended with a chorus of demons that surrounded the evil Don Giovanni and swept him off to Hell. A few bars of a simple melody, and applause and "Bravos" surged in waves at the curtain calls and flowers for the divas.

I applauded, but Roddy, oddly, did not, not even when his favorite soprano curtsied with lush bouquets cradled in each arm.

My husband applauded no one, not the sopranos, not the famous baritone who sang Don Giovanni. I nudged his shoulder, but he held back, as if waiting for a cue. My husband was not fussy. Spoiling a white glove could not be why he stood stock still as the house lights shone and the audience began its exit.

The auditorium emptied at the same brisk pace as our Diamond Horseshoe, and Roddy and I ought to be pulling on overshoes, soon to drive off in our waiting carriage. "Shall we...?" I asked.

"Not yet, Val. Something has come up. We're waiting until everyone has gone."

Emphasis on *"everyone."* The house emptied, and only then did I learn what had stopped my husband cold at the Metropolitan Opera on this second night of January, 1899. He raised his left hand to me, palm up, and his "smeared" glove fingertips showed a dark rust color. He pointed to the stain on the pale beige carpet, a darkness that spread from the very bottom of the partition and onto our carpet—also dark rusty red.

"A leak," I said. "Something has leaked…from the next box…red wine?"

Roddy shook his head and kept his gaze on my face as I puzzled out the possibility until, at last, I whispered, "Is it…is it blood?"

A curt nod, and my husband insisted I stay put while he sought help.

I stood alone while the house lights dimmed and went dark. My heart hammered. Somewhere in the cavernous opera house, Roddy searched for an official while the house was shutting down. I stood in total darkness.

Was it fifteen minutes? Thirty? Footsteps, and finally, "Mrs. DeVere?"

"—right here, Mr. DeVere."

My husband brought two men, one carrying a lighted kerosene lantern and wearing workman's overalls. The other wore a formal suit and opera slippers.

"—introducing Mr. Hoff," Roddy said. "And Janko, who has the lantern." Roddy pointed at the carpet. "If you'll look down here...." Heads lowered, and Janko turned a knob on the lantern. Yellow light flared, purpling the stain.

Mr. Hoff ran a hand across his balding head. "Very well," he said, "we must have a look in box...box—"

"Eighteen," said Roddy.

"Precisely."

I insisted on going too.

Mr. Hoff knocked at the box door. "A formality," he said. Then, "Janko, if you will...."

The door opened, and, in the confusion of the moment, the courtesy was mine—the lady first. The scene flashed like the opera come to the box—the *Commendatore* in the pooling blood, crisscrossed with the man in the chair... crooked but slumped, his white shirtfront darkened. He looked about my papa's age. Glass shards flashed in the lantern light, and he did not move. Bathed in blood, soaked in blood, he was alone. And he was dead.

Chapter Two

TUESDAY'S BREAKFAST STARTED LATE. I barely slept, and Roddy had a restless night. We sat across from one another at the antique breakfast table with our usual tea, coffee, and juice, Roddy in a maroon robe, I wrapped a blue woolen sacque pulled tight for the warmth that somehow failed me. The wall clock struck ten a.m., ten intrusive beats of its mechanical heart. The windowpanes had frosted, and the outdoor temperature dipped well below freezing. I shivered despite the warmth of our breakfast nook. Our French bulldog, Velvet, dozed in her bed at the foot of the table.

"All night, Roddy…eyes closed or open, I kept seeing the lantern light and broken glass, and his shirtfront…. soaked in blood. He was soaked…blood dark as…as your robe."

"My dressing gown…." Roddy flushed. "Thoughtless of me, I'll change right away."

"No, don't leave. Take my hand."

Across the table, Roddy's warm palm covered my icy fingers. "Forgive me, Val," he said. I should have stopped you from going into that box…. You should not have seen… what you saw."

"You saw it too. And the others…the worker with the lantern and the other man…Hart?"

"Hoff."

"They saw it…saw him." I swallowed, my voice a whisper. "Death…death is not new to me, Roddy. Remember Papa…his cough…he coughed blood…his last hours…." My husband nodded, pressing my hand. "And the mines," I said, "the fires, accidents …bodies crushed…burned…the funerals that I remember…."

"Val, don't…."

I tried to take a deep breath. "The silver mines," I said, "teach lessons about deadly danger. 'Never deny it,' Papa said, 'and never forget.' But Roddy…the opera and Diamond Horseshoe and the blood. That man…he reminded me of Papa."

"Val, don't."

Roddy's hand gripped mine tighter. I heard myself begin to ramble. "…and they were noisy until they left. They all left him, we heard them go. It was quiet…quiet as a—"

"—don't, Val."

"—quiet as a tomb. The opera box, a tomb." My shrill laughter rose, and I wiped tears on a sleeve and sipped coffee. My husband looked alarmed. "Roddy," I said, "he must have tried to get out of his chair to go for help. His body was… crooked in the chair. You saw he was crooked."

"I did."

"He must have tried…."

"Yes, he probably tried to find help."

"Too late," I said. "He bled to death, all alone…so close to us. Our box beside him…right beside him, and we didn't help."

"Val…."

"He died alone. My papa feared dying alone."

"But he didn't. You were with him. We were with him in Virginia City…."

"We'd have tried to help if we knew…the next box over…not a sound but the music…."

"Only the opera," Roddy said.

I swallowed, my throat dry. "And Roddy, I thought that man would never let us go…Hoff. All those questions…as if we knew the man who…who bled…."

"Perished," Roddy said.

"Perished," I echoed. "And questions…who ought to be notified…next of kin." My chin trembled, and I reached again for my coffee cup. "As if we knew…. How could we know?"

"Probably the Wendells…the rental…."

"We didn't know." I sipped and put the cup down. "I was afraid Noland would drive home without us."

"He would never do such a thing."

"I hope not…midnight. Was it midnight?"

"Nearly." Roddy held both my hands in his. The opera official, I clearly remembered, had led us from the Horseshoe by lantern light and seen us into our carriage—the one-and-only carriage left under the *porte cochere* with our anxious coachman on the box seat.

"Val, we ought to have some breakfast. It'll do us good."

The footman, Bronson, had approached to inquire about breakfast. I asked for dry toast, and Roddy requested a three-minute egg. The kitchen doubtless had readied the customary hearty winter meal, but not today.

Roddy rubbed his unshaven cheeks and paused to sip his tea. "I think Maurice Hoff was as shocked as we were, Val. He manages the opera company, not the house. He's highly respected, and I was lucky to find him in the darkness. He probably dreaded being alone with…alone in the Diamond Horseshoe when we left."

"He'd have the workman, Janko—"

"— who might not speak English."

True, the workman was possibly a newcomer to these shores. He had not spoken a word. Roddy and I grew quiet as the footman appeared with the toast and soft-boiled egg, both served on the Royal Doulton china from my in-laws—Royal Albert Old Country Roses.

"Painted roses in winter," I murmured. "…the dead of winter." Our dog stirred, went to her emptied feed bowl, licked twice, and returned to her bed.

Roddy salted his egg and urged us to "pamper" ourselves today. The winter grippe and croup were "going around," and we ought to rest up.

"We'll have a quiet day," Roddy said, "but let's order the later editions of the newspapers. You needn't read the accounts, Val. You can leave that to me. I'll send Bronson out for all the papers, and he can walk Velvet too. I have papers to review for a case coming up against a saloon accused of fouling its beer and whiskey."

"The Temperance people again?"

Roddy nodded. "A new wrinkle...trying to shut the place down by charging their alcohol is tainted. A false charge, but we'll go to court."

My husband reached for his tea. It seemed a twist of fate that lawyer Roderick DeVere defended saloons, taverns, and other "oases" targeted by Temperance zealots, all the while pursuing his *bon-vivant* hobby that first brought us together. The sip-and-savor cocktails that shocked his parents were the pastime that often put Roddy in demand in the city.

"And I'll scan the newspapers," Roddy said, "and look up the Wendells' travel itinerary for the name of...of the deceased."

"—the deceased," I said, recalling my husband's duty to the DeVere family friends. "You'll need to wire the Wendells," I said, "about the—"

"—the unfortunate occurrence."

"I gripped Roddy's free hand. "Just so you understand," I said, "it might be some time before I'm ready for the opera."

"I completely understand. We'll work it out, Val."

We left it at that. Breakfast over, we dressed for a day at home without callers. Calista encouraged soft woolens for comfort. She had put away my opera gown and laid the

"Pleiades" necklace in its rosewood box. One of my diamond hoop earrings was missing, probably somewhere in the carriage. It seems I hadn't fastened it tightly. Calista would see about it. Perhaps our coachman or groom could find it.

Roddy appeared in dark brown fabrics that would not show printers' ink from newspapers just off the press. At midmorning, a hand-written message arrived from M. Hoff, assuring us of "complete restoration with upmost promptness."

"Rug cleaning, I suppose," I said, "or replacement. What else would 'restoration' mean?" At that moment, Roddy was busy scanning the Wendells' schedule and weighing whether to wire Rio, or wherever the Cunard line took the couple on the third day of January. He had found the name of the man who died.

"Do you want to hear his name?"

My husband was really asking whether emotion would get the better of me. "I do."

"It's Rankin. The Wendells' box was rented for the remainder of the season to Mr. Leon Lee Rankin."

"The Coal King," I said.

"The 'late' Coal King," Roddy said softly.

The hours dragged until evening, when Bronson brought an armful of the final edition newspapers into the drawing room where we sat with Velvet stretched out on the sofa between us.

"Roddy," I said, "I'll take my share of these papers. I'm ready." The footman had set them on a table.

"You're sure?" My husband looked eager to take my pulse, but I reached for the stack and grabbed the *Times*, the *World*, and the *Sun*.

Roddy took the *Herald*, his favorite. "Here it is, Val. First page, 'Apoplexy Claims Life of Coal Chief! Succumbs at Grand Opera!'"

"Apoplexy?"

Roddy read aloud, "'Star Coal Company President, Mr. Leon Rankin of Suggs Run, West Virginia, and Palm Beach, Florida… believed to be fifty-two years of age… wintering in New York…attended to business as advance in coal rates engineered by the coal trust'…."

"Roddy, what exactly is apoplexy?"

My husband glanced at the ceiling to gather his thoughts. "Anger, most often, but it can mean a hemorrhage."

"So he bled to death?" I said. "He hemorrhaged and bled to death?"

"So it seems."

"But his friends…" I said. "The whole group left the box. We heard them go."

"Yes, but Rankin stayed on."

"They left him all alone…" I said.

The sorrow began welling in my chest, but Roddy snapped the newspaper open, then shut. "Val," he said, "Consider this… Perhaps Mr. Rankin insisted on staying for the entire performance by himself. Perhaps to get his money's worth. Remember the 'princely' sum he paid the Wendells."

Roddy gently lifted the newspapers from my lap and laid them on the table. "Let's call it a day," he said. "The *Herald* is quite enough for now. We both could use a decent night's sleep. Let's go..."

Roddy stood and took my hand as if asking me to dance, but there would be no waltz tonight.

○

Wednesday morning, 9:00 a.m., found us once again across the William IV antique table. Roddy was wearing a paisley robe in bronze tones, and my blue sacque felt warm enough. I had lain awake, but Roddy looked rested. A new batch of papers lay neatly before us, untouched. "Time enough, Val, after we have a bite."

If only our footman hadn't startled us with today's special from the kitchen: blood sausage.

I gagged.

"Thank you, Bronson," Roddy said calmly, "but Mrs. DeVere will begin with toast again this morning, and I'll have another three-minute egg." He glanced down at Velvet, whose kibble bowl was licked clean. "Perhaps," he said, "Velvet might enjoy the sausage later today."

The footman bowed and withdrew. Velvet shifted from her bed, stretched, and lapped a hearty drink of water.

"Sweet rescue dog," I said. She nuzzled my ankle and lay down for a nap, ignoring the gong of the Junghans German wall clock that my mother-in-law brought from

Vienna, insisting that it "belonged" on our breakfast nook wall. I envisioned the clock in storage, along with a good many antique "pieces," as Eleanor called the furnishings that became mine after our wedding. Roddy's parents had abruptly moved into the part of the house that had been Roddy's private apartment in his bachelor days. My in-laws now lived in our building, around the corner of 62nd Street, where they had their private entrance. They had taken a few "pieces," but my husband and I lived with Eleanor DeVere's taste in furniture.

I planned major redecoration, in due course. For the moment, I thought only of bland breakfast toast and, for once, appreciated the feeble coffee that bore no relation to the bracing campfire brew that I loved in the West.

The footman brought my toast and Roddy's egg and refilled our drinks. Breakfast lasted two minutes, then we reached for the papers.

"You're sure, Val?"

Last night, lying awake, I remembered Papa's gentle chiding when I moped as a child. "Little girl," he'd say, "don't act like you're raised on sour milk." He meant, perk up, get going. I liked the silver miners' saying—"Quit spittin' on the pick-ax and get to work."

I would not recite those words at our breakfast table but reached for the morning papers. "Roddy," I said, "It's a new day. You take the *Herald*, and I'll have the *Journal*." We scanned the usual headlines--*'Poisoning Case,' 'Trust Companies Slapped' 'Caucus Is in Doubt.'*

"Here it is, Roddy, '*Coal King Dethroned by Death!!!*'" The photograph of Leon L. Rankin showed a bearded, narrow face, sunken cheeks, and fiercely dark eyes.

Roddy sipped his tea, but my cup stayed at arm's length. "Listen to this…'Coal, my life blood,' declared young Leon Lee Rankin early in stellar career… Miner from youth…down-and-out in West Virginia, bound to rise high despite small stature…a teetotaler…swore coal tipple his sole tippling…coal and rail lines too'…." I looked up. "Something about a bank and a railroad I never heard of…The Barret and Nitro Line."

"Probably a short line to the New York Central or the Pennsylvania," Roddy said. "Coal moves on rails."

I put my cup down and read on. "'…divorced, early career touching New Orleans…recent venture in Florida…planned hotel in Palm Beach…competition with Flagler."

Roddy's eyebrows raised at the name of the wealthiest railroader, Henry Flagler, who had become a prominent hotelier. Before my husband could speak, I found scathing lines in the *Journal* obituary. "'Rankin the spoliator…jackal and betrayer,'" I read aloud. "'Called cold-blooded impoverisher of families…pirate.'" I took a deep breath. "Think of it, Roddy, the man bleeds to death in an opera box, and the *Journal* prints 'jackal' and 'pirate.'"

"Sells papers, Val, but no surprise. Self-made men are envied and loathed. Think of the 'Copper King,' the 'Corn King.' Think of Rockefeller. And your father too—"

"—my father was revered." My Irish temper rose before I remembered the banker who had hated Patrick Mackle, filed a lawsuit, and ended up in a lunatic asylum when the case was dropped. "My father knew mines and the miners," I said, "and he respected everyone, no matter where they came from. And he cared about safety, and—"

"—and he mined silver, Val, not coal. Coal is a different beast."

At "beast," Velvet stirred and sat up at Roddy's knee. He patted her head and looked again at the morning *Herald*. "Two survivors," he said, "a sister, Miss Glenna May Rankin of Palm Beach, Florida, and a son, Lewis, no age or location. No funeral plans or memorial service known at this time."

We both grew quiet. Mortality again at breakfast.

Roddy put down the newspaper. "The papers tell their tales, Val, but I must speak to Hoff."

"Oh?"

"Maurice Hoff has nothing to do with the *parterre* boxes, but he can tell me something more about the bod...about the arrangements after we left."

"So you can wire the Wendells?"

Roddy nodded. "I have a committee meeting early this afternoon, a proposal for a sanitary patrol near the wharves. The ice and slush and trash are out of control, and something must be done. And I'll stop at the Murray Hill Hotel... something about a Scotch whisky cocktail on approval. But first, I must see Hoff."

My husband pushed back the light brown wave that had charmed me from the beginning. A puckish grin played at the corner of his mouth. "Hoff is a legend in his time...

knows where to spend a dollar and save a nickel. He's put the Met in the league with La Scala, and he supposedly 'delights in difficulties.'"

Roddy toyed with a spoon. "He's also trusted with secrets. Neither the *Herald* nor *Journal* reported that Rankin died in the Diamond Horseshoe, and I'd wager the other papers missed that 'ripe' detail. Hoff is a master at publicity, what gets into the news—and what's buried."

"Buried…? Did you say 'buried?'"

We managed a nervous laugh. Napkins down, breakfast was over. "I'll pay a call on Hoff this morning," said Roddy. "And you, my dear? I suggest another restful day."

"On the contrary, Roddy. I need to get my mind off the… the opera. So, I'm going…to the Ladies Mile."

"Shopping?"

My husband knew I seldom ventured into the department store district between Fifteenth and Twenty-third Streets. "I'll visit a few stores."

"For purchases?" He paused. "Or is it an 'inspection' tour, Val?" Roddy's skill in cross-examination began to surface. "For that club you've joined, isn't it? The women socialists."

"The National Consumers League," I said, "is not political, not unless decent pay and working conditions are 'political.'" My voice rose, and Velvet's ears perked. "The League is new this year, and I am pleased to join. Right now it feels like…like pioneering in the city…like my western self on a new frontier."

I met my husband's wary gaze. "Roddy, you swore you did not want a 'lady' from a pattern book.

"I meant it—"

"—and you knew from the beginning in Virginia City… deep in the silver mine with Papa. You saw me straddle my horse and handle a wagonload of lumber…a pair of draft horses, and I held the reins."

"You did."

"And when New York Society gives me the cold shoulder and feels sorry for you marrying the Wild West instead of a debutante?"

"—it's their loss."

"—and no matter how many etiquette books your mother sends me, you don't care."

"—not a wit."

Eleanor DeVere tallied her disapproval with each new manners manual on a lengthening shelf in my boudoir. Some proved useful as "rules of the road," but her efforts to reform her son's Wild West wife had foundered. She pushed, and I pushed back.

Roddy kissed my fingers. "Which department store will you scrutinize this morning?"

"Not the store. I'll focus on the working conditions of the young women behind the counters. The Consumers League is looking into women's work, and my committee will report on retail jobs. Reform is in the air, and progress too. I'll start with Macy's. If there's time, Lord & Taylor. I ought to be back by mid-afternoon."

We prepared for the day. Calista selected my tailor-made suit, and I approved the menu for tonight's dinner. Roddy telephoned our stable to order the cabriolet brought around for himself and a closed carriage for me. I asked that the brougham be searched for my missing earring. A footman was instructed to walk Velvet and reminded that her fleece coat must be snug in this wintry cold.

Ready to go separate ways, Roddy and I were bundled up in hats, coats, boots, and gloves, ready for the front entrance, where our butler, Sands, would wish us good day and open the massive oak door to usher us into the crisp, cold winter air. The carriages stood at the curb, and Sands waited, a model of propriety in his swallowtail morning coat.

Somehow, he looked uneasy, as if the envelope on the silver tray in his outstretched arm had brought contagion. "A message that was delivered just in the last minutes, sir... and ma'am."

"Perhaps we can attend to it later in the day?" I said, already warm in the swathes of wool and fur.

Sands cleared his throat. "The messenger," he said, "seemed quite hasty. The envelope is addressed to both Mr. and Mrs. DeVere."

Roddy held up gloved fingers, as did I. Such nuisance.

"Sands," Roddy said, "please open it and give me the message inside...no, don't bother with the paper knife, just your thumb...fine, thanks."

Sands stepped aside, though he would hear every word my husband spoke as he read from the folded sheet.

"What is it?" I whispered to Roddy.

Roddy read softly, "'—to call upon you without delay in reference to an occurrence on the night of January second...'"

"The opera," I murmured. "Whose signature is that?"

"Bernard J. Gork," Roddy said, "and he wants to talk to us."

"Bernard who?"

Roddy bent close to my bonneted ear. "Bernard Gork," he said, "is the New York City Commissioner of Police."

Chapter Three

A POLICE OFFICIAL VISITING our home? "Must we, Roddy?"

My husband nodded a firm *yes*. He suggested that Mr. Gork be invited here this late afternoon and dashed off a hasty reply. Sands opened the door to see me off to Sixth Avenue to R. H. Macy & Company…Macy's.

Within an hour I had stepped from the carriage onto the sidewalk in front of the department store's great show windows. Weeks ago, they featured Santa's Elves in the North Pole Workshop, and I had joined the crowd with Cassie and her children one December evening. In front of the plate glass, we marveled at the miniature Elves that crafted toys and loaded Santa's sleigh, while a tiny train circled the scene, its locomotive puffing snowy white clouds.

These same windows now displayed life-size mannequin "ladies" dressed in red-white-and-blue frocks and jackets. They held mallets on a croquet court that was edged with tulips and tiny flags—fashions for a patriotic springtime at the crest of the wartime victory over Spain. The Spanish-American War had officially ended last August, but spirits ran high, and a huge celebration was scheduled for next September in the city. Roddy served on a planning committee that met frequently, the Dewey Committee, named in honor of the Admiral who defeated the Spanish fleet in Manila Bay. Months of patriotic fervor continued to this day. The croquet mallets were painted with stars and stripes.

The frigid air nipped my nose, but the window was a welcome distraction from the horrors of the past two days. The frocks and lightweight jackets also focused my thoughts on the task ahead. In minutes, I went inside and checked my hat and coat. My friend Cassie had suggested that salesgirls in handbags or china might be easiest to meet, but I decided to "shop" for the spring season in the ladies clothing department.

My etiquette manuals advised, "Do not endlessly consume the time of the clerk," and "do not volunteer criticism upon the goods." Also "refrain from bargaining about price," which was a moot point because modern department stores allowed no haggling.

I came here to take notes on the "salesgirls" who dressed smartly, smiled valiantly across the racks and counters, and stood on rock-hard floors for hours without complaint. Rumors circulated about pitiful wages and trifling offences that cost them jobs. I had agreed to gather facts of the matter.

The Macy's managers knew nothing about this amateur espionage.

Why did I, Valentine Mackle DeVere, agree to "spy" on salesclerks in a New York department store? Cassie called the scheme destiny, but I preferred coincidence. A few months ago, somewhat by chance, I had sat through a meeting of the new National Consumers League and heard a fiery speech by its new General Secretary, Mrs. Florence Kelley, an ample, no-nonsense woman who reminded me of ranch women in the West.

Mrs. Kelley had inspected factories and tenements in Chicago, and she denounced bosses who worked employees to the bone and paid starvation wages. "What I saw," she thundered, "encumbered the earth with error," but she vowed the "error" could be corrected with action and new laws. Seated in the rear of the meeting room, I had heard Mrs. Kelley's scorching voice trumpet high-minded words about "humane working conditions" and "enlightened laws and courts" and "our best Republic."

Her speech had reminded me of the Sunday sermons in the Presbyterian Church with Papa in Virginia City. Somehow, my past met the present—and pointed to the future when my friend, Daisy Harriman (Mrs. Borden J.), also at the meeting, urged me to get involved. Daisy had already joined the Consumers League, and she said to me, "Valentine, a new century is soon upon us, and we owe it to the future to work for a better day for all."

The "all" was abundantly clear to Mrs. Kelley, and perhaps to Daisy, but my push to membership was a rebel yell against my mother-in-law's campaign to move me into a ladylike hobby. Just days after the League meeting, Eleanor had brought me a stack of dainty Egyptian cotton tea towels, skeins of embroidery thread, needles, and a model sampler "exhibiting the grace and beauty possible to obtain in designs for initials and monograms." She also supplied an instruction booklet "for the beginner and novice," wished me well, and promised to oversee my progress achieving "grace and beauty" in needlework.

Every little girl learns her way with a needle and thread, but some of us yield elegant sewing to those more ready, willing, and adept—and patient. Not me. The embroidery kit was stashed in the far reaches of a cabinet. I immediately joined the Consumers League and volunteered for the Retail Clerk Committee.

"May I help you?"

I turned to see an ivory-complexioned young woman with upswept dark hair approach from a rack of jackets. She smiled, folded her hands, and asked, "If I may be of assistance, if you please...?" Her clothing echoed the red-white-blue motif in the front window, a navy skirt and a red-and-white dimity shirtwaist with turn-back cuffs. Smart, up to date.

My papa would say, 'First break ground, then the bedrock.' "New jackets...." I said. "Springtime will arrive before we know it." I hoped the words were not too stagy.

"Perhaps you would like to see what's new this year...? My name is Miss Marler, and let me show you...." She plucked out a red jacket with white piping and double rows of military buttons. "The flag sets the pace for spring," she said. "The soldier boys are coming back from the war, and we show our thanks."

"Oh, yes," I said. "We are all so proud."

"The new jackets salute the flag—with fashion flair."

Did Macy's tell the saleswomen what to say? I had no idea. "Very nice," I said.

"—and Macy's offers custom alterations, as needed, for a modest charge."

"So tempting," I said. Getting nowhere fast.

Just then, two young women approached the rack...customers. With winter coats unbuttoned, they pulled off their gloves and pawed at the jackets. The taller one frowned, and her round-faced companion laughed. Their jaws worked, and I sniffed mint...chewing gum. They pulled the jacket sleeves close to their faces, all the while laughing and chewing.

Miss Marler's eyes darted back and forth. "Excuse me." She approached the twosome. "Ladies, I will be with you shortly." She slipped between the women and the jackets, a deft move that sent the pair elsewhere, still cheerful, still snapping their gum.

"My apologies, Mrs...."

"DeVere," I said. "I am Mrs. DeVere." The young woman's eyes had darkened with anxiety, and I saw my chance. "It must be difficult to protect the merchandise...."

"And to please the customers at the same time," she said.

"'The customer is always right,' Miss Marler," I said. "Isn't that the rule?"

"Actually," she said, Macy's also has its rule for the sales floor, and we must follow it…." She hesitated, and I cocked an ear when she leaned forward. "Here it is: 'Be everywhere, do everything—and don't forget to astonish the customer.'"

"That is…astonishing," I murmured. "I can't imagine—"

"—oh, don't get me wrong, Mrs. DeVere. It is a privilege…." Anxiety darkened her eyes again. "…a great privilege to be employed by the Macy Company. 'Many are called, but few are….'"

"'Chosen?'"

She flushed. "No disrespect. I worship at church every Sunday. I would teach Sunday school if I had the…the strength." Beneath the flush, her ivory complexion looked sallow, and her slender frame struck me as seriously thin. She turned to scan the racks surrounding us, as if to eye a promising sale, but in vain.

"I'm afraid that I'm taking too much of your time," I said.

"Not at all. January weeks are so slow…after Christmas. But new ready-to-wear comes in, and the store has 'expectations.'"

"Expectations? I don't understand," I said. "Do you mean you are expected to sell—"

"—a quota," she said. "We have our quota…and fines if we don't…." She broke off.

"Miss Marler," I said, "I believe my wardrobe needs to be freshened with a new jacket this afternoon. Perhaps two jackets. And if you could personally assist me in planning for spring? I will need a number of new things, and if I could rely upon your help…?"

She looked pitifully grateful. "At your service, Mrs. DeVere."

"Miss Marler," I said, "I will see you very soon again."

"Jackets? You bought jackets?"

"A red one, Roddy, and a navy blue. Macy's will deliver them. And I opened a charge account."

My husband shook his head and mumbled something about my charity donation to Macy's. He had come home earlier and brought out his wheeled cart, a tea wagon he converted to a bar cart with bottles, fruit, an ice bucket, and glassware. He had been "experimenting" at the request of certain hotel, he said, and would I care to sip his latest effort? I nodded. Sandwiches waited on nearby trays, but Roddy now mixed what he called a Jack Frost cocktail. I think you might like it, Val."

I watched my husband's hands play over a bottle, lemons, the ice bucket tongs, glasses…and finally the fizzy selzer.

Jack Frost Sour (for two)
Ingredients:

- 1 lemon
- 2 ounces applejack
- 2 teaspoon sugar
- 2 ponies fresh cream
- Selzer
- Ice

Directions:
1. Fill shaker with ice.
2. Squeeze lemon juice in shaker.
3. Add applejack, sugar, and cream.
4. Shake vigorously
5. Strain in equal amounts into 2 tall tumblers filled with ice.
6. Top each tumbler with selzer and stir gently.

We touched glasses and sipped. "Roddy it's delicious. The hotel will be a favorite for its 'Jack Frost.'" I sipped again. "But no ladies can enjoy the cocktail…only the gentlemen."

"Now, Val, let's not start again…not now."

We had gone round and round about the iron-bound "rule" that cocktails were off limits to ladies. We could quench thirsts with endless wines and liqueurs and occasionally enjoy punch, but whiskey drinks were strictly forbidden. To me, the whiskey problem matched the ban on ladies' votes. One day soon, we would vote and order cocktails and not bat an eye. At a hotel bar, I planned to lead a revolt, but not just yet. Timing, timing….

A grandfather clock struck 3:15 p.m., and our visitor, the Police Commissioner would be here at four. It was snowing when I left Macy's, so I had come straight home. We sat with our drinks and sandwiches, Velvet shuttling back and forth between us, hoping for a morsel of chicken.

I pinched a bit for the dog. "What about your meetings? Did you see Mr. Hoff?"

"I did...and got an earful. After we drove off at midnight, Hoff went upstairs and ordered Janko to wrap the... the deceased...in a tarpaulin and lock the box. My guess about the workman was right, so Hoff's order was in gestures...a pantomime."

"—because Janko speaks no English?"

Roddy nodded. "Hoff called it a godsend that Janko just 'got off the boat' and is a willing worker. He carried the... the tarpaulin downstairs to the Seventh Avenue entrance."

"The back door...the service entrance?"

"Yes, then Hoff went outdoors with the lantern—coatless in the cold—and waved down a night patrolman, who rallied officers from the nearest precinct house to lend a hand. The police wagon came and took the... tarpaulin downtown to the morgue. Calling cards in the deceased's formal suit identified Rankin, the "Coal King," and the news immediately reached the police command and the mayor. Hoff was interviewed yesterday, I believe by the Police Commissioner."

"He didn't say?"

"No."

I pushed away my sandwich plate and put down my drink. "So, Mr. Hoff felt you needed the explanation about the...tarpaulin."

"Much more, Val. He apologized profusely for the damage to our box and the Wendells' too. He promised prompt restoration and offered his own *parterre* box for our use... until our Box 17 is 'refreshed.' He also took the box keys away from the usher and assigned him to other duties on performance nights.

Roddy sipped his drink. "Hoff dreads publicity about Leon Rankin's death, Val. He worries terribly about opera finances, and he fears bad publicity could send the company into a slump...afraid the board would slash the budget and he'll be disgraced."

"Could it happen?"

"It could. The Metropolitan Opera is the pinnacle of Maurice Hoff's career. He made his reputation in theatre management, then leaped at the chance to manage the Opera when the board took a chance on him."

My husband paused. "The ownership has shifted in recent years. Annual assessments have risen sharply, and quite a few old stalwarts sold their shares and got out. A public scandal like bankruptcy would be out of the question for the Opera, but the current financing is a patchwork. The income and expenses teeter on the edge, and Hoff feels like a target. The season ticketholders gripe about the noise from the boxes and threaten to boycott. The box holders say the 'groundlings' have no right to complain."

"And Mr. Hoff feels caught in the middle."

Roddy nodded. "The opera is so costly to produce, and fewer box holders attend regularly. Their boxes are often filled with renters."

"So the box holders are...landlords. Like the Wendells...."

Roddy winced. "Don't let my father or mother hear you say so, Val. They take pride in never renting...not even during their downturn. Mother stood firm. She follows Mrs. Astor's example to the letter—either invite guests to enjoy your box, or let it be vacant."

Roddy rubbed his eyes. "Charles Wendell is among those who have chosen to recover expenses—and more. He's not alone. Box rentals have doubled these last few seasons, and Hoff fears the Horseshoe is becoming something of a way station."

"I see."

"But luck was with him last Monday night, because the box on the other side of the...the 'unfortunate event' was not occupied."

"Box 19," I said.

Roddy nodded. The clock struck another quarter hour, and he signaled the footman to take the trays and wheel his cart to the butler's pantry. "Drink up, Val. In thirty minutes, the Police Commissioner will be at the door, and a few more things about Hoff and the opera...."

Roddy pulled his chair closer to me and lowered his voice. "A few patrons in the Diamond Horseshoe actually do love the music and care passionately about the opera. Two gentlemen are especially important to Maurice Hoff. He needs their unwavering support. One is the president of the Opera, and you have met him—Mr. Augustus Juilliard."

I recalled a gentleman with beautifully tonsured hair and moustache. He had hoped I might speak French, the native tongue of his family. I had disappointed him.

Roddy said, "The other is Mr. J.P. Morgan."

"A financier."

"Not *a* financier, Val. Morgan is *the* financier. The house of Morgan is a keystone of finance in this country, and J.P. Morgan is a keystone of the Opera. His *parterre* box is number thirty-five, smack in the center."

"But nowhere near the box where, last Monday night...I mean, nowhere near our box."

"No."

"Then why bring up Mr. J.P. Morgan's name?" My irritation rose, the afternoon cut short by this intrusive police official who was about to drag us into discussion of a shocking event that had nothing to do with us.

I also sensed that nasty gossip could infect the household. Mr. Sands took pride in his discretion as a butler, but he would feel duty bound to tell the housekeeper, Mrs. Thwaite, that the caller was a city Police Commissioner.

We had "inherited" Mrs. Thwaite from her longtime service to Roddy's parents, and she would beeline to Eleanor DeVere with the news that a police official had visited her sainted son and his Wild West wife. Mrs. Thwaite would imply that "Mrs. Roderick," as she called me, had once again "upset" the household. The housekeeper already begrudged my paying servants' better-than-average wages and offering days off and vacations. She made common cause with Eleanor, who loathed defending me from her friends who thought Roddy had married a socialist. ("Household budgets are a most sensitive matter, dear Valentine, and it won't do to upset the 'apple cart.'")

"Roddy," I said wearily, "We are bystanders...were bystanders. The Wendells' opera box is not our business. Why is the Police Commissioner coming here? What's the point?" We gave our empty glasses to the footman and waited.

Based on the facts as we knew them that afternoon, my husband thought Commissioner Bernard Gork would request our discretion—our silence—in the matter of Mr. Leon Rankin's demise. There would be no reason for Messrs. Julliard or Morgan, or any other Diamond Horseshoe box holder to be disturbed by news of a death that occurred in a Metropolitan Opera House *parterre* box on January 2, 1899.

"He'll request our silence, Val. I'm sure of it."

We prepared to receive the Police Commissioner on that basis. In the next moments, we would learn how wrong we were.

Chapter Four

SANDS CLICKED HIS HEELS together and announced, "Mr. Bernard Gork to see you, madam...sir."

Roddy stood, while I remained seated in a Louis period chair. Our Corinthian reception room was no favorite, but its massive columns and filigree scrolls served whatever purpose my mother-in-law had in mind when she planned the formal space.

"Mr. Gork, welcome," said Roddy. "I am Mr. DeVere... and may I present Mrs. DeVere."

A gaunt figure with a long jaw and heavy eyes, Bernard Gork rubbed his hands together to warm his fingers. Sands had taken his overcoat, hat, and gloves. He bowed slightly to me and shook Roddy's hand. His heavy tweeds, bulging necktie, and wide whiskers seemed an effort at enlargement, as did his heavy police shoes, the only item linking him to law enforcement. I had noticed his bitten fingernails and a heavy signet ring with a large red stone. His tight smile revealed a gold front tooth.

"Won't you sit down?"

My husband gestured to a nearby chair, but the Commissioner stepped sideways into a tufted armchair several feet outside our seating area.

Did he miss his cue? We shifted our own chairs in his direction for courtesy.

"My thanks to you, Mr. and Mrs. DeVere, for your time this afternoon."

"Not at all, Mr. Gork," Roddy said. "I believe a snowy evening is in store for us, so your visit is well timed."

"Difficult…" the Commissioner began. Did he mean the weather? He rubbed his whiskers. "A difficult situation…." We waited. "You might know," he said, "that the mayor appoints the city's Police Commissioner…his honor, Mayor Robert Van Wyck, appoints the Commissioner."

Roddy had told me that Mayor Van Wyck was embroiled in a shady scheme to monopolize ice, which, given the winter, I found amusing.

"People confuse the Commissioner with the Chief of Police," Gork said, "and that would be a mistake. The Commissioner does not arrest anybody. He oversees the department and offers advice. My predecessor gave the wrong impression—"

"—you must mean Mr. Roosevelt," Roddy said, "now Governor Theodore Roosevelt."

"People believe he was the chief, a definite mistake. He was not ever the police chief in those days. The chief now is—"

"—William Devery," Roddy said. A silent moment followed. If Bernard Gork knew that Chief Devery had called on us in this house just a few months ago, he gave no sign of it.

He smoothed his whiskers and folded his hands. "The mayor has made a request...some information came to his office...and to Mulberry Street."

"Police headquarters," I said, feeling I'd better put in a word before becoming an audience for the two men.

"Yes, Mulberry Street is also involved...the mayor and Mulberry Street...and also the Coroner...."

I glanced at Roddy. The Commissioner's tone had changed on the word, coroner.

He sat at the edge of his chair cushion. "The opera," he said, "is too rich for my blood. My wife follows who's who, the ladies' finery and jewels. Me, I go to the ballpark and follow the prizefights."

He tugged his whiskers. "But the mayor requested that I visit the Metropolitan Opera house yesterday afternoon, and so I did. And I paid another visit a couple hours ago. Now I'm here."

The silence grew awkward. I asked, "Were you given a tour? The interior is very fancy."

"Ma'am, to be truthful, I paid no attention to the insides of the building. Both times, my purpose was to meet with Mr. Maurice Hoff and tell him that everything would go smooth as possible. My purpose was to ask a few questions and tell him not to worry."

"And you did?" Roddy sounded bemused.

"That was my purpose."

Roddy said, "But you do know that someone died at the opera last Monday night…? A well-known businessman died…Mr. Leon Rankin."

"Which is why I am here this afternoon, Mr. DeVere."

"Perhaps Mr. Hoff informed you," I said, "that Mr. DeVere and I were present at the time…?"

He twisted his signet ring and nodded. I prepared to hear the Commissioner ask for our silence about the death in the Diamond Horseshoe.

I was in for a shock.

So was Roddy.

"The death was not from natural causes."

He had blurted the words, looking past us at the columns. "The man bled to death because he was attacked… stabbed in the neck…in a big artery. The coroner looked over the body…examined the body. The death was homicide."

Somewhere a steam radiator hissed, but I felt an icy draft. Roddy asked to hear the word once again, and Bernard Gork repeated, "For sure, no question about it. Homicide."

"The newspapers," I said, "reported 'apoplexy.'"

"And so they did," he said, "and so they will…for the sake of all concerned."

Roddy said, "The law requires an inquest. The law requires that the body not be interred before an inquest."

"The law in this instance, Mr. DeVere, needs to be… and will be…flexible."

My lawyer husband looked startled.

"Mr. Gork," I said, "whatever you mean by 'flexible,' let me assure you that neither Mr. DeVere nor I have knowledge of the circumstances in the death at the opera box. I assume," I continued, "that you have called upon us to request our... discretion in the matter...our silence as the investigation proceeds. Am I correct?"

The Commissioner tugged at his collar. "Not exactly, ma'am. That's just the half of it."

A hallway clock struck five p.m. I fought the urge to stand up and walk around the room. I wanted to wrap up and go out into the snow. Roddy shifted in his chair and crossed his legs, restless.

"Commissioner Gork," he said, "I believe the snowfall this evening might slow down the carriage traffic. You surely have other plans, and we don't mean to detain you."

He seemed deaf to Roddy's hint.

"I speak for the mayor and police headquarters," he said. "I am here as the Police Commissioner...officially. Maybe you've visited Mulberry Street, Mr. DeVere?"

"On several occasions."

"Then you saw the reporters...thick as flies around police headquarters, twenty-four hours a day, no letup."

Roddy said, "New York is a newspaper town...." "

"The news hounds get their tips, Mr. DeVere, but this is not a case for the police."

The man spoke sideways, as if expecting us to know what he struggled to say.

"Mr. Gork," said Roddy, "I was told that police officers retrieved and transported Mr. Leon Rankin's body from the opera house to the morgue. Mr. Hoff told me so when I met with him earlier today. So, the police are already involved, are they not?"

The Commissioner drew a handkerchief from a breast pocket, wiped his eyes, folded the handkerchief several times over, and carefully pocketed it. "The mayor's people," he said, "...the opera bigwigs...business bigwigs and Chief Devery too...the idea is an investigation on the q.t....on the quiet...a civilian investigation." Bernard Gork's heavy eyes drooped, and he spoke to the Persian carpet on the floor. "Your names came up," he said. "...Mr. and Mrs. DeVere, the both of you."

"'Came up?'" I said. "What does that mean?"

"Your names..." he repeated. "From Chief Devery and a detective...Finlay."

Roddy shot me a sharp glance. Last fall, Detective Sergeant Colin Finlay sought our help in a case involving deaths in Central Park. We had helped. My mother-in-law, if she knew, would never forgive me.

"Commissioner Gork," Roddy said, "a homicide requires an inquest and a report. The Coroner—"

"—the Coroner has been spoken to," Mr. Devere." The Commissioner moistened his lips, his words spoken once again to the carpet. "A body can be disinterred, and a report can be amended."

He raised his eyes to the columns. "I can't say I know the rhyme or reason for all this, but it's like a tunnel that's dug from the opera to a big bank…money and music like they're welded together. I wish I knew more. Mayor Van Wyck hopes you can lend a hand. The city will be grateful for whatever you can do. New York does not need another scandal, not with the big doings in a few months…for Admiral Dewey."

"That's not until September," said Roddy. "I happen to be on a planning committee."

"The newspapers know how to string out a murder story, Mr. DeVere, a little at a time. The city got past the riots and Tammany Hall, and the country feels good about Admiral Dewey and the war."

"Indeed it does, Commissioner Gork," Roddy said. "However, the sort of investigation you propose—"

"—I do not propose, Mr. DeVere. I represent the greater good of New York City." He tapped a knuckle against his gold tooth.

"I fear this conversation can go no further," Roddy said. He shifted, ready to stand.

Bernard Gork, however, pushed back in his chair, entrenched in the cushion, socially clueless.

"Commissioner Gork," I began, sitting forward, "we can wish you a good evening…."

He did not take the hint. Closing his eyes, he dug two fingers into his trousers watch pocket. Roddy and I exchanged a glance.

"If you need to know the time, Commissioner…." Roddy said.

Bernard Gork grunted, working his fingers into the heavy tweed pocket until, at last, he retrieved a small object wrapped in tissue paper. Setting it on his knee, he unfolded the tissue to reveal—my missing earring.

I stared, then laughed. Surprise became confusion. No question, the diamond hoop that nestled in tissue on the man's knee was mine. The police commissioner did not move, nor speak. In the silence, the twinkling display on the man's trouser leg looked grotesque. Where did he get hold of my earring? And why didn't he pass it to me?

Surely, I was not to grab it off his leg. I stole a glance at Roddy, who looked as perplexed as I felt.

"Mr. Gork..." I began, "you seem to have found an earring of mine that has been missing for the last few days."

"Missing since the night of Monday, January second, I was told." He sounded official. Sands peered from an open doorway, ready to bring the official's overcoat and hat, but the earring kept us in our seats.

Roddy said, "Mrs. DeVere confirms the earring is hers."

"I do," I said. "Our coachman and groom have been asked to search our carriage in case the earring came loose inside."

The Commissioner looked back and forth from Roddy to me but did not touch the earring. "It was discovered, Mrs. DeVere," he said, "inside an opera box."

"Oh, our Box 17," I said. "I slipped it off briefly during the *entre*...between the acts. I thought it was fastened securely."

The Commissioner pulled at his whiskers. "Ma'am," he said, "the earring was found in...inside a different opera box."

"Eighteen?" my husband asked.

The Commissioner yanked at his whiskers.

"Box eighteen," Roddy said, "where Mr. Rankin died?"

Bernard Gork nodded at the carpet.

"Mr. Gork," my husband asked, "did you learn about the earring from Mr. Maurice Hoff? Did Mr. Hoff put it into your hands?"

"For safe keeping, yes," he mumbled.

"The ownership is verified," Roddy said, "so please do return the earring to Mrs. DeVere."

I held out my palm. The Commissioner's face turned scarlet.

"I would like nothing better," he said.

"I'll keep it safe…." I said, but the hand that unwrapped the earring wrapped it back up and tucked it into the watch pocket.

Roddy started to protest, but the Commissioner stood and began to button his tweed jacket. "Ma'am," he said, "material evidence must be secured. The law is firm on that point." He cleared his throat. "The mayor wants you to know the city will be grateful for whatever you can do to help. Also, Chief Devery and Detective Finlay send their regards."

Chapter Five

"MY EARRING...." I SAID, "'material evidence'...evidence of what?" I stood ramrod straight in the reception room as Sands ushered the Commissioner to the front door, which finally clicked shut. The next moments became a babel between the two of us.

"Regards from 'Big Bill' Devery...that's rich," said Roddy. "The Chief of police is crooked as...crooked as they come." He stood, hands shoved into his pockets.

"I could have explained," I said. "I could have showed the Commissioner the matching one—"

"—I had thought better of Maurice Hoff."

"—a white gold hoop with diamonds would take two minutes," I said, "the matching earring—"

"—Hoff could have shown me that earring when we talked late this morning...gentlemanly thing to do."

"Decent thing," I said.

"And Bernard Gork will go straight to City Hall and to Mulberry Street to tell Devery and the mayor. He won't risk the telephone or a messenger. He'll want credit for his... errands. He insults us twice over."

"Roddy, what is 'material' evidence?"

My husband did not answer but abruptly took my arm. "Val, we need to talk."

"Not here," I said, "not with these blighted Corinthian columns."

"Blighted?"

"Like marble armed guards," I said.

Roddy looked confused.

"Never mind," I said, "let's sit...somewhere else."

A footman approached like a referee. Would we wish aperitifs, he inquired, or would Mr. DeVere prefer to tend to refreshments himself? Our whiskey cocktail rule was one-at-a-time, which meant Italian red vermouth for me, Amontillado sherry for Roddy. "A fire has been laid upstairs," the footman said, "in the 'Green' sitting room."

In moments, we sat in matching plump Bergere chairs before a crackling fire.. The forest green chairs and black granite fireplace usually assured comfort, but not today, not now. The onyx mantle clock would soon strike six o'clock. Our wine glowed on a walnut table, untouched. We grew silent.

"Insanity..." Roddy murmured. "Insane...all of it.... But let's try to reason...be reasonable."

"My earring, Roddy," I said, "...was a simple white gold hoop with tiny diamonds. It must have slipped off when

I stepped into the box...in the dark...at the sight of...of Rankin. I didn't feel it drop. Didn't hear it. How could I?"

Shivering, I sipped the sweet red vermouth from cut-glass crystal, but my mind's eye saw blood and broken glass...my earring in the shards.

"Val, are you with me?"

I put down my glass and took two slow, deep breaths. "For two days," I said, "Mr. Hoff has had the earring...so, why didn't he show it to you today? Why?"

Roddy rubbed his chin. "Possibly...quite possibly, he didn't have it—not yet. The Wendells' box was locked and stayed locked after the...the episode. Hoff would have taken his time deciding how to proceed. The stained carpet, the champagne bottles, and broken glass would raise questions. For secrecy, Hoff would be very careful. Let's give him the benefit of the doubt. If the Wendells' box was finally cleaned out this afternoon, the earring could have been found and turned in after I left...probably by Janko."

"Hoff could have sent it here by a messenger."

Roddy sipped his wine. "In a manner of speaking," he said, "Maurice Hoff did exactly that."

"The police commissioner." I shook my head. "But why?"

Roddy shrugged. "I very much doubt that Maurice Hoff knows who owns the earring, Val. But Hoff is a shrewd man. He needn't tell the Commissioner the details of the Diamond Horseshoe homicide, but he would wish to seem cooperative."

"So, he offered up my earring."

"...as an interesting object found near the body. It could be any lady friend's earring. Hoff would let the Commissioner make sense of it."

"To show cooperation."

Roddy nodded. "Bernard Gork probably thought he ought to seize it to exert authority. We saw the man's discomfort here, and the opera house is no prizefight gym. The Commissioner would bluster, and Hoff yield...a convenient fit." Roddy held his wine glass but peered at the fire. "Misplaced bluster..." he said, "especially given his preposterous request."

"You're mulling over the 'q.t.' investigation, aren't you?" My husband nodded but kept his eyes on the flickering flames.

"Roddy," I said, "why did you insist on inviting Commissioner Gork this afternoon?"

He turned toward me. "Because of the Dewey celebration."

Yet once again, Admiral George Dewey. Lately, it seemed next September's celebration had wormed into every talk.

"It's shaping up to be a three-day gala, Val," Roddy said, "morning-to-night, parades, speeches, city hall, fireworks in the harbor...all five boroughs, crowds in the hundreds of thousands." He sipped his sherry. "Excited crowds, drinking and milling about...every saloon in the city will be jampacked...drunken brawls...and I'll be in the courtroom defending every brewer and whiskey distiller against an onslaught of Temperance lawsuits. And who knows what else...."

Roddy leaned toward me. "Here's the point. We'll need the full support of the police department, including the Commissioner. It means extra shifts, extra money from the city budget...the whole ball of wax. This was no time to risk insulting Bernard Gork."

"I suppose not."

"And there's more 'q.t.' business...the opera box...boxes. The opera hasn't been on the same footing since the fire."

"What fire?"

Roddy sighed, as if I needed tutoring on yet another historical event in my adopted city.

"The scenery caught fire one hot summer afternoon about seven years ago...a painter's stogie lighted the flats, and the whole interior was gutted. The building had been guaranteed fireproof, so the insurance coverage was minimal. A good many of the original stockholders wanted out after the fire, and they got out. My father would have been one of them, but mother wouldn't hear of it. Her question was always—"

"—'What would Mrs. Astor do?'"

Roddy paused briefly, and a smile played at his lips. "Indeed, 'What would Mrs. Astor do?' The reigning Queen of box number seven."

"Or is it eight? Or nine?"

We both laughed. "The 'q.t.,'" I said, "what exactly does it mean?"

"It's Latin...*quae tacdenda*...not to speak, keep it quiet." My husband grew serious. "It shouldn't be dismissed."

"Roddy, don't tell me you're duty-bound to Charles Wendell. The Wendells' box is not that important. A cleaning, new carpet—"

"—It's not just the Wendells' box, Val. It's the opera, the opera house, and the property. The Diamond Horseshoe supports all of it, and if rumors circulate about a death, especially a murder, a good many shareholders will use the excuse to pull out. The 'murder box' will become a ghoulish favorite for cheap thrill seekers, and the ladies of Society will find another balcony to display jewels and gowns."

"Including Mrs. Astor?"

"That's no joke. When it first opened, the Metropolitan Opera House was ridiculed as a yellow brick brewery. If the shareholders call it quits, the legal wrangling over the building and the property will go on for years, and the rancor would infect the city at all levels." He added, "Opera lovers who can afford it will travel to Milan or Vienna."

A hall clock chimed. "Val," Roddy said, "I'm thinking of the gravity of the police commissioner's proposal…a criminal investigation outside the criminal justice system." He shifted his gaze from the fire to me. "Do you realize the magnitude…the risk of the undertaking….do you?" He looked into my eyes. "The old days when New Yorkers took the law into their own hands, Val…those days are long gone." He reached for his wine. "Perhaps in other parts of the country—"

"—you mean the West, don't you…my West?" He blinked. "Sheriff's posses…vigilantes…?" He nodded slightly.

"...because New York gets its ideas from Buffalo Bill's Wild West Shows on Staten Island."

I stood, went to the fireplace, grabbed a poker, and pushed at a log that needed no tending. The fire snapped. I sat back down.

"Val, I apologize. I'm trying to think straight. Maybe if I had studied Real Estate law at Columbia...."

"Instead of whiskey law?"

"Ouch." Roddy sipped his sherry. "Stereotyping," he said. "We both bring our 'baggage,' don't we?"

I squeezed his hand. My husband already worked on the "q.t." in our Golden Age of Cocktails. He was often summoned in strict confidence to mix special drinks for clubs, resorts, hotels, even railroads. His name did not appear on any cocktail menu, but his reputation as an expert "mixologist" put him in high demand. Roddy also served on a number of committees, including the Patriarchs, the city fathers. We joked that he was the youngest of the "Fathers," most of whom had gone gray years ago. We spent the next minutes sipping our wine.

At last, my husband said, "Suppose that, instead of an investigation, we were to...let's say, to make 'inquiries' about the circumstances of Leon Rankin death...."

"Inquiries..." I repeated. "To keep the opera from going bust? To keep peace in the in the Diamond Horseshoe boxes?"

"In part," he said.

"What's the other part?"

My husband finished his wine. "For extra protection," he said, "yours...and mine...ours." He turned to face me. "You asked about the meaning of 'material' evidence, Val. It's evidence that matters in law, in court...when a jury of one's peers weighs the evidence and hears the prosecution's theory of the case. A woman's earring...it could belong to a friend of the murder victim. Or it could point to complicity in a criminal case. 'Material' evidence can be the bright, shiny object that overrides all reason and fact."

Chapter Six

HOW COULD AN EARRING complicate life, a simple ornament that fell because I was nosy—and then careless? The jewelry meant nothing to me, and yet became "material evidence."

"Who was in the opera box with Leon Rankin the night he died, Roddy?" How could we find out?"

The questions dogged us at dinner, from the lemony soup to the fish mousse and the Quails Figaro, a dozen tiny poached birds that were "*to be served immediately when lifted from the cooking liquor,*" as I recalled from the morning's consultation about dinner.

"Do we agree, Roddy," I asked, "that after Rankin's group left the box, we heard other sounds, as if someone had forgotten a hat?"

"Or a walking stick? Yes, I remember. It took place during the first scene of the second act...the group's departure, a quiet moment, and then more sounds...the one who returned."

"Or ones…who returned to Box 18 with homicidal intention. Or perhaps for a confrontation that quickly turned deadly."

The questions stayed with us outdoors in the thick nighttime snow, where we marched up and down our deserted Fifth Avenue block for an hour, while my husband berated himself for drawing a blank about the entire group, the three men, one woman, and the "Coal King."

"I was furious about their noise, Val," he said. "I was barely civil."

Back indoors, we chafed our hands before the fire in the front drawing room, while Roddy still searched his memory. "I spoke my piece to the whole group during the *entr'acte*, and I noticed champagne glasses…so offensive at the opera. I recall brief pleasantries for politeness sake… but I'm not sure which man was Rankin."

My husband held palms out before the fire. "The Diamond Horseshoe lighting was bright enough," he continued, "but all I recall is four men in evening dress, and a woman with hair in coils."

"But her earrings…?"

Roddy flushed. "Val, I don't exactly remember her earrings…or yours. You adjusted your earring after the *entr'acte* when you listened against our box wall. You looked beautiful, and your eyes sparkled…and your Pleiades diamonds ….?" He broke off.

"Don't worry, Roddy. I didn't know it was missing until Calista noticed. I'll never wear diamond hoops again. Not ever." I touched both ear lobes to feel the smooth stones I'd worn since dinner. Garnets? Opals? I couldn't remember. "We should have listened to Cassie," I said. "She foresaw something 'ugly.'"

"Val...."

"She did. Her 'sixth sense' warned us about January days."

"My dear...." Roddy was about to choose his words carefully, but I could predict the sentiments. "Cassandra is a lovely person, Val, and a good friend, but her imagination can run wild. This city has had quite enough of spiritualism. My parents remember Madame Blavatsky and her Egyptian hieroglyphics...zodiacs and a reincarnated Maltese cat... the town got its fill."

"Roddy—"

"—I know, Cassandra is a new generation, and some of her forecasts have come about, by coincidence. Purely by coincidence." He frowned and squinted. "Let's not veer off course."

This was no time to debate Cassie Forster's intuition. At times, my friend touched objects and sensed meanings that crossed time and space. My earring...? if Cassie's manicured fingers touched the ring of diamonds, what else might she have felt?

Roddy rubbed his fingers. "I asked Hoff whether the opera keeps a registry of guests in the Diamond Horseshoe just in case Charles Wendell wants to follow up with another rental. Hoff said not unless a box is reserved for particular persons. For all the recent press coverage, there's not a word about Rankin's friends or associates. And believe me, I did look."

I murmured about the newspapers' reference to Glenna May Rankin, the deceased's sister, and his son, Lewis, but I'd heard so very little with my ear pressed against the box partition during the *entr'acte*—the ear pressed close and the earring tucked in my palm for the moment. On that stalled note, Roddy and I went upstairs and said good night.

The day dawned bright and sunny, as if Mother Nature apologized for the snowfall, which was Papa's saying after blizzards on Nevada's Mount Davidson halted work in Virginia City, which perches on the mountainside about six thousand feet above sea level. Newcomers always got short-winded.

Roddy appeared at breakfast looking cheerful. "Val, look at this...."

"What is it?"

He slapped down an opera program from last December. "*La Traviata*," he said. The dog raised her head, sniffed, found nothing edible, and settled down.

My husband smiled as if he had landed a fish at a trout stream. "Good thing I kept a few programs," he said. "Notice the advertisements."

"For pianos," I said, turning the pages. "Here's Steinway, of course, and Knabe & Co. ...'workmanship, durability....'"

"Keep looking."

I detested guessing games, but Roddy's mood lifted my spirits. "Here's Runkel Brothers' Fine Vanilla Chocolate...."

"On the right side of that page, Val."

"Oh, I see it," I said. "'Star Coal...Leon L. Rankin, President...Offices...Trinity Building, 111 Broadway...and other offices too."

"And the wharf."

I read aloud, "'Foot of 23rd Street, East River.'"

"So, Rankin supported the opera," I said, "...commercially."

"For business, Val. Every upper East Side household buys tons of coal...houses like ours, a ton every week in cold weather."

"Roddy," I said, "I understand the butler takes charge of household supplies, but is our coal bin filled with—"

"—Rankin's Star Coal? No, ours is Hechscher's...my parents' preference."

My in-laws, yet again. The footman appeared, and I asked for the beans-and bacon hash I had enjoyed in the West. For Roddy, scrambled eggs, ham, toast, marmalade. He sipped his tea, and my weak coffee signaled a recovery from the last two morbid mornings, when I had welcomed the pale liquid. One of these days the kitchen would brew me a decent cup, but nothing compared to the campfire coffee and sourdough biscuits at the break of day when the sun flared over the peak, and each day so new....

Roddy's words focused the moment. "I'll go to the Trinity Building this morning," he said, "and if necessary, to the wharf. A Star Coal clerk must know something about Rankin's friends or associates."

"Doubtful that you'll hear about friends," I said, "for a man that's called a 'jackel.'"

"We'll see. And Val, about the carpet in our box… I could ask my mother…but…."

"Roddy, I have an idea. I'm not ready to attend the opera, but I can chat with the ushers and maids who work in the building. I'll say that I've come to see about new carpets for our box…maybe both boxes, since Mr. Hoff promised us 'complete restoration.' Someone might remember Rankin and his guests. Calista can go with me."

"Not Cassandra?"

"Cassie? Not today." I was tempted, but an errand at the opera house required undivided attention. My otherworldly friend might see an "aura" in the Diamond Horseshoe. I wouldn't take the chance. "Not this time, Roddy. This lady and her lady's maid on a winter afternoon."

"Mrs. DeVere, we have a plan."

By midmorning, New York City's Department of Street Cleaning showed the proud results of fast and furious snow clearance. Banks of snow mounded high on both sides of the pavement because the shovels flew before dawn. Footmen from every household had shoveled and scattered cinders on the stairs and front sidewalks, but Calista and I stepped cautiously outdoors into the cold afternoon, both bundled in dark wools and snow boots.

"Ma'am," my maid said, "in Greece, we slipped on olives that dropped from the trees. Here, a person can skid on a banana peel in the summertime, or on ice in winter…so let's not slip."

"Not!" I echoed. Calista Adrianakis was ever willing to pair up with me for outdoor errands. She had worked for years in all weathers on a coastal steamer, a stewardess assisting cabin passengers, no matter how thick the ice on wintry decks or how heavy the seas. Her trim figure moved efficiently, and her judgment guided my clothing choices. I counted on her.

Each breath sent little clouds as Calista and I left the hansom cab just after two p.m. at the entrance to the yellow brick opera house on Fortieth Street. The Metropolitan Opera did look like a commercial building, if not a brewery, perhaps a hotel. The front doors were locked, but I rapped on the window glass of the Louis Sherry restaurant inside at street level. If memory served, the dining room connected to an interior staircase to the *parterre* balcony, and the cooks and pastry chef would surely see us and open the door to the outdoor Ladies Entrance.

So they did, ushering us into a dining room filling with rich aromas from ovens and stovetop pots and pans. Not yet set for dinner, the tabletops stood bare. An aproned young woman approached and said, "Ladies, the restaurant will open at five p.m."

"For reasons of décor," I said, "I must see about my *parterre* box...the "Diamond Horseshoe." She softened at the magic words and offered my companion a seat at a table while waiting for me. "...and a cup of tea?"

I left Calista at a small corner table, crossed the room to the main staircase, took hold of my skirts, and climbed up to the Horseshoe corridor. At its center, I scanned the box numbers and name plates in dim light...Huntington, Livingston, Vanderbilt.... No one was in sight, and I began to retrace my steps when—

"You there...."

A box door had opened, and a rail-thin figure with a feather duster emerged, turned a key in the door lock and limped toward me. Her housemaid's uniform hung from frail shoulders, and a crooked name badge that said Sylvia... Sylvia Lilely.

"Could I help you, lady?"

She squinted as if to see through dimmed eyes, a woman old enough to be a great-grandmother.

"I am Mrs. DeVere," I said.

"You can't fool me," she said. "I know Mrs. DeVere by her voice. I helped her many times. Who might you be?"

"...Mrs. Roderick DeVere," I said. "Mrs. Roderick...."

A long pause, then "Oh, then, Junior...." She squinted close. "What's it you're after?"

"The DeVere box," I said.

"Box 17," she said, as if proud to know the number. "We're not to go in there now...not in 17 or 18 either."

"The Wendells' box," I said.

"—from Academy of Music times," she said. "I helped Mr. and Mrs. Josiah Wendell when the opera was at the Academy...before they came here, uptown. I'm here ever since." She twisted the feather duster. "I straighten up the saloons and the boxes...some of them, you'd be surprised."

"By the decorations?"

"By what you find." Her feather duster twirled.

I said, "Perhaps you know the gentleman who has rented Mr. Charles Wendell's box this winter?"

"We're not to go inside."

"I understand," I said, "but if you saw him...saw his guests...."

"Not like the Wendells, not one bit." She peered closer. "You better talk to Antony D."

"Who is—?"

"—Antony D.'s the one. If he's here...he sneaks downstairs, listens when they practice their singing...can't get enough of it. Wait here, and I'll see."

Left alone, I crossed the corridor to Boxes 17 and 18. The Wendell name plate had been shined bright. Pasteboard cards—'**Please do not enter**'—were push-pinned to both box doors. In the distance, a piano sounded, and voices up and down a scale. Then another scale, higher, and another....

"Mrs. DeVere?"

I turned to see a swarthy figure. "Oh," I said, "you're the usher who opens our door…when my husband and I attend the opera."

"I am Antony Dessey."

This stocky young man with a mass of curls and a dark caramel complexion bowed and stood on the balls of his feet. His broad face and warm brown eyes looked open to my questions, but his butler's apron and rubber gloves meant he was at work.

"Sylvia tells me you have a question, madam."

"About carpets," I said, "for these two boxes."

"—with apologies, but Boxes 17 and 18 are not to be opened at this time. We are under strict orders. We have no keys to those boxes." He peeled off one glove. "Your own box, I regret to say, is under repair."

"And Box 18, the Wendell box…."

"Also under repair."

I pointed to the brass nameplate. "Perhaps you polished this name plate?"

His smile showed a gap between two bright front teeth. "I believe Mr. DeVere asked me to do so…he shouldn't have needed to ask. I ought to have polished the plate before it tarnished."

"No need to apologize," I said.

"Even so…." He stood at full height, as if formally attired for the opera. "We ushers are responsible," he said, "for patrons' well-being. On that point, Mr. Hoff is definite."

"Mr. Hoff? He supervises the ushers?"

Antony smiled. "Custodians who also wish to be ushers are interviewed by Mr. Hoff. On opera nights and matinées, we line up for his inspection."

"But otherwise, your duties are...."

"...polishing, brushing...whatever they need."

I pointed to the two boxes. "The repairs," I said, "...are you at work on Box 17? Or Box 18?" I tried to sound casual.

He shook his head. "No. I wish I was," he said, "because the music sounds best in a box." He broke off. "Oh, do you hear the chorus? It's rehearsal...*The Barber of Seville*. Perhaps you will attend. The 'Barber' is a baritone. He rehearsed this noontime while I worked in the auditorium...just listen to those voices...listen...." He looked lost in the choral music. His voice, I had noticed, sounded soft and rounded, not like New York.

Quietly I said. "Mr....Antony, do you open the boxes for each performance?"

He reluctantly turned to me. "Certain boxes for each evening performance, yes." He glanced at his gloved hand. "The brass handrails need polish in the afternoons, so we hear all the rehearsals." His brown eyes clouded. "Ma'am, we do our jobs, but we listen to the music too. Why work as a custodian or usher if you don't love the music? The only better place is on the stage."

Did he mean to listen or perform? He began pulling his glove on, a sign that our talk was to end. "Last Monday night for *Don Giovanni*," I said quickly, "you opened our box...and also Box 18, which was rented this winter season to Mr. Rankin."

Both gloves on, Antony rocked back on his heels. "The gentleman in Box 18," he said, "has passed away, but we are not to speak of it." He added, "I did a little something special for his party on *Don Giovanni* night, and I hope his final hours were the better for my small effort."

Roddy has encouraged me to open space for others' voices. I waited.

Antony rocked forward, flexing his fingers. The rubber gloves squeaked. "Mr. Rankin asked for flower vases filled with ice…really, champagne buckets. And glasses and the bottles too. He took me aside on *La Traviata* night…the last night of December, to ask the favor. It was supposed to snow, but it didn't."

"December thirty-first," I said, "New Year's Eve."

"I think so…yes, he wanted the champagne opened and cooled when his party arrived…highly unusual…out of order. He said the *Don Giovanni* night would be very special and could I do him the big favor. I managed to do it. A small favor. If you'll excuse me now…perhaps I will see you and Mr. DeVere and open your box for *The Barber of Seville*. The repair will be done, I am sure."

He disappeared, a piano sounded, and operatic voices swelled. Antony was back on duty, the maid Sylvia nowhere in sight, and Calista waited for me downstairs. I went down, and we went home.

I had barely got my coat and gloves off before Roddy leaned close and murmured "Hell's Kitchen." He had been waiting impatiently for me in an anteroom near the foyer.

He said, "A Baptist church in Hell's Kitchen, and the service is tomorrow."

"What service," I asked. "What kitchen?"

"It's a neighborhood, Val…on the west side…cheap lodging houses…and a Baptist church. A memorial service for Leon Rankin will take place in the morning…ten a.m. A clerk at the Trinity Building told me…fellow named Taggart. Elmer Taggart. Let's sit down."

I settled on a rococo sofa, and Roddy pulled up a chair. Our dog trotted in, and I lifted her beside me on the sofa. She licked my hand. "It's not a funeral?"

"No," said Roddy. "A memorial service only…no casket."

"No casket, no body." I let out a big breath. "We don't know where the deceased Mr. Rankin is…."

"No, we don't know," Roddy said.

The room went quiet. The dog snuggled beside me. "You learned about the service at the Star Coal office…on Broadway?"

"The headquarters, yes. Busy place, all four telephones ringing, and messengers running in and out, and telegrams. The coal comes into the city by train and ship, and customers worry their furnaces will go cold."

"Because of Rankin's death?"

"Star Coal is a major supplier, Val, and publicity about the death has rattled households and businesses too. The clerks were assuring customers their coal will be delivered, no interruptions."

I rubbed Velvet's ears, and she almost purred. "Who will attend the service?" I asked. "The Star Coal clerks and managers, I would imagine…."

"And surely Leon Rankin's sister and his son," Roddy said.

"Glenna May Rankin from Florida," I said, "…and son Lewis, whatever his age, wherever he lives. The papers didn't say, did they?"

"No."

"If he's an adult," I said, "maybe he's in the Star Coal business."

"We'll probably find out."

"We?" I said.

"—because Mr. and Mrs. Roderick DeVere will be at the Calvary Baptist Church in the morning." Roddy spoke with a tang in his words. "Let's hope the late Mr. Rankin's opera guests attend their host's memorial service. We need a good daytime look at them…for an inquiry on the 'q.t.'"

Chapter Seven

A FINE BAPTIST CHURCH had risen on the Upper West Side, Roddy said, with a rose window and handsome arches, but the church in Hell's Kitchen was another story. We passed blocks of snaggle-toothed wood and brick buildings strung along on West 46th Street, boardinghouses and storage sheds, a livery stable, and a butcher. The Calvary Baptist Church stood bravely, a modest structure of stone and red brick, though the cross atop its steeple slanted as if it might topple.

"Was Rankin a Baptist?" I had asked. Roddy didn't know. The newspapers had not reported a religious affiliation. The street had not been cleared, and at 9:30 we stepped from our carriage into mushy snow. Roddy asked Noland to circle the blocks slowly, to keep the horses moving and we would meet the carriage after the service.

We climbed the cement front stairs and entered a sanctuary that smelled of mildew and rusty pipes. Large wood crosses hung on whitewashed side walls, and dusty windowpanes filtered dull light onto a dozen rows of hard pews. No one was present. A pulpit with a massive Bible stood on a raised platform at the front, and a door in the far corner was shut. Why this sad outpost to commemorate the "Coal King" who could well afford Tiffany windows?

A rear pew would let us see everyone who walked down the center aisle. In minutes, a thin man entered from the door by the pulpit. He held a wood chair that he placed by the door, then hastened down the aisle to station himself at the main door. A sexton? He wore no clerical collar.

A moment later, the entrance opened behind us, and an older, veiled woman slowly moved up the aisle. She wore a broadtail mink coat that engulfed her tiny frame, and she stepped gingerly in high-heeled black boots that looked quite new. She also leaned heavily on her escort's arm for balance. Roddy whispered, "Val, that man is Elmer Taggart, the Star Coal clerk. The lady is probably Rankin's sister." Seated in a front pew, she hunched inside her coat. The church was not warm. We kept coats on too. The clerk looked uncertain about what to do. She patted the seat beside her, and he sat.

The next minutes saw ten or twelve men walk heavily forward, hats in hand and buttoned into thick coats with fleece or sealskin collars. I wondered which one might be Lewis Rankin, the deceased's son. Was he the jowly younger man with mutton-chop whiskers, or the portly fellow with a goatee who slapped his gloves against a thigh as he walked?

Or perhaps the starchy one who eyed the pews disdainfully, as if sitting in any of them was beneath him.

Those three took the middle pews, along with several others, probably employees of Star Coal or other Rankin businesses. Front pews were always held for family and closest friends. Someone coughed, and boot soles shuffled. I glanced at my little gold Cartier watch (a gift from Roddy) on its chain deep inside the folds of my black mourning attire. Two minutes before ten a.m. A pipe organ would have been calming.

At that instant, growling voices erupted behind us at the church entrance, and two men walked stiffly side by side up the aisle, one clutching his top hat, the other a fedora. They slowed their pace midway, seeming reluctant to break off their heated words. Surprise...they went to the very front and sat in the pew opposite the lady in broadtail mink. Their heads turned in her direction and nodded, as if to doff hats that were already off. She did not appear to acknowledge their presence.

The door by the pulpit opened, and a tall, pale young minister in clerical garb appeared with a stout woman in a black bombazine gown and religious crosses dangling from each ear. I fingered my own earrings, black pearls, both intact. The woman sat on the wood chair. A deaconess? Did Baptists include women in mourning rites? The minister stepped to the pulpit and cleared his throat to speak, but at that moment a man and woman entered the church and walked quickly forward, seeming together but separate. Her heavy black silks rustled, her perfume thickened the air, and the ostrich plumes on her wide-brimmed hat floated and waved. She sat by herself in an empty pew, while her companion—if he was a companion—marched up to the very front, as if to commandeer the pulpit, then swung left, yanked off his fur cap, and sat in the same pew as the two arguing men, but at a distance. The three men nodded at each other like bristling dogs. None of the three looked young enough to be Leon Rankin's son. The lady in broadtail did not move.

"Dear friends and family, I am Reverend Calkins, and today we gather in memory of our brother, Leon Lee Rankin. The Calvary Baptist Church welcomes one and all...." He continued, "...saddened by the passing, rejoicing that his soul...at long last, at rest...in the arms of...."

Reverend Calkins led a prayer and delivered a short eulogy that sounded from a seminary handbook, what Papa called "boilerplate." If Leon Rankin ever worshipped here, one would not know it from this pastor.

Fumbling in a robe pocket, he retrieved a paper and a pair of wire-frame spectacles, which he adjusted before studying the paper. "Regrettable circumstances prevent Mr. Lewis Rankin from joining us today," he announced.

I nudged Roddy at this first useful bit of information, that Leon's son was a "Mister," meaning at least eighteen years of age.

"...and Miss Glenna May Rankin...beloved sister of Leon Lee.... Aunt of Leon's dear son, Lewis.... Miss Glenna

May will represent the Rankin family this morning." The minister nodded to the figure in the broadtail coat.

An awkward moment passed while he pored over the paper. "To recall the works and days," he said, "we will hear tributes from those who knew Leon in life. We call upon Mr. Jeremy Dent...is Mr. Dent among us? Mr. Dent?"

The space felt eerily quiet until one of the two bristling men arose from the front pew and turned, nodded to the lady in the mink coat, and fixed us all with a hard stare. His opened greatcoat showed a brocade vest and a tie with a diamond stickpin that caught the light. A thin black moustache streaked a long face with brooding eyes and a rat-trap mouth. Mr. Jeremy Dent reminded me of a Civil War photograph of soldiers ready to fire a cannon.

"Leon and I go back," he said, "before a lot of things... history, you might say...boys in the hills and hollers...West Virginia." His tone rose defiantly. "We fished and shot squirrels. Fifty-fifty, we split up what we caught and shot. It wasn't sport. It was food." His jaw tightened.

I glanced sideways at a whitewashed wall. To depend on this stern man for food.... Pity his family, if he had a family.

"Leon's folks settled in Suggs Run," he continued, "and my family in Barret. We both went to Barret School, and Leon took to math, ran numbers in his head, way ahead of the teacher. He got hold of her math book and swallowed it in a day or two. And he tied a rock on a string and took it outside along property lines and said he was measuring for a survey. Some thought he was touched in the head."

Jeremy Dent scowled. "Railroads and coal, West Virginia is coal mines. And railroads. And hard feelings. The Barret rail line ran along the Barret River. The Dents settled first… Grandpappy owned the land along the river, and Dents laid track to the Keymont mine, which was new at the time."

He paused and fingered his stick pin. "But a river in flood time, what a flood can do…over the banks…the washout…." He broke off. "The Dents," he said, "came from a long line of storekeepers and ought to have kept to themselves, minded the store. Anyway, Leon and I grew up and lost touch. I did not go down in the mines with him. I heard that he mined coal and also learned about accounting. The Keymont people took to him, and when the Barret River flooded out the rail line, it was Leon that came to see us and offered a deal. The Dents took it. Before we knew what was up, the Barret & Nitro Railroad Company hauled coal, and Leon Rankin was treasurer."

Jeremy Dent's eyes seemed fixed on the men in the middle pews. "The Star Coal Company," he said, "got its start in the Barret & Nitro Railroad. Leon Rankin got his start from track laid by the Dent family men. I did not lay eyes on Leon or talk to him for many years, but this New York visit was supposed to let bygones be bygone. So, gentlemen, let Leon Lee Rankin rest in peace."

The minister, who had been standing at the side, skipped forward with his paper as Jeremy Dent sat down. I breathed deeply and rolled my shoulders. The men in the middle pews stirred, as if they, too, had felt the bitter taste of Dent's words.

"Thank you, Mr. Dent, for your warmest appreciation. And now…." The minister stammered. "Now may we hear from…from Mr. John Griggs, a good friend of…of many years…."

The second "bristling" man sprang up, flung down his overcoat, and stepped in front of the pulpit. Of medium height, he was bald and paunchy, his suit coat straining at the buttons. He struck the sort of pose recommended in mail-order lessons on leadership. John Griggs reminded me of a pompous haberdasher in Virginia City. Papa had bought extra shirts because he felt sorry for the man.

"We of the banking business," he began, "are often regarded with suspicion by our friends and neighbors. A banker's lot is seldom a happy one." He paused as if to share his unhappiness. "The Griggs Banking Company," he said, "was founded by my late father in Pittsburgh, Pennsylvania. Upon his passing, it was my honor to succeed him as president of the company."

He slid one palm into his waistcoat, a pose I had seen in portraits of Napoleon Bonaparte. "As I learned," he said, "a most important loan on the Griggs books was to the Barret & Nitro Railroad Company, with collateral being a locomotive from the Baldwin Company…and the hopper wagons too. Very good collateral, you must understand."

He looked at the tiny woman in the broadtail mink coat. "You brother did me a great favor," he said, "and I will proclaim it…a great favor to the Griggs Bank." His arm swept high. "We know that rumors can start a panic…that people fear a bank will fail...their hard-earned money disappear." He paused as if waiting for a response, seeming to forget that finance was not a topic for a church memorial.

"...and so the rumors spread like poison, and depositors lined up for blocks to withdraw their savings...for whole city blocks." He faced Glenna Rankin and spoke solely to her. "No bank worth its salt would keep that much money in its vault. It might as well be stashed in a coffee tin. The money is loaned and invested, but people don't understand, so the withdrawals kept on for days, and we were low on cash. We could have failed, but Leon Rankin arranged a fast loan from Keymont Coal...and the Griggs bank lived for another day."

He suddenly clasped his hands together and almost hugged himself. The bluster had turned into something like an entreaty. "When the Griggs Banking Company lost its lease on life, it wasn't clear that Leon Rankin was the responsible party. A bank's lifetime is not guaranteed. It wasn't clear, and who am I to judge?"

John Griggs reminded me, just then, of a pudgy young English teacher in Virginia City. He had endured the big boys' heckling and dodged their spitballs. Amused but embarrassed, the rest of us cheered when he fled at midyear. The cheering, however, felt hollow, the same feeling this minute in the church as I watched this man struggle.

"The coal business differs from the banking business," Griggs continued, "and the benefit of the doubt is best. It is true, Miss Rankin, that some say your brother and I parted ways on bad terms. This visit to New York City gives the lie to such opinions. Mr. Leon Rankin showed himself to be the best host. May he rest for all eternity."

Griggs leaned closer toward Leon Rankin's sister. I thought he might try to join her, but Reverend Calkins, to my surprise, took command and nudged him to the pew with Jeremy Dent and the third "bristling" man.

Before the minister could consult his paper, a fair-haired man rose from the pew, stood, faced us, planted his legs far apart, and folded his arms across a sunken chest. "Amos Nathan Suggs," he announced in rasping tones, "from Suggs Run…Suggs Run."

The name from newspaper obituaries, I recalled, along with New Orleans and Palm Beach, Florida.

"You'll find it on the map because the railroad passes through Barret and goes near the Keymont mine." He glowered. "But Mordecai Suggs came first, before the Rankins and the Dents, either one…long before any of them." Amos Suggs's fearless blue eyes distracted me from a face with off-center features, a thin nose and wide mouth, a narrow forehead and sharp chin. His shoulders could not quite square, and his neck seemed both scrawny and thick. His complexion struck me as a faded suntan. The double-breasted black suit he wore looked made to measure, but somehow Suggs's body defied the tailoring.

He peered into the distance of his family's past. "Mordecai Suggs came first," he said again, "and every Suggs thereafter cut timber and raised hogs…the women kept chickens and gardens…all before the coal."

He tightened his arms. "So, Leon and me, we went into the mine together. Way down, you squat, you crawl, you hope to God the timbers hold, and you work your pick and shovel. The rock will rub your shoulders raw, but you meet your quota, load up the wagons, take it one day at a time."

His lips pressed together. "Leon got promoted to foreman, but we still went down together. Eight of us, me and Leon and six more men in a shaft. By rights, the cave-in should have killed us all. Dust and thunder, that's what it was. I got free, couldn't see one thing, no lights, no way out... crawled on my belly...and heard Leon call out, 'Help me, help me.' But coal dust meant an explosion any minute... one spark, and boom. But I stopped."

He looked up at the rafters of the church, as if the beams were timbers in the coal mine of his past. "Leon got pinned under rocks, both legs... couldn't recollect how, not to this day, but I pushed and dragged, and we made it out. The other six...my two cousins, Len and Vern, good men...Keymont closed the shaft, sealed it up. My cousins...gone...." He blinked and wiped his eyes on his sleeve.

"Why the cave-in? Some say it's the Lord's will, but folks did talk. Leon was foreman, and he studied coal mining mathematics, and he wasn't going down in the mines much longer. No matter what, sooner or later he was going upstairs in the office."

Amos Suggs took a long look at all of us in the pews. "He took me with him," he said simply. "Leon said I brought him luck, like a brother, and better off wherever life took me...took us. All these years building up Star Coal, I was with him, and New Orleans and the last few years in Florida...Palm Beach, Florida. A different world, Palm Beach." He paused.

"Leon came to New York on business, but this trip was for a good time, and he showed us a good time. We none of us know when it's our final time. One thing sure, none of us knew Leon's time had come."

Pivoting, he sat, and Reverend Calkins beckoned to the women in the bombazine gown. "Mrs. Ferber will sing for us," he announced as she rose from the wood chair, came forward, and blew a pitch pipe. A favorite Baptist hymn," the minister said, "'There Is Power in the Blood.'"

The sacred and profane jostled in my mind as she sang in a quavering soprano. On high notes, her earrings danced, and I looked away. After a closing prayer, Reverend Calkins invited all present to visit with one another in the vestibule and to sign the album held by the sexton.

I recalled no vestibule in this church and doubted that anyone would linger to exchange pleasantries in the Arctic air. Roddy and I stood and waited until everyone had filed out—the veiled Glenna May Rankin escorted by the clerk, and then John Griggs with his top hat and Jeremy Dent holding his fedora, each coldly eyeing the other. Amos Suggs came next, pausing at the pew where the perfumed woman with the wide-brimmed hat fastened her silks. She took his arm, though she and Suggs looked estranged as they came toward us down the aisle. Her hair had slipped from the hat, and peculiar yellow curls—really, coils—caught my eye. Her teardrop earrings jounced. Roddy looked hard at her as she passed us, and he nudged me, but the dozen men from the middle pews crowded the aisle and blocked my view. I caught sight of the minister at the doorway. He had somehow come around from the outside and shook hands with the men but bowed to the lady in mink and the woman in the ostrich-plumed hat.

Roddy and I were the last to leave. Several hansom cabs at the street awaited the men in the middle rows, and they were off and gone, as was the woman in the huge hat, who took a cab by herself. The only remaining carriage was ours, but a glistening, shellacked horse-drawn omnibus opened its doors for those who had sat in the front pew. A groom helped the veiled lady in mink inside, and the men followed, last of all the Star Coal clerk. The sexton, shivering in his thin coat, held the memorial album for our signature, and Roddy signed for both of us while I looked closely at the signatures. A quick gracious word to Reverend Calkins, and Roddy and I stepped quickly into our carriage. "Noland," my husband said, "please follow that omnibus. I believe the passengers are going to a hotel."

Chapter Eight

RODDY GUESSED THE BREVOORT Hotel or the Hoffman House, but the omnibus made its way to 59th Street to the entrance to the Plaza, where we watched brass-buttoned doormen helping passengers into the hotel. A tangle of carriages and delivery wagons stalled us long enough to see each person step from the shellacked 'bus and disappear into the hotel's front door. Except for the Star Coal clerk, every person we had seen in the front pews of the Calvary Baptist Church was presumably headed to the elevator and a private room.

Roddy and I went home, just a few blocks up Fifth Avenue. Noland took the horses and carriage to the stable where Apollo and Atlas were kept. At Roddy's suggestion, we quickly changed from mourning black to clothing for afternoon teatime at the Plaza.

"What makes you certain that Glenna May Rankin will have tea with us?" I asked. We sat over warmed-up stew in a nook off a drawing room as a clock struck one p.m. Velvet sat at our feet, hoping for her share.

"I'm not at all 'certain,' Val, but her brother's opera box is a concern, and she might be persuaded by a kindly note of invitation." He added, "If we could talk to her before she goes back to Florida…."

"Or if she would talk to us," I said, sipping my glass of water. "So strange this morning, those three men nodding toward her face, which was veiled. But she looked straight forward and gave them all the cold shoulder. I thought the banker was about to sit down beside her. The pew had plenty of room."

"It did." Roddy put down his spoon. "And why was the Star Coal clerk her escort? If she grew up with her brother in West Virginia, she ought to know two of them…Amos Suggs and—"

"—and Jeremy Dent," I said.

Roddy pushed his chair back. "When I visited the Star Coal office, the clerk told me about the memorial service, but made no mention of Rankin's sister."

"Or where Leon Rankin is to be buried…."

"Or is already interred," Roddy said, "because the morgue is no final resting place."

I shuddered. "Not a single word from the minister or the three men about a cemetery or a family plot…or mausoleum."

"No."

"—and the woman in the ostrich plumes, Roddy...the hair in coils.... You recognized her, didn't you? ...the woman who was in the opera box with Rankin?"

"A possibility, Val...." My husband often resisted the obvious, which irked me no end.

"Coils," I said, "are not in fashion." My voice rose, and the dog scratched an ear. "Her hair," I said, "looked like lacquered bedsprings. You noticed her hair in the opera box. If she was in the Rankin party at *Don Giovanni*, then the three men who spoke at the church were most likely also—"

"—most likely," Roddy repeated, "but not conclusively."

Roddy had asked me not to mistake his patient calculations for confusion. I tried, most of the time.

"Leon Rankin's sister," he said, "might help us clarify the situation...and explain the reason for the memorial service in Hell's Kitchen.

"...such a sad church," I said, "not like a monastery that's meant to be plain...more like...poor." Our dog began sniffing the carpet for crumbs.

Roddy scratched her back. "So, Val, a note to Miss Rankin to suggest tea at the Plaza this afternoon...."

In minutes, I sat at my writing desk with *Manners, Culture, and Dress of the Best American Society*, which insisted on "heavy, plain, white, unruled paper, folded once" and a "square envelope to match." I read: "Endeavor to make your style clear, precise, elegant, and appropriate."

I endeavored. "Our sympathies...regrets that we did not make acquaintance this morning at the church...hesitate to intrude…your dear late brother …Metropolitan Opera box…my husband's obligation…the Plaza Hotel tearoom at…at three p.m. this afternoon."

"Done, Roddy," I said. "Signed, sealed, and—"

"—delivered in the next hour. I'll send a footman to the Plaza and hope he'll bring an answer."

The footman returned without an answer. "I waited in the lobby, sir…ma'am, and a bellhop delivered the note to Miss Rankin's suite—"

"Not a room, but a suite?" I asked.

He nodded. "I said that a response was requested, but the bellhop came back empty handed."

"Thank you, Chalmers."

So, bundled in furs and taking a chance, we set off for the Plaza at two p.m., walking as quickly as the lumpy packed snow permitted. We reached the Plaza tearoom at 2:50, slightly out of breath, our fingertips and noses chilled.

Roddy requested a table for four in the center of the room. "We should be visible, Val. Let's hope Miss Rankin feels curious or obliged."

"Or bored in her suite," I added.

We sipped tea but delayed the tiered tray of scones and finger sandwiches until our "guest" arrived. On our third cup, after four o'clock, I was ready to go home. No one resembling the petite Miss Rankin had appeared. The room had filled with hotel guests and others eager to escape the cold. I found myself peering at ladies' earrings and fingering my own. Calista had asked whether I planned to replace the lost hoop. I said no, and she murmured that a lost earring meant bad luck in her native Greece, but maybe not in America. I had no reply.

The clink of silver against china mixed with cheerful conversation. "Roddy," I said, "let's go before it gets dark and the sidewalks ice up."

He signaled to the waiter, but at that minute, I tapped his arm. "There she is… Miss Rankin."

Unveiled, the petite figure at the entrance scanned the tearoom with the gaze of a schoolteacher who brooked no nonsense. Wearing a black-on-black dress and jacket, she leaned on a stout cane as a tearoom attendant brought her to our table.

On his feet, Roddy pulled out a chair. "Miss Rankin…." He bowed and introduced us.

She sat, ignored his bow, hooked her cane over the empty chair, and pressed two fingers of my extended hand. Her knuckles were gnarled…from age? Illness? Or the hard work of a lifetime? Fierce eyes and a tanned, narrow face reminded me of her brother's newspaper photograph, but her supple mouth was nowhere in the photo of Leon Rankin. With silver-gray upswept hair and dark brown eyes, she appeared resolute. Her brother had died at fifty-two years of age, I recalled, but whether Glenna May was younger or older was anybody's guess.

"So kind of you to join us," Roddy said, "at this difficult time." The waiter appeared. "And will you have tea?"

Unfolding her napkin, she barely nodded.

"Ceylon oolong, please," Roddy said, "and service for a light afternoon tea."

The waiter disappeared. We Westerners were not "big" on light conversation, but it was my turn. "Miss Rankin," I said, "our New York winter must be quite a change from Florida.... I believe you live in Florida? Palm Beach?"

"The last three years down there," she said, "when Leon took a notion to build in Palm Beach."

"And before that," Roddy said, "West Virginia?"

"Born and raised," she said, then reached into a sleeve and produced my note. She put it on the table as if to critique my handwriting, which was no point of pride.

Roddy seemed about to speak, but I followed a hunch. "Isn't West Virginia called The Mountain State?" I asked. "I grew up in Colorado and Nevada."

Those brown eyes did not twinkle. She said, "That's Rocky Mountains," and fell silent. So much for common ground.

Two waiters appeared with a teapot, cream, lemon wedges, a tray of scones and sandwiches, and little plates. The next minutes were spent pouring, choosing, sipping, and tasting. Miss Rankin broke apart a scone and looked ready to dip it into her tea. Instead, she took a bite and moved my note to the side.

"I regret that we did not make acquaintance at the memorial service this morning," Roddy said. His somber words were drowned by sudden laughter from a nearby table, and our guest looked resigned.

I said, "It must be difficult…being the only family member here…the only one…."

She slowly roused herself as if to answer a call. "There used to be scores of Rankins," she said. "The Rankins settled all over…mountains, ridges, foothills…all over…until diphtheria."

I could have choked. "Diphtheria," I cried. "My mother died of diphtheria. I never knew her."

She suddenly touched my hand, her brown eyes softer. "It rages in," she said gently, "comes on like a storm, and nothing to do but pray. There's hardly a man left to dig the graves."

We fell silent, sipping our tea, huddled from merriment at other tables.

"Quietly Roddy said. "We regret to add to your concerns, Miss Rankin, but the opera box—"

"—my brother wanted his own box," she said abruptly. "He didn't like to own things outright as a rule, but he wanted his own box…if it was for sale. He said a 'deal' was in the works."

"But friends of ours rented to him for this season," Roddy said. "Mr. and Mrs. Wendell are out of the country, and I agreed to care for their box. If another member of the Rankin family ought to be consulted …perhaps Mr. Lewis Rankin?"

"My nephew," she said, and her mouth moved as if tasting something sweet and sour. "Perhaps you know that my brother is divorced from Lewis's mother, wherever she is…."

We paused. Miss Rankin changed the subject.

"Lewis was with us in Palm Beach for Christmas," she said, "but he's visiting in New Orleans now...and going off to hunt wild pigs in Louisiana, and then I don't know what all...or where."

She reached for her tea. "When the news came to Palm Beach about...my brother's passing...." She lifted her cup. "I got the express train right away, but I thought, what would my brother want? He would want his son to be spared any bad news about his daddy's health, just like Leon made us do at Christmas. He said not to talk about it."

She sipped her tea, and Roddy glanced at me. "Mr. Rankin's health...?" I said.

Her teacup snapped down in its saucer. "My brother always said, 'What do doctors know?' He called them quacks. He said, 'Take what they say with a grain of sand.'"

"Sand?" said Roddy. "Not 'salt'?"

"Florida doctors," she said. "There's miles of sand down there." She paused. "The Christmas weather was nice, and the Royal Poinciana Hotel put out a feast every night. Lewis played golf and went fishing in the ocean. My brother would want his son to remember last Christmas, not get dragged through that service this morning. I sent Lewis a telegram. One of us with blood boiling ought to be plenty."

"—at the Calvary Baptist Church," I said.

"A church that's out of the way, so the newspapers wouldn't come. Mr. Taggart knows about Reverend Calkins's church because it's a Star Coal charity church. A winter's free coal is persuasion enough. The minister was glad to help out.

"And I knew who would come," she said, so I was ready. They were all here to make amends in New York, banquets and actresses paid for by my brother."

"You mean stage plays?" Roddy asked.

"I said 'actresses.' She paused. "I tried talking sense to my brother, but he went ahead." She tugged a black handkerchief from a sleeve and dabbed at her eyes. "I tried to get him to go to a New York doctor. I heard about a contrivance that measures the pressure of blood inside the body. Some Italian doctor...it fits on your arm like a cuff and does not hurt one bit. Leon said nothing doing. Now we've lost him. The apoplexy killed him."

My husband and I sat quietly, not moving. It felt sacrilegious to eat or drink.

"Leon was my baby brother," she said. "There's just two years between us, but he was the baby. Folks couldn't reckon with him because he was different."

"How different?" Roddy prodded gently.

Miss Rankin's brown eyes looked faraway, and a little smile played at the corner of her mouth. "There's a saying about a goodhearted man, he'd give you the shirt off his back. Leon made fun of it. 'Shirtless? What good if I'm shirtless?'"

She smiled more broadly. "He meant he'd help folks when the time came that he could give out shirts to everybody in need...or in want. Scripture says, 'a time to plant, a time to pluck up what is planted' and 'a time to every purpose under the heaven.' He'd quote it by heart. Leon saw his purpose. The Rankins have gumption. Folks talked when I went on to high school. 'Foolery,' they called it."

"In Suggs Run?" I tried to picture it.

She scoffed. "Barretville High School," she said, "...four miles from Suggs Run, and across the Barret River, and I set out in the dark, rode a mule the four miles to the river landing, tied up the mule and paddled across...unless the river was up too high."

"You had a boat?" Roddy asked.

"Half boat, half raft. Most days, the current wasn't too fast. The school was close enough to walk when I got across. I carried my books and school clothes in a sack, and a teacher let me change before the first bell. I'd change back after the last bell and wind my way back. Took five years, but I got my high school diploma, which certified me to teach school, which I did for many years."

Her brown eyes shone. "The Suggs Run pupils learned their 'three R's' in my schoolroom, lots of them by the name of Suggs and Dent. We Rankins...when we set our minds, our minds are set...barring sickness or the unforeseen."

Glenna May tapped her walking cane on the empty chair. "That," she said, "was unforeseen." She looked from Roddy to me. "Never needed a cane in West Virginia. But in Florida, I skidded on a big red flower called a hibiscus... turned an ankle but good."

Roddy said, "My mother suffered a sprain several years ago. It took a long time to heal. She did not like to use my father's cane."

News to me, my mother-in-law hobbling on my father-in-law's cane. Three years and seven months married to Roddy, and what else was I to learn about Eleanor and Rufus DeVere? Distracted by the thought of Eleanor choosing among Rufus's many canes and walking sticks, I snapped back to hear Glenna May respond to whatever Roddy had asked.

"...no, we Rankins weren't much for farming. A garden patch, a few chickens, but Leon said our flock mainly kept the foxes fed. He said coal would be our crop, and we better be the ones to reap it. Without my brother's gumption, we'd have been like the Suggs folks, salting a hog or two for the winter, or the Dents...too busy frittering their good fortune away."

"Good fortune?" I asked.

"The money they got from the riverfront land and the washed-out railroad. My brother brought them more money than they would ever see in five lifetimes. Where did it go? Flashy jewelry and Easter bonnets and whatnot. I believe the Sears and Roebuck mail-order company got most of it. The Dents are spenders."

"Then the Dent family had no connection to Mr. Griggs's bank," Roddy said.

Her voice tightened "Mr. John Griggs...Leon called him 'Weepy' Griggs...not to his face, of course."

Roddy glanced at me. "Weepy?" I asked. "Like tears?"

"Some womenfolk are not cut out for school teaching," Glenna May said. "And my brother said some men better stay out of the bank business."

"Mr. Griggs?" I murmured. She nodded.

A waiter stopped at the table. The finger sandwiches lay untouched, the bread dry and sunken. Would we care for another pot of tea?

"Tea, Miss Rankin?"

"No thanks. I ought to be going along." She gazed around the tearoom. "My brother wasn't much for tea...but maybe he came in here to think about the hotel he planned for Florida...maybe he sat right here." She tucked her handkerchief into her sleeve and appraised the space with new regard. "One thing sure, the Rankin hotel suites would be bigger."

"Oh?" Roddy said.

"Leon grumbled his Plaza suite gave him cramps. I said, 'Leon, build yourself a mansion up there in New York. Whatever you pay the Plaza for that suite, you could have yourself a palace.'"

She shook her head, and wisps of silver-gray caught the light. "He said the location suited him, but I beg to differ. Fact is, the bellhops and the maids fussed over him like he was family. So did theatre actresses. I think he tried not to feel lonesome."

She pushed back her sleeves, as if at a blackboard with chalk. "And the doorman called him 'Colonel Rankin.' Why men like to be called 'Colonel' is beyond me, but I'll tell you, I never felt so close to my brother as upstairs in his suite... his clothes and shoes...especially his shoes...all handmade. Back in West Virginia, it was different...."

She looked to the side, her eyes welling. "I'm to meet Mr. Taggart for dinner. He has papers for me to sign... more papers, just like Leon always put in front of me. 'Just write your name in big enough letters,' he'd say. 'Put down Glenna May Rankin here...and here...and here," till my fingers cramped. Anyway, Mr. Taggart promises to teach me about the Star Coal Company, and I will be his pupil... the teacher becomes a pupil...but no mule, no river to cross." She folded my note, tucked it into a sleeve, gathered her napkin and leaned in.

Our heads bent toward her.

"I don't mind telling you...my brother is now laid to rest in the Calvary Church cemetery."

Roddy gasped, and my jaw dropped. My husband managed to echo Miss Rankin's words, as if he hadn't heard what he heard. In my mind, Leon Rankin's body hadn't left the morgue. I suspected Roddy felt the same.

"A poky graveyard out back of the church," Glenna May said. "It's like the family plots around Suggs Run. Mr. Taggart made arrangements, and the minister found space enough. The ground was frozen like a rock, but they managed."

"But for peace of mind," I said, "wouldn't Mr. Rankin be at rest near you in Florida?" I asked.

"—with salt water three feet down? No ma'am."

"Or West Virginia?" Roddy asked, as if Leon Rankin's body had become portable.

Glenna May Rankin's hands tightened to hard fists. "West Virginia," she said, "but not Suggs Run...not near

Keymont or a Star Coal mine, and that's pretty much the whole state, one way or another. If you listened, you heard Jeremy Dent this morning, and for once, he had it right—there's coal mines and railroads and hard feelings... feelings that stay hard." She looked at Roddy. "You know about hard coal?"

"Anthracite," Roddy said. "It burns hottest."

She nodded, stood, reached for her cane, and said, "Feelings," she said, "burning hot as anthracite coal."

Chapter Nine

WE WALKED HOME IN darkness from the Plaza, the temperature dropping with every block we passed. Coats off, we skipped upstairs to our favorite Bergere chairs. Velvet vaulted on her hind legs and settled between us as a footman lighted the fireplace birch logs and went to fetch Roddy's wheeled cart. "I think we're up for Whisky Skins, Val."

"What?"

"A standard drink," he said, but I have tweaked it a bit." My husband requested a thermos of hot water, and I stood before the fire rubbing my hands. In moments, I heard a cork pop, pouring, stirring, and a warm glass was put into my hand.

"Salud, Val."

"Salud, my dear Roderick." We sipped, welcoming the warmth. My papa always liked his nip of Irish whiskey, and I hadn't known about smoky spirits from the Scottish Isles. "Yum," I said.

Whisky Skin Cocktail

Ingredients
- 2 ounces scotch whisky
- 4 ounces water at boiling point
- 1 teaspoon sugar
- Lemon peel

Directions:
1. Pour water and sugar into tumbler.
2. Add whisky.
3. Squeeze peel to release citrus oil, add, and serve.

We sipped the hot drinks before the fire. "Rankin's sister offered no information about the opera box after all," I said to Roddy.

"I'll wire Charles in the morning," he said, "but the Wendells' box is the least of Glenna May's worries."

"What a jolt," I said, "that Leon Rankin has been buried in the Calvary churchyard cemetery."

"It made sense from his sister's outlook," Roddy said, "no publicity, and no 'hard feelings' if his body were taken back to West Virginia." Roddy sipped his drink "Ghoulish to say this, perhaps, but the frozen ground could be helpful…."

My husband said nothing more. Leon Rankin, now six feet under, would be a prime candidate for the Coroner's inquest if our inquiry on the "q.t." made headway before the spring thaw. I pictured the Commissioner of Police returning my earring with an apology, and my donation of the diamond hoop pair to charity. I also imagined the Commissioner showing my earring to the chief of police and the mayor, fingering the diamonds and guessing why Valentine DeVere's earring was found lying near Leon Rankin's dead body.

Roddy added a log to the fire, and I rubbed Velvet's ears, which she liked, purring like a cat. I said, "Glenna May is grief-stricken...comforted in her brother's Plaza suite, but truly mourning his loss."

"She might be the only one...except for his son," Roddy replied, shifting in his chair. "Miss Rankin's feelings for young Lewis seemed mixed, but her scorn for the homefolks was obvious. Quite simply, the Dents had squandered their windfall, and the Suggs clan was shiftless."

"And the banker..." I said, "'Weepy' Griggs...her brother despised the man, and Glenna May seemed to agree." I sipped my drink. "She said that 'actresses' and hotel workers kept her brother from feeling lonely, but she did not seem to know the woman with the blonde 'coils.'"

"And yet," Roddy said, "the woman entered the church with Amos Suggs, and he escorted her out." He turned to me. "Of course, a gentleman extends courtesies to a lady—"

"—but the woman in the pew was...a spectacle, too much perfume, and that hat.... Those charcoal ostrich plumes bobbed like pennants in a breeze. Whoever she is, she wants to be noticed."

"The puzzle," Roddy said, "is why those three men were Rankin's guests. None of them voiced any affection for the man, nor for one another. Both Dent and Suggs sounded bitter, and the banker seemed grateful but needy...or grateful because he is needy. He looked 'weepy.' He did."

I gazed at the fire. "Whatever did she mean by making 'amends'? Whose 'amends?'" The flames danced, and our dog fell asleep and snored. "Roddy," I said, "have you heard of the medical device Miss Rankin mentioned? The Italian doctor who invented a 'cuff' to measure the pressure of one's blood?"

He put his drink on a side table and nodded. "I have. It's called a...." He looked at the coffered ceiling and seemed to sound out a word. "...a sphygmomanometer. Don't ask me to repeat it, Val. And yes, it's a real advance in medicine."

"How do you know about it?"

"My mother...."

Roddy said no more, but 'mother' said plenty. Eleanor DeVere devoted untold hours to a major hobby, her health. As for the inventor's birthplace, Leonardo Da Vinci might qualify, but all Italians nowadays were, in her view, low life "garlic eaters."

"Leon Rankin's blood pressure," Roddy said, "might have been dangerously high. His sister was worried. She wanted him to be tested."

"But he refused, and his sister thinks his blood pressure caused the burst artery...the apoplexy that killed him."

"Triggered by the stress of the men's visit," Roddy added, "and whatever 'dues' were paid to the lady friend in the hat."

"But Glenna May has no suspicion that her brother's death was a homicide."

"No," Roddy said. "For now, it's just as well that she harbor no such thought."

A moment passed, and the fire needed poking, though neither of us moved. "So, chances are," I said, "that three persons in the opera box with Leon Rankin believe that he died of apoplexy…a burst artery in his neck."

Roddy nodded. "And the fourth person knows he was murdered because that person returned to the box and stabbed him…unless…."

"Unless what?"

"Unless the one who committed the actual deed also conspired with someone else. Or some ones."

"Unless, unless, unless…." Restless, I stood, grabbed a poker and jabbed at the fire. "Roddy, we can play a guessing game until the snow melts and the flowers bloom, but we can't let our 'inquiry' about Leon Rankin's death take over every waking minute of the day. Or that cursed earring…I've been looking at women's ears and touching mine over and again. I've asked Calista to tighten my earrings, and now they pinch."

"Why not stop wearing them?"

"Because a lady with naked ear lobes would fire up the gossip mills. The word that Mrs. Roderick DeVere neglects her appearance will reach your mother in a heartbeat, and Society will dish its slurs about the primitive Wild West. Papa's advice to 'pick your fights' means big fights, not piffles."

I fought the urge to ask Roddy where, in police custody, my earring might be stored. In the Commissioner's desk drawer? The chief's? Under lock and key in a vault? Possibilities multiplied until a clock chimed, and Roddy reminded me of a dinner party in two days.

"The Drakes?" I asked.

"The Stadlers…."

"Already?"

My husband tried not to frown at my error. "Val, it's been nearly a year. We had them last, remember?"

I remembered because my hostess jaws had cramped from smiling. The blue ribbon for dullest could be awarded to Hornby and Philippa Stadler. I wanted to ask, must we? But I knew better. Roddy insisted the loom of social obligations wove New York together, that business alone could not do the job.

I promised to keep better track of our social calendar, to stop depending on reminders from Calista or needing to send apologetic notes and flowers to hostesses who were always forgiving but forever kept score. Despite my efforts, the merits of the social calendar remained a sore spot between Roderick and Valentine DeVere.

My husband spread the logs so the flames would shrink to embers. We would now dress for dinner and dine. "One more thing, Val…" Roddy said. "I assume you are planning another visit to Macy's?"

"I am."

Roddy finished his drink. "It sounds to me," he said, "as though you plan to pry out information by filling your wardrobe from Macy's."

"'Pry' isn't the word, Roddy. I can't simply interrogate a salesclerk. I need her confidence. The clerks have sales quotas to fill, and spending too much time with a 'dud' customer is probably a black mark against them."

"And so," Roddy said, "the Macy Company will profit from your purchases, and the clerk will not be terminated. Is this a new idea of charity?"

I would not take that "bait" but simply shook my head. "My Consumers League committee meets in a few days," I said, "and each member is expected to present a report."

"And I will pay another call on Elmer Taggart in the Star Coal office. He introduced himself as a clerk, but no ordinary office clerk would escort Miss Rankin to her brother's memorial service, much less tutor her about the coal business over dinner at the Plaza Hotel. And speaking of dinner, my dear…shall we?"

He took my arm, and our dog sprang up. The three of us prepared to be fed.

Chapter Ten

AN OVERCAST SKY THE next day signaled warmer weather that turned the snow to slush and icicles dripping from eaves. Icy water got into my boots and chilled my toes when I stood on the sidewalk, yet again, to face a show window at Macy's Department Store. The red-white-blue color scheme now covered ladies' springtime tennis clothing. With racquets in hand, the life-like mannequins showed off red ankle-length skirts with short blue jackets, white shirtwaists, bowties patterned with red and blue stars, and straw hats with blue chinstraps. Fuzzy white tennis balls scattered over a pea green court with a short net for an afternoon match.

In moments, I had checked my coat and boarded the elevator to ladies ready-to-wear on the second floor, where a few customers browsed, an older woman who was cloaked in raccoon fur and a mother-daughter pair who seemed to enjoy a private joke. The department looked more heavily stocked than on my first visit. The tennis ensembles clustered with the croquet clothes and racks of flower-print day dresses. I did not see Miss Marler in the thicket of clothing, nor did she appear when I suddenly sneezed.

A high voice called, "*Gesundheit*," but no salesclerk appeared. The merchandise nearly blocked the aisles. Department stores now hired psychologists for advice about consumers' shopping habits, so racks of cotton morning dresses printed with yellow daisies and purple tulips probably boosted spring sales.

Voices rose nearby. "...polished cotton...mercerized, isn't it?"

I saw no one.

A short laugh, then, "Will this dye hold? A customer complained the skirt faded and I didn't warn her. She tattled on me, and I got an earful...thought they'd fire me on the spot."

"They might...."

"...I'd be gone like Louella was...sick as a dog, and not a cent if you're not on the floor every minute."

"So the poor thing came in...."

"And the customer bellyached, and that was it...." The voice lowered but stayed audible. "...and she can't get on at Lord & Taylor or Altman's, either one...."

"...black-balled, that's what."

I stifled another sneeze and heard sympathetic cluckings, and then, "...dime a dozen, that's us...legs cramp up something terrible some nights...."

"...should see my veins...all this standing on cement floors...and staying after hours...."

"...and not one nickel extra."

"...not a penny...but better up here than first floor near the big doors...the noise, dust, cold drafts...gets into your lungs."

"So, we're lucky up here...?"

"...long's we meet the quota and don't get fined. Let's hope our millionaires show up soon...I am ready, willing, and able...."

Laughter, and a tickling in my nose. Once again, I sneezed.

"Bless you."

Around the rack, a thin, familiar woman appeared. "Why, Mrs. DeVere...."

"Miss Marler."

Her thin face flared a deep scarlet. "I'm so sorry," she said, "I didn't see you. I hope you didn't hear...I mean, I hope that...that...." Her voice sounded strangled.

"Miss Marler," I said, "I'm pleased to see you again. And by coincidence, I plan to take tennis lessons when the weather permits." I smiled my broadest smile. "As I recall, Miss Marler, you told me the Macy's motto—that the customer must be 'astonished.' So, consider me 'astonished.' And now, what do you suggest for my tennis game....?"

⁂

One eyebrow cocked, Roddy asked, "So you failed to mention your lessons in Newport?"

"The Macy's salesclerk did not need to hear that I take tennis lessons on the ladies' court each summer at the Newport Casino, Roddy. "And please, no snide cracks about my purchases when the Macy's wagon makes the delivery."

The early evening hour found us at home with our dog in a blue-toned drawing room with Velvet's favorite suede bed beside a Louis sofa. She had been walked, her paws dried, and her dinner devoured. Roddy had come home before me, and I joined him. We sat with glasses of sherry this evening.

"I learned a great deal from 'hiding' in the dresses for five minutes, Roddy. The saleswomen's working conditions are sickening...literally sickening. I was nearly in tears, but the women I overheard ought to be the ones weeping. What they endure is outrageous, and I suspect there's more for me to learn. I will give my report at the Consumers League meeting. Something must be done. We'll see about it...if only we women had the vote right now—"

"—Val, let's not talk about women's votes. I know how you feel. I don't disagree...not really. The problem is timing, and please, no quotes about 'time's winged chariot.'"

Roddy's fretful gaze stopped me. Women's suffrage pulsed in our marriage like a chronic condition. With a brief pause, I yielded to the moment. "Mr. Taggart?" I said. "You visited the Star Coal office?"

"I did indeed. Mr. Elmer Taggart is no mere clerk. I misjudged him. He is the comptroller of the Star Coal Company and its affiliates."

"Oh...," I cried, "the money man...the man who counts the dollars in, dollars out, dollars owed."

"The very one," Roddy said. "The payroll, the accounts payable and receivable, and the monthly income statements too. And the comptroller also oversees the periodic audits."

"Big job."

"Huge," Roddy said.

The man who escorted Miss Rankin up the church aisle had made no impression when I focused on Glenna May's veil, her mink, and shiny boots. At her signal, he sat beside her during the service and escorted her outside to the omnibus. But I well knew how important his job. My papa had called his trusted comptroller the hub and spokes of the Mackle Mining Company.

"He simply told you he's the comptroller?"

"Not at first. I presented my card and asked for a few minutes at his convenience. He obliged. I think he was glad to duck out of the hubbub for a few minutes. The customers still need assurance that Rankin's death will not interrupt coal supplies, and the Trinity Building office was running full steam...telephones ringing, typewriters clacking, messengers rushing about. The office boys scrambled when someone opened a window, and papers blew out of wire baskets. He apologized for the bustle...promised things would soon quiet down.

"Anyway, Mr. Taggart invited me into his office, as private as etched glass partitions allow. He said 'Mr. Leon' frowned on private offices at Star Coal and insisted on a 'fishbowl' to keep everybody in sight." Roddy paused. "Taggart seems a quiet sort, but in full command of the clerks and office boys. They knew what to do, and they hustled. As sudden as it was, Rankin's death has not hurt the business."

Roddy swirled his wine. "But Rankin's recent social life has thrown Taggart off his game...the out-of-town guests, the extravagant entertainment. He seemed relieved that I didn't present an unexpected invoice, past due."

"For the opera box?"

"No, the Wendells' box rental had been paid, and tickets to Broadway shows and after-hours dinners...all claimed as business expenses charged to Star Coal. But unforeseen new bills keep popping up, and Taggart asked me about certain...customs."

"Customs? What customs?"

Roddy brushed dog hair off his sleeve. "Elmer Taggart," he said, "is a man at ease with ledgers and figures, happiest in a green eyeshade. He got his start as an office boy from a town near the Canadian border and worked his way up. His job is his life. He seemed tempted to open a discussion with me...looked at my card twice, three times—"

"—and took a chance on Mr. Roderick Windham DeVere, Esquire, attired in a bespoke suit of clothes...and a good listener?"

"Whatsoever...." My husband slightly flushed.

Roddy sipped and put his glass down. "I mentioned our tea with Miss Rankin, which helped put him at ease. He obviously approves of her stay in her late brother's suite, which Rankin rented for years for his business trips to the city. He'd inspect the mines and rail lines in West Virginia and go to New Orleans, then come north to New York… or he'd go to Florida and then take a 'flying trip' north and show up at the Trinity Building. Taggart was always waiting in the office."

"Comptroller on duty."

Roddy nodded. "And he is confident that Mr. Leon would approve of his handling during these troublesome days. I'd guess that he idolized the 'Coal King' as a business genius, a man of the world.

"But socially, Taggart feels at a loss…clueless. Rankin's social life bewildered him and made his job harder. For the past two years, a certain private apartment on West 26th Street has been leased to Star Coal, and Rankin insisted that it appear in the annual audit as a company rental. The comptroller kept misgivings to himself. But lately, his 'in' basket is overflowing with surprise bills…silk shirts and ties…florists, theatre receipts…a gentleman's opera cape from Brooks Brothers…railroad passes…."

"For the men at the church service?"

"Yes, for them. Minor expenses for Star Coal, but concerning to the comptroller. And now the Plaza guestrooms…. Rankin booked rooms at the Plaza for three men… all charged to Star Coal. And their meals, also paid by the company."

"The same men at the church service…?"

Roddy nodded. "All meant for their stay in the city, but no departure date was set for Rankin's guests. Leon took control of the schedule and insisted that all charges be settled by the company, but without a termination date. Now, the bills are coming in from the Plaza and jewelers, and from invoices from Rector's and Murray's Roman Gardens."

"The 'lobster palaces?'" Roddy nodded. Another sore spot between us, those shady late-night restaurants known as lobster palaces, which my husband frequented in his bachelor days.

"The bills indicate that Mr. Dent is especially fond of Rector's…night after night. The other men dine at Delmonico's."

"No expense spared?"

"None," Roddy said. "And something else…bills from a dressmaker and a milliner."

"—for a woman," I said. "All charged to the company?"

"Yes. I advised Taggart that these bills are highly irregular."

Despite myself, I laughed at the picture of the man in a green eyeshade facing bills for ostrich plumes and champagne suppers.

Roddy's somber face, however, stopped all mirth.

"Something else, Val," he said.

"What?"

"The Plaza tea yesterday afternoon.…Taggart will tutor Miss Rankin about the coal business before she leaves for Palm Beach…several more days in New York."

I nodded.

"He also had a message for her...about the many documents she had signed at her beloved brother's behest."

"She told us about them."

"—about signing them, Val, but no idea what her signature meant."

Roddy's gaze had a stormy look around the eyes. "Unknown to Miss Glenna May Rankin, she has been named the Vice-President of Keymont and Star Coal. With her brother's death, she officially becomes the president. If Leon's murder is linked to his sister, then—"

"—then her life might also be...might be at risk...." My husband nodded, and we said no more.

Chapter Eleven

"WHAT DOES A LADY wear to a lobster palace?" I asked Calista the next morning after breakfast.

Not one iota of surprise from my unflappable maid. "You're planning to dine at a 'lobster palace,' ma'am?"

"I am... I mean, we are...Mr. DeVere and myself...tonight."

"I see." Her glance fell to the several volumes on the nearby desk as we stood in my boudoir—*Sensible Etiquette*, *American Etiquette*, and *The Well-Bred Girl in Society*. (No girl "well bred" in the West.)

"These books are useless, Calista. Lots of advice for 'visits' or 'dinner parties' or 'balls,' but nothing about restaurants, let alone a lobster palace."

My maid paused. "Occasionally," she said, "I was asked for recommendations by passengers who journeyed to the city on the coastal steamers...especially ladies from the South. They wanted something risqué but not scandalous."

"That's it," I said, "something risqué."

"Yes, ma'am. Give me a few minutes."

"Take your time, Calista. We have all day."

Wishing life's time away was wrong, my papa often warned, but the daylight hours passed quickly as I drafted my scorching report on department store salesladies' torments and reviewed recent documents from the Mackle Trust, posted from a law firm in Virginia City, Nevada. Roddy spent the afternoon with my friend Cassie's husband, Dudley Forster, a scientist who knows a good deal about pyrotechnic chemistry and also advised the Dewey committee about fireworks. Roddy took Velvet with him to the Forsters' home, knowing that Cassie and Dudley's two children would be thrilled by a visit from our dog. Vice versa for the dog.

Our cook was told that we would dine out this evening, and I suggested to Sands that the kitchen staff be given the evening off. The butler cautioned that impromptu free time for servants might set an "unfortunate" precedent, but I held firm and did not insult him by blurting, "Nonsense."

That night, as our clocks struck ten p.m., I descended the stairs wearing a broché satin and chiffon gown with a deeply scooped neckline and a hat set at a rakish angle. Calista proposed a pair of rose gold earrings that would not pinch. Roddy stood in the foyer in evening dress, top hat, and a fur-lined overcoat. Smiling, he held open my blue iris mink cloak.

Swathed in fur, with long gloves buttoned, I nodded to Roddy, who took up his ebony walking stick and gestured to Sands, who opened the door. Noland prepared to drive us to Rector's Restaurant at Longacre Square. The air felt moist, and our coachman remarked on this "January thaw." He flicked the reins, and Apollo and Atlas, the matched high-stepping Hackneys, plunged ahead to speed us on our way.

Just past eleven o'clock we reached a building that might have been a bank, except for the overarching sculpture of a winged griffin, part eagle and part lion. "Charles Rector's symbol," Roddy murmured as a doorman sprang to our carriage door.

"Look up, Val. Mr. Edison would be proud."

High above our heads at the entrance, electrical lightbulbs spelled out RECTOR'S, and we entered the building through the newest clever "thing," a revolving door, the first in New York City.

The gold and green dining room outmatched Aladdin's cave. Baroque gilded pier-glass mirrors reflected and amplified the scene to a vanishing point. Burnished panels of ornately-carved wood glowed in incandescent light from chandeliers and pearly wall sconces, and ranks of potted palms against the edges of the room somehow suggested intimacy. A grand staircase beckoned to an upstairs dining room, but Roddy murmured that the ground floor was Rector's more formal dining room.

"And more likely to attract a man with a new opera cape, Val." Roddy inquired about a recent, frequent patron, Mr. Jeremy Dent.

"Mr. Dent, sir? Let me see." The maître d'hotel hesitated, then brightened. "Why, yes, Mr. Dent has found favor with us in recent evenings." Roddy said we hoped Mr. Dent would join us as our guest this evening, and would he please seat us at Mr. Dent's preferred table?

He slipped the man a banknote, and we were seated at a table for four in sight of a corner sculpture that looked like a Statue of Liberty draped in a see-through peignoir. Her left arm hoisted a cocktail instead of a torch. The heavy silver and oversize china gleamed against a tablecloth whiter than new-fallen snow, and surrounding tables were set for new arrivals as waiters cleared and reset the tables with sleight-of-hand speed.

"Champagne to start, Val?"

"To start," I said.

"You understand that we are here at an early hour for the late supper…?"

"Fully understood."

A waiter appeared at Roddy's elbow, and with whispered words, a bottle of champagne arrived and wine sparkled in two gold-rimmed glasses. "Salud, Val. Here's hoping our 'guest' appears."

This late night supper at Rector's was my husband's idea. If Jeremy Dent joined us, we hoped to learn more about him, about his 'friends' at the church service, and about "Coal King" Rankin. Perhaps we would also learn something more about his sister, Glenna May.

Roddy ordered an oyster cocktail while we waited and sipped champagne. Inches from my handsome husband, I felt more and more vexed as he speared oysters with a tiny fork, as if Rector's succulent oyster cocktail was a familiar dish.

In truth, the lobster palace prompted uneasy thoughts of a certain young man who had been a law student with a *bon-vivant* hobby mixing cocktails, and a bachelor 'stage door Johnny' at lobster palaces—in other words, my husband before I entered the picture, my husband as a New York playboy.

The Roddy I first met that winter when his parents took him West to "dry out," but I learned about his years of private schooling with a tutor, followed by college and law school at Columbia University. Recently, however, during dinner at our own table, I learned that, in his younger days, my husband had frequented New York restaurants where champagne flowed like tap water and every night was a riotous "Mardi Gras" into the wee hours—in short, lobster palaces. Not only that, but my Roddy had been a stage door Johnny. He met Broadway chorus girls after the shows, presented them with bouquets of fresh flowers and took them for carriage rides in Central Park, then for feasts at Martin's Café or Murray's Roman Gardens…or Rector's.

My husband had been a playboy in this very restaurant. He told me so himself. Not in so many words, but clearly and without apology. He put it down to youth and a few "wild oats." I wondered how many banknotes he had slipped to various maître d's and waiters in those years.

"How many?" I asked, posing the question before I realized I had spoken aloud.

"How many what?" Roddy leaned close, all attention on me.

"Banknotes," I said, "when you brought chorus girls here."

He took my hand. "Val, no...Valentine DeVere, my love... please don't think..." Just then, he broke off and looked up as his hand gripped mine. "Here we go, Val...."

In seconds, Roddy was on his feet with his arm out for a handshake. "Mr. Dent? Mr. Jeremy Dent...if you will please join us, sir...please do us the honor...."

Jeremy Dent blinked, uncertain, but my charming husband clasped the man's palm with one hand and cupped Dent's elbow with the other, drawing him closer to the table, a tactic I had admired more than once.

Dent was not alone. A split second ahead of the waiter, my husband pulled out a chair for his young woman companion. "So pleased that we might meet and enjoy ourselves," Roddy continued, "and waiter, champagne for all..... We're not too late to toast the New Year.... I am Roderick DeVere at your service, and may I introduce my wife...."

In the West, I'd say the two were corralled. Hesitantly they sat, the long-faced Jeremy Dent with the razor thin moustache and a mouth like a rat trap, and a round-featured young woman whose upswept hair shone raspberry pink in the light. Her sea blue gown of pleats and flounces cinched tight at the waist, and her deepest "V" neckline over an ample powdered bosom defined the word, "*décolletage.*" Her earrings dangled in tiny coin cascades that nearly reached her shoulders. Dent introduced her as Miss Millie…or was it Tillie? A nearby table had broken into laughter so I wasn't certain. I nodded and smiled.

Champagne and glasses appeared as if by magic, and the waiter poured, refilled, poured once again. Roddy whispered a few words to the waiter and reached into his trouser pocket.

Was I seeing things, or was a banknote slipped to the man?

Seated, Dent rolled his shoulders like a peacock fanning "feathers" to show off his purplish gray evening suit, a double-breasted waistcoat of lilac satin brocade, and a scarf the color of a ripe plum. Diamonds glittered in each shirt stud, and an amethyst stickpin flickered an inch beneath the knot of his tie. I recognized his violet boutonniere as a "snowball." In recent years, I had socialized with Old New York gentlemen who wore their wildest stylish clothing like a second skin. On Dent, the formal wear looked like camouflage.

"…and regrets that we did not have an opportunity to become acquainted after the church service the other morning," Roddy was saying, "but the frigid air made it impossible." He leaned toward Dent. "Impossibly cold, wasn't it?"

"…cold day," the man said, as if tiptoeing on alien ground.

The waiter refilled the glasses and brought another bottle. Roddy turned to the young woman. "My wife and I attended a memorial service a few days ago," he explained, "and Mr. Dent spoke so passionately about the deceased… someone he had known for many years. He was most impressive…and everyone in the church appreciated every word… didn't we, my dear?"

"We did indeed." I lowered my voice for sincerity. "We were so…moved," I said.

Miss Tilly…or Milly sat forward and said, "That new front door moved us."

Roddy smiled at her. "The revolving door," he said.

"Moved us like a merry-go-round…I got a little bit dizzy."

"Newfangled contraption," Dent said. "Probably got a patent on the thing, probably set him up for life."

"…someone from Philadelphia, I believe," Roddy said. We all raised our glasses and sipped. Just then a group of six burst past us, chattering and wafting perfume and cigars. "The night is young," Roddy said, "so let us toast the evening and turn our thoughts to supper, shall we?"

We raised our glasses once again, and I noticed two champagne bottles in use—the waiter pouring for Dent and his lady friend from one bottle, the other for Roddy and me.

Acrobatic waiter," I murmured.

"Nothing beats Rector's," Jeremy Dent said. "They got a chef from Paris, France. Cost seven thousand dollars to bring him over here."

"Then let him cook for us tonight!" Roddy exclaimed. "Here come our menu cards, so let us begin!" Buoyant, my husband played to the table. He flashed a toothy grin at Jeremy Dent as the waiter gave each of us a Late Supper Card, with colorful pictures of fish and fowl surrounding the "Hot" and "Cold" dishes. "If you please," Roddy said, "do allow me to be your host this entire evening."

His gambit was our best chance to glean information, and I must help out. "Mr. Dent," I said, "if you have recently dined at Rector's, could you suggest a particular dish? A favorite?" I added, "A bit confusing, so many choices...."

"Oh yes, Jeremy, what do you think best?" his companion cooed. She drank and pointed to her empty glass, which the waiter promptly refilled and, at Roddy's nod, brought another bottle.

Dent drained his glass, and the waiter poured again. "Make mine a mignon filet of beef, well done," he said without a glance at the serried ranks of French foods on the menu.

"Not lobster?" Miss Millie asked. "Not lobster thermidor? At Murray's Roman Gardens, they bring you the whole lobster, claws and all."

The teasing bordered on taunting, and Dent glowered before Roddy stepped in. "A good beefsteak fills the bill," my husband said. "You ladies pick and choose, but I'll join Mr. Dent in a mignon of beef, cooked all the way through. We gentlemen know something about beef, do we not, sir?"

In Jeremy Dent's short nod, I detected a hint of fellowship.

The dining room was boisterous by the time a squad of waiters lifted silver domes over Miss Millie's lobster croquettes, my chicken breast, and the two plates of incinerated beefsteaks. Roddy ordered more wines, both red and white, and once again, a waiter poured from separate bottles for our guests. As we lifted knives and forks to begin, my husband pointed out the surrounding tables of the city's luminaries.

"—to your left, Mr. Dent, a world-famous vaudeville performer, and on the other side of him, the gambler who won his yacht with a pair of sixes...you remember him.... And there's Mr. Belmont, who swept every category at the last Horse Show.... And see the couple other there? That's Diamond Jim Brady and the famous actress and singer, Lillian Russell.... Don't dare challenge Diamond Jim to an eating contest. He'll beat you every time."

Roddy set down his knife and fork. "So there you have it, all New York at supper. But I've talked a great deal, and we'd be pleased to hear about your doings, wouldn't we, my dear?"

"Very much so," I said. "If I remember correctly from the church, I believe you spoke of store-keeping...."

"The lady's got a memory, DeVere." His voice sounded slightly slushy.

Roddy squeezed my hand under the table and said, "She sure does." I took a cue for silence. Jeremy Dent had finished his meal, mopped the plate with bread, and washed it down with red wine. Waiters deftly switched our plates with menus for desserts and liqueurs.

"Merchants..." Jeremy Dent said. "The Dents got started trading and peddling.... You heard of Daniel Boone? David Crockett?"

"You bet we have," Roddy said.

"...followed right after 'em...the Big Sandy and the Tug Rivers...and the forks...and the Barret. The Dents peddled along the rivers and set up storekeeping in due time. Drygoods, cookware, beans and the like.... Jedediah Dent knew his tinware. The name, Dent, meant something... means something to this day on the Barret River...and the gospel of Jedediah Dent still rings true."

"Gospel?" Miss Millie's eyes opened wider. "What gospel is that?"

Dent leered. "'Get rich,'" he said. "'Get rich quick as you can, sharp as you need to be. Do unto others if you must, but to the Dents, be true.'"

Roddy's laugh died. The man was serious.

"Do you still rely on the rivers?" I asked. "It seems like the railroad is everywhere nowadays."

"Nowadays, lady," he said, "but don't rub it in."

"Oh, I didn't mean to offend," I said softly.

I didn't think he heard me. "You got the story in the church...the rail line washed out. Some say the river turned against us Dents. I'll tell you who turned...what's the word? Turncoat, that's it."

"Strong word," Roddy said.

"Whose coat?" asked Millie, who seemed roused from her stupor. "A fur coat? Was it fur?"

Ignoring his companion, Dent pounded a fist on the tablecloth. "Traitor," that's it...showed his true colors."

"Do you mean Leon Rankin?" Roddy asked with quiet intensity.

"—thinks he paid us off with theatre shows and the fancy hotel...sleigh rides in Central Park...and the opera... caterwauling... couldn't hardly stand it. *Romeo and Juliette* the night after Christmas, and right after New Years, it was *Don Jovial*...something like that.... Got out of there early, all of us except him." Dent wiped spittle from his lips. "Betrayed us," he said. "Betrayed us, one and all."

"How so?" Roddy asked, still low-keyed.

"...sticks in the craw to this day...sign the papers and get rich, just like swapping." He snapped his fingers. "And there goes the Barret River land, the Dents' land... legal gobbledygook." He finished his wine, his face now florid. "It's what Leon didn't say to my pappy...didn't tell my pappy when he signed."

"And what was that?" Roddy asked.

"...the rail line...the Barret Railroad."

"Rebuilt after the flooding, wasn't it?" Roddy said.

"Cut us out...cut us like he knew it would...thought it up, planned it that way. No sooner the ink dried, and we watched gravel hauled in, and steel and all the rest... land settled way back by Dents. And Leon kept his big secret. All that time, he had his big secret."

Millie said, "I love a secret...."

"What secret was that?" Roddy asked.

Jeremy Dent peered at Roddy as if his eyes struggled to focus. "You know about it…" he said. "The newspapers when he died…about the Barret and Nitro Railroad. Leon had it all planned…two railroads…one plus one, and get rich…sell stock and get rich."

"They merged," Roddy said softly. "The Barret and the Nitro line became a new company, traded on Wall Street."

"Richer than before…stock market…more fancy paper. But I'll get lawyers…yes, I will…fight for Dents' own share. We're not done." He looked at Roddy. "Town's full of lawyers," he said. "You a lawyer?"

"Not that kind," my husband murmured.

Dent banged the table, and a couple nearby glanced our way. "Leon Rankin," he said, "was a rat."

"…scare the daylights out of me," Millie murmured. "Rats…spiders too.…"

Dent leaned close to Roddy. "Rotten as he was to the Dents," he said, "he did worse to Suggs."

"Amos Suggs?" Roddy asked. "The man who saved his life in the coal mine?"

"Treated like diddly-squat. Like a beggar. You want to know what's what, you talk to Suggs… 'course, Florida's where you got to go."

"To the hotel construction site?" Roddy asked.

"Treated like dirt." He fingered the new menu. "What's this?"

"Liqueurs," Roddy said, "and sweets."

Dent gripped the menu with both hands. "Liqueurs..." he said, "glass the size of a thimble...well, I say, bring the bottle and a big tall glass...ice too. We can toast the rat. Here's to Leon Rankin...." He squinted at the menu and read, "'Desserts.'" His laughter grated and rattled. "Leon," he said, "that's what he finally got coming... got his dessert."

Chapter Twelve

WE GOT HOME FROM Rector's after three a.m. and went straight to our beds. I slept like a stone and woke when the winter sun blazed through my boudoir window. In robe and slippers, I tiptoed to the breakfast room just as the dreadful Junghans clock banged the half-hour, ten-thirty a.m.

At the table, my newly shaved husband rose for a quick kiss. "Good morning, dearest Val." A toast plate dotted with crumbs meant Roddy had been up a while.

I sat. "Roddy, did you slip the waiter a banknote last night at Rector's?"

"Guilty as charged, my love. Our sly waiter made certain that you and I imbibed a good deal of mineral water." He grinned. "No pounding headaches for us this morning, though I would wager Jeremy Dent needs a bromide or the 'hair of the dog that bit'...bit him hard, Val, but well worth it. And now, breakfast. Shall we?"

I nodded. Three thick books lay opened on the table along with the newspapers, and Roddy pushed them aside. The footman brought my coffee and refilled Roddy's tea. Napping in her bed, Velvet opened her eyes, sniffed, and waited for tidbits from our morning meal, eggs and Canadian bacon for Roddy and "chuck wagon" hash for me. Also grapefruit, a treat shipped from Florida in wintertime. We ate as if famished.

"I should have alerted you last evening, Val. I feared you'd tell the waiter your champagne tasted like mineral water."

"I was too focused on Dent...and Millie, or Tillie...and relieved when you and the maître d' finally put them into a hansom cab."

"It was shabby of me to 'overdose' the young woman, Val, but I saw no other way to get Dent 'oiled' and loosen his tongue. By the time he drank a tumbler of Grand Marnier, the man was babbling. He could barely stumble outdoors to a cab."

"—but still raving about Leon Rankin and the railroad."

Roddy nodded. "A grudge that runs deep...like those mountain feuds, the Hatfields and...."

"...the McCoys," I said, "except that diphtheria struck down the Rankin clan, and so the fury has been centered on Leon."

Roddy signaled the footman for more tea, I for coffee. "Roddy, what are those tomes?"

"Law books...on incorporation, trusts...joint-stock companies. I got up early to bone up...in case I speak with Taggart again." Roddy drummed his fingers. "After the memorial service and last night's dinner, I can easily foresee a lawyer persuading Jeremy Dent that his family has a rightful claim against Star Coal or the Florida hotel. Or both."

"—or against the Barret and Nitro Railroad?"

"Especially against the rail line." Palms down on the tabletop, Roddy said, "The Dents' grudge started with the sale of their riverfront land…and the rebuilt Barret Railroad. But their fury boiled when the two rail lines combined, and the value surged…as is often the case."

The math sounded familiar from papa's mining days. "Greater than the sum of the parts," I said.

My husband nodded and stirred milk into his tea. "Merged lines can increase the market share tremendously. Fortunes are made, especially if the new railroad connects to a big line, like the New York Central." He sipped. "It's a trick that Jay Gould mastered years ago, and they called him the Mephistopheles of Wall Street."

"So, the Barret & Nitro line was Leon Rankin's devilish maneuver," I said. "And the Dents felt short-changed."

"Blindsided, Val. Cut out of the deal."

"And furious when they figured out what Rankin had pulled." I imagined the Dents in their store, gathered around a pot-bellied stove and stewing over the riches they would never see. Every locomotive hauling coal in sight of their store would be a galling reminder. "The coal wagons," I said, "…would have 'Barret and Nitro' painted on the sides?"

"Yes, the 'B&N.'

"Outrageous," I said. "I'd feel the same way."

"But that's business, Val. It happens."

Nevada's V&T short line railroad, I recalled, wound around Mount Davidson from Reno and Carson City to our dear Virginia City. It hauled supplies to serve the Comstock Lode silver mines. It added passenger service too. We loved it. The sound of the V&T steam whistle was music to our ears.

To the West Virginia storekeepers, the same sound became a jeering reminder of riches stolen and gone forever, and the Dents left high and dry on the riverbanks.

"The Dents have stoked their rage for years, Roddy, but did Jeremy Dent kill Leon Rankin? Did he go back into the opera box and stab him to death? And if he did, how could we possibly find out?"

Roddy sipped his tea. "I wish we knew something about Rankin's son."

"Lewis...."

"If the family feud crosses generations," Roddy said, "it would not cease at Leon's death." He tapped a spoon against his saucer. "Add Glenna May...not only a Rankin, but she'd be rich...and a target."

"She's something else, Roddy...a schoolmarm...a strict schoolmarm who drilled the three "R's" into a roomful of balky, sullen girls and boys...kids who don't forget, no matter how old." I added, "Kids named Dent...and Suggs...."

"Suggs..." Roddy rubbed his chin. "And what did the half-soused Jeremy Dent mean that Rankin 'did worse' to Amos Suggs?"

"...the man who rescued Rankin and was promised he'd be 'better off' if he followed Rankin like a 'brother.' He said 'brother,' didn't he?"

"He did."

"It sounds as though Suggs has gone back to Florida," I said. "He was at work on the hotel building, wasn't he? Outdoors in Florida? His face looked like faded bronze in the church."

The footman cleared our plates. "I'll try to research the Barret and the Nitro Railroads this afternoon," Roddy said, "but I'm also due for an inspection of the wharf area...a surprise visit before we file a report. And you?"

I sensed that my husband was already absorbed in his plans. "A ladies meeting," I said, deliberately vague, "downtown...Noland will drive."

"Excellent...."

I stood up first, as etiquette required, and Roddy sprang from his chair as if a school bell had sounded. One day soon, I would convince my husband that if he stood first, I would take no offence. On the contrary, thumbing our noses at certain iron rules of etiquette would free both of us. The twentieth century was at the doorstep, and high time to usher in a few changes, long overdue.

※

A few household duties came first. As usual, I must approve the menu for tonight's dinner, though the dishes were already underway and overseen by the cook who had ruled the DeVere kitchen since Roddy's boyhood. His parents bestowed the cook upon us, then hired a new chef for their apartment. With the menu presented by the butler, my daily review was usually mere courtesy, though I sometimes nixed a few doozies, such as parsley kidneys or stuffed ox tail. They sneaked in among the dishes copied from the famed French chef, Escoffier. I only wished the "Chef of Kings, and King of Chefs" knew sourdough biscuits and campfire coffee.

I approved tonight's pea soup with mint, rib chops *en casserole*, chateau potatoes, a mysterious *Salade Lorette*, and apple pie. Sands bowed out, but the housekeeper, Mrs. Thwaite, appeared to report a telephone conversation with a carpet dealer who proposed to deliver samples for my selection.

"For our opera box, Mrs. Thwaite?" I asked.

"The purpose, Mrs. Devere, is not for me to know. Nor to say."

The woman's pinched lips matched her pinched nose in distaste for her former employers' Wild West daughter-in-law. She loomed large in her stout shoes and long gray housekeeper's dress. My friend Cassie's housekeeper wore an identical uniform, and the keys that dangled from a ring on her belt jingled like bells. On Mrs. Thwaite's belt, the keys looked ready for cell doors.

"I will be pleased to examine the carpet samples later today, Mrs. Thwaite," I said. "...and will there be something else...?"

"A problem with the new maid you hired, Mrs. Devere. A 'Mattie' who was employed here after her dismissal from a nearby house."

"Mattie Sue Joiner," I said. The young maid's complicated story was not for the housekeeper's ears. "She may not be with us for long," I said, "but I hope her work is satisfactory."

"I am afraid, Mrs. DeVere, that her strange method of cleaning the marble floors has set a very poor example for the house."

"Oh?"

She did not kneel to scrub, and she eschewed the time-honored mop."

The housekeeper patted her bosom, as if overcome by 'vapors.' "The young woman," she said, "wrapped cleaning cloths around her shoes and moved her feet.... She skated across your floors."

"She skated...." I fought laughter. "But the floors," I finally asked, "...the floors are cleaned, aren't they?"

She ignored my question. "I hope you agree, Mrs. DeVere," she said, "that work is not play and must not be mistaken, the one for the other."

I nodded solemnly. "I must be about my day, Mrs. Thwaite. I shall speak to Mattie," I said, "but it happens that the meaning of 'work,' especially women's work, is very much on my mind at the present time."

The housekeeper marched off, and within the hour I was bundled up and off to the brougham that stood at our curb. The air felt colder, and the blanketed Apollo and Atlas stamped and snorted as I stepped into the carriage. I agreed with Noland that our "January thaw" was disappointing.

"Henry Street, Noland," I said, "number 265 Henry Street."

The coachman's salute doubtless masked his dread of returning to the Lower East Side address. Once before, he had driven me far downtown into a maze of pushcarts, vendors, and ragged children. On that cold October day, a pounding rain had filled the gutters and given the coachman the grippe that sent him to bed for days.

The same narrow streets would be rutted with refrozen snow today, but the air was clear, and the coachman heavily outfitted. The Henry Street address made space available for my Consumers League meeting on working conditions for women in retail jobs. My Macy's report was tucked into a calfskin folio. Three or four ladies would join me on the ground-floor of the old Federal style building informally dubbed "The Nurses Settlement." Two trained nurses, Lillian Wald and Mary Brewster, launched the effort to bring healthcare and counsel to a mixed neighborhood of immigrant families, and a flock of young women nurses had joined them. Philanthropy helped them purchase the building and put it into good repair.

"So brave of them," I had told Roddy, "and they promote schooling…and kindergartens too…and playgrounds to get the children off the treacherous streets." He listened, but had not actually seen those children, as I had, on that fateful morning when, inside 265 Henry Street, I heard Mrs. Florence Kelley's thunderous speech that summoned all who heard it to join the movement for fair wages and safe working conditions for women.

Just before 1:00 p.m., I climbed the stone front steps to enter a space scented with furniture wax and iodine. A young nurse directed me to a meeting room. "...the door past the dispensary, ma'am, you'll find your four friends."

I tiptoed past a nurse dabbing salve onto a tearful boy's scraped cheek. ("Snowballs," I heard her say, "ought not to have rocks inside....") Through the opened door, four women sat around a small table, including Daisy Harriman, a social friend.

"Valentine DeVere!"

Daisy's greeting struck the same pleasant note as when she drew my name in the summer tennis tournament at Newport, where her backhand tricked me every time. She sailed her catboat in the harbor and won ribbons for horsemanship. The Harrimans lived in Mount Kisco, but frequently appeared at social events in the city. Word recently spread that Daisy Harriman had turned her attention to the plight of workers' low wages and injuries. A charter member of the Consumers League, she welcomed her "scandalous" new reputation.

"Splendid to see you again, Valentine...Mrs. Roderick DeVere."

I quickly pulled off my gloves, opened my coat, and took a seat on a bentwood chair.

"Do let me introduce Mrs. Chadwick Bourne...Paulina Bourne...high time you two become acquainted."

I greeted a stately, gray-eyed woman whose smile looked tightly rationed. She extended her hand, cool to the touch, and said, "...so pleased...have heard so much...." She glanced a bit sideways, as if to appraise my hair...no, my earring. The woman narrowed her eyes to inspect my ear lobes. On impulse, I reached for the agates that Calista had selected and fastened to my ears, then folded my hands and outstared Paulina Bourne's searchlight gaze.

Was the gossip mill grinding about me? Or did my imagination run amuck?

Daisy kept on smiling "...and Mrs. Coleman Ordway... Felicia...and her daughter, Mabel Ordway Crouder.... It's Mrs. Crouder, now that Mabel and Stephen Crouder have so recently tied the knot."

Mabel Crouder's ring finger sparkled with diamonds, and her cheeks flushed a lovely, soft pink. Was this new bride, perhaps, seventeen years of age? At most, eighteen.

Lines on the bride's mother's face gave Felicia Ordway a tabby-cat expression, reminding me of a "mouser" that my papa got for our house on "B" Street in Virginia City. Thoughts of life in that house warmed my heart and stirred friendly feelings toward Mrs. Ordway. Neither she nor her daughter seemed interested in my earrings.

"To work, shall we?" said Daisy, who chaired our committee. "We're hoping that Mrs. Kelley might stop by, but the General Secretary of the Consumers League is a busy woman! So, Paulina, if you please...."

The stately Paulina Bourne unfolded a sheet of paper, smoothed it on the pine tabletop, and spoke in a voice as cool as her handclasp. "My information," she said, "comes directly from sales ladies employed by Lord & Taylor." She glanced at each of us, touched her throat, and continued. "A so-called 'living wage' to meet expenses of lodging, food, and clothing must be $9.00 weekly, but the ladies in the shoe and the lingerie departments earn less than $7.50."

She paused to let our mental arithmetic take hold. "Another category of employment," she said, "is the 'stock girl,' who earns $4.50 per week."

"Appalling," Mabel Crouder murmured. We all nodded.

"Of course," Paulina Bourne continued, "her clothing expenses would be negligible, since she toils behind the scenes, out of the sight of all customers."

No one commented, until I said, "A winter coat...surely a 'stock girl' needs a warm coat...and good boots." Paulina cast her gray-eyed gaze on me and murmured about the Salvation Army.

Daisy quickly called upon the mother-daughter pair, as if to ward off a chill. "Felicia...Mabel...I believe you have something about conditions at Siegel-Cooper."

"Indeed we do! Don't we, Mabel?" Her daughter nodded and produced sheets of personal stationary with handwriting rivaling an engraver's finest P's and Q's. "Our report," she announced, is titled, 'Problems at the Siegel-Cooper Department Store.'"

The Siegel salesgirls..." Mabel began, "...and they like to be called 'girls'...they must purchase their meal from the store, and the meal costs eighteen cents, so they cannot afford to take the horsecars, but must walk outdoors in all weathers. And they must eat these meals in a drab backroom and sit on chairs without cushions."

Felicia added, "Chairs like these...." We chuckled. The Thonet bentwood chairs were never meant for comfort.

Daisy nodded to me, and my handwritten sheets told the grim story I had heard and overheard from Miss Marler and her co-worker in Macy's ready-to-wear. Reading aloud, I felt thankful for lessons in composition and elocution at the Fourth Ward School in Virginia City. As for penmanship, I settled for legible.

"Thank you, Valentine, and so we have it, ladies," Daisy concluded, "three strong reports ready for the Consumers League typewriter." She collected our pages. "I understand that other committees are reviewing conditions in the textile mills and the garment industry, and the evidence is mounting." She smiled brightly. "And now," she said, "an announcement.... Here it is...the League expects a visit from Mother Jones!"

The mother and daughter exchanged a puzzled glance. "Who," I asked, "is Mother Jones?"

Daisy gave a wily smile. "Her real name is Mary Harris, but she goes by Mother Jones. Mrs. Kelley praises her to the heavens. She rallies coal miners to promote unions, and she is coming to New York to raise funds for the union cause."

"Labor unions...." Paulina Bourne looked as though she might need smelling salts.

Daisy took no notice. "And you'll especially want to meet her, Valentine. You come from a mining region, so Mother Jones will be your cup of tea." She flashed her nicest smile. "And you mustn't be alarmed by the dreadful thing they call her. Pay no attention."

"What do 'they' call her?" I asked.

Mrs. Borden J. Harriman leaned across the table and winked. "They call her 'the most dangerous woman in America.'"

Chapter Thirteen

IN THE FADING LIGHT of the setting sun, the 'most dangerous woman' buzzed in mind like an out-of-season housefly. Once or twice, I touched the agate earrings, which started to pinch. I planned to take an active part in The Consumers League, but Daisy Harriman's notion that the "dangerous" Mother Jones would be my "cup of tea" rankled. What made the Jones woman "dangerous?" Is it possible that my "Wild West" past somehow linked me to treacherous women, like Pearl Hart, the "Lady Bandit" who robbed stagecoaches in Arizona? Or Laura Bullion, the "Rose of the Wild Bunch," convicted of robbery. Also prostitution.

A quicker wit would have scotched the idea of a cozy "cup of tea." I practiced several "should-have-saids" in the carriage until the cold air bit my forehead when Noland helped me step down in front of the chateau that was my home.

"A good evening to you, ma'am," he said.

"Good evening, Noland."

Our coachman would carefully tend the Hackneys, warm them in the stable, clean their icy hooves, and exchange their blankets and hoods for their linen night clothing. And feed them. The horses would be cosseted in steam heat.

So would I.... I who had climbed jutting rocks on my own in cold weather in the West just a few years ago. I, who had searched hours for water and found a bare canteen full in a mud hole trodden by bears and other beasts.

Our butler, Sands, took my arm up the front steps. "Mr. DeVere hopes you will join him without delay in the *Crème* drawing room," he said, but my mood had darkened as I peeled off my coat, traded boots for slippers, and made my way to the drawing room.

"My love...." Roddy stood to greet me, one hand around a crystal cocktail glass with tinkling ice. "Your favorite," he said, "an Old-fashioned, this time with rye instead of bourbon. Tell me what you think."

The Old Fashioned

Ingredients

- 2 oz. rye
- 2 dashes Angostura bitters
- 1 sugar cube
- Maraschino cherry
- club soda

Directions
1. Place the sugar cube in an Old Fashioned glass.
2. Wet it down with Angostura bitters and a short splash of club soda.
3. Crush the sugar with a wooden muddler, then rotate the glass so that the sugar grains and bitters give it a liquid lining.
4. Add Maraschino cherry.
5. Add large ice cube or cubes.
6. Pour in the whiskey.
7. Add selzer (soda) water.
8. Garnish with an orange twist.

Roddy paused while I sipped. "What's the verdict?" he asked.

"Delicious," I said dutifully." The drink felt somehow off schedule.

"Val, has something happened? You look distressed. Did your meeting go...?

"The meeting was fine, Roddy. I'm a bit...out of sorts. January doldrums."

This was no time to ask if insane rumors circulated about my earring and Rankin's dead body. Roddy's mother would be the first to get wind of it, and her son would be a pipeline to me. My husband hesitated while I held the cocktail glass.

"Shall we sit for a minute, Val?"

I perched on a chair facing the cold fireplace. "Why no fire, Roddy? And why are we to sit for just a 'minute?'"

"Val, can we take a breath? One breath?"

I loosened one earring and leaned for his kiss…then lingered for another kiss, and another. I put down the glass. Roddy kissed me again and again, and so it went.

"Let's go upstairs," I said, "and have our own time…together."

My husband slowly, regretfully drew back. "My dear… nothing I'd like better…."

"Then, let's…or why not?"

Roddy sighed. "…because we have an invitation…or rather, a summons. Miss Glenna May Rankin hopes we will join her for dinner at the Plaza…tonight." He slipped out his pocket watch. "…in less than two hours. A 'matter of great importance,' according to her telegram."

"She sent a telegram?"

Roddy nodded. "If she does not hear otherwise, she'll expect us."

"Why us?" I asked.

"She's Rankin's sister, Val. It might be important.

"What about our dinner?"

"I've had a word with Sands."

I abandoned the Old-Fashioned. "Roddy, if I had toiled for hours in a hot kitchen and was told that the effort was null and void, I would be furious. Tomorrow, we give the kitchen staff the day off. Sands must be instructed to tell the kitchen that tomorrow is a holiday. He won't like it, but if he won't tell the cook, I will."

"Val—"

"—I know, there I go again."

Over the next hour, I submitted to the "ladies combination garment" and a forest green velvet dinner gown with modest lace trim, which Calista thought suitable for a hotel dinner with a woman in mourning. A simple garnet necklace and a garnet button for each ear won over emeralds from the DeVere vault. A new pair of long kidskin gloves, and I was ready.

With our horses stabled for the night, Roddy ordered a hansom cab, and by 7:15, both in fur and wool, we made our way to the Plaza Hotel, where a uniformed bellman met us at the front entrance, verified our names, and escorted us to the elevator, whose white-gloved operator whisked us to "Floor number seven…Colonel Rankin's suite. Watch your step, if you please."

The maid who opened suite door **Number One** took our coats, invited us to be seated, murmured that Miss Rankin would join us, and disappeared behind a far door.

We entered a parlor of woodwork and draperies, of Havana silk sofas and armchairs, of paneling in light mahogany and gold-framed etchings on the walls featuring castles and scenes of fox hunting. It must have felt deluxe for a man from Suggs Run, West Virginia.

Seated on a sofa, we both glanced toward a far corner where a table was set for three, silver and glassware sparkling on a white tablecloth.

"Mr. and Mrs. DeVere, hello to you."

Glenna May appeared from an inner room, the maid at her heels. She raised one hand in greeting, the other gripping her cane. A tiny figure in black, her only jewelry was a jet necklace.

"Don't get up," she said. "Let's sit for a spell." Moving to a chair opposite us, she hooked the cane over the chair arm. "Would you favor filtered water? The ice comes the size of river rocks."

In moments, the maid appeared and set down a tray with glasses, a carafe, and a bowl of colossal ice cubes and silver tongs.

"Clear plant ice," Glenna May said. "They freeze it in a factory. Time was, they'd only cut it off lakes and ponds in winter. My brother got interested in the ice business. Coal and ice, winter and summer…Leon spent time in New Orleans studying factory ice they make with ammonia. He decided against it."

The maid poured and retreated. Impatient to hear about the matter of "great importance," we sipped and waited. I knew Roddy would begin with pointed small talk. "Mrs. Devere and I are happy to join you this evening," he said. It's fortunate that your telegram reached us."

I said, "Perhaps the luck of the Irish."

"The Rankins," she said dryly, "came from Scotland."

The room went silent. Somewhere a clock struck eight p.m., and Glenna May pointed to a disc-like device on a nearby stand. "Press a button on that thingamajig," she said, "and our dinner comes to us right here. Whatever you want, the button gets you newspapers or a hairdresser, all sorts of cold or warm dishes...drinks too." She pointed to the table set with silver and glassware. "It's only fair to give you a dinner, so we'll start right off. I asked them to make us something good. They'll bring it when I push the button."

She reached for her cane, but Roddy said, "If you please, Miss Rankin, do permit me...."

My husband pushed, and the wheeled carts arrived with a bevy of waiters to seat us and serve salted almonds and gherkins, roasted sliced turkey, mashed potatoes, stewed turnips, and cauliflower fritters. Offered wine, we declined. Roddy and I sat on either side of Glenna May, just as we had two days ago at tea.

"And one last thing," Glenna May said, pointing to a covered crock. "That's my brother's favorite dessert, bread pudding with rum sauce. They made it for him in Palm Beach."

We nodded in respect to the pudding, and the waiters withdrew. Often ravenous by this time, I had no appetite. We soldiered through the meal until finally, at the pudding, Glenna May announced, "The reason I wanted you to come here is John Griggs."

"The banker," Roddy said.

"Used to be. Not anymore." Her silver-gray hair glinted in the light. "He waylaid me today. I think he waited in the lobby for when Mr. Taggart left and I went out for a breath of fresh air. I gave the elevator man a dollar not to ride him up here."

Roddy frowned. "Does he continue to be a Plaza guest?"

She shook her head. "No more, no Dent or Griggs, either one."

"And Mr. Suggs?"

She shook her head. "Amos went back south to work on the hotel, and Mr. Taggart said I could stop those two from mooching on my late brother...I mean, the Star Coal Company. Both Griggs and Jeremy Dent are on their own. I told the maid, 'Do not open the door for either one, no matter what.'" She spooned her pudding. "Dent...he's likely too busy with women and fancy tailors to bother me just now. Griggs, now...that's different."

Glenna May looked up and paused. "Years back, I had a sweet-natured black and tan coon hound. Never once did he tree a raccoon, but he'd look at you something pitiful. If you didn't give him a bite to eat, he'd growl and bare his teeth." She looked from Roddy to me. "John Griggs puts me in mind of that dog."

I smothered a smile, but Roddy said, "Miss Rankin, is there a special reason why Mr. Griggs goes to such length to speak with you...wait for you in the lobby?"

She said, "I hardly go out, cold as it is, but a body needs fresh air. First thing in the morning, Mr. Taggart comes with a satchel of papers, and we sit right here at this table...right here."

She knocked on the table with the end of her spoon. "We go over everything I need to know...over and over about Star Coal and Keymont too, and other enterprises... even the opera box."

"The Metropolitan...." I began.

She nodded. "Leon was far along to owning a box. He told me at Christmas, he signed papers."

Roddy looked startled. "Papers?"

"Leon said the opera was good for business. The official owner would be Star Coal."

Roddy paused with his pudding spoon in hand. "Miss Rankin, have you seen the signed 'papers?' Perhaps when working with Mr. Taggart?"

She fingered her necklace. "A whole lot of papers," she said. "The charity churches…a home for deaf children.… I don't recollect the opera in particular. Mainly, I pay attention to the coal companies and the B&N Railroad. And Keymont Bank."

"Bank?" Roddy asked.

"Keymont Bank," she replied. "There's Keymont Coal and a bank too. My brother got attracted that way. I must've signed twenty-five papers. My Taggart showed me papers with my own name in ink."

"Your signature?" I asked.

"Mine for sure," she said. "Nothing to brag about, but I am a trustee of the Keymont Bank. The assets.… My brother had showed me. They look considerable."

Roddy had put down his spoon and narrowed his eyes. "Miss Rankin," he said, "we regret that your brother's sudden passing has brought us together. From what you say, Mr. Griggs is not welcome. The Plaza management could easily see that he does not trouble you." Roddy paused. "Is there something else of particular concern?"

Glenna May's fingers tightened into fists, her knuckles almost as white as the tablecloth. "My brother saved his hide in Pittsburgh. The Griggs Bank was sinking into the Allegheny River, and Leon kept it going for a good long while, but the bank was not charity. Leon said 'weepy' John Griggs had better learn to stand on his own two feet, or else."

She shrugged. "So, by and by, that bank was no more, and now John Griggs figures me for…what's the word? A 'soft touch?' That's it. With Leon gone, he thinks a woman will be his soft touch. If my brother was alive, John Griggs would not be sneaking into a hotel lobby to tug at his sleeve and whine."

Roddy lowered his gaze to the table, his jaw tight. I peered at a fox hunting scene on the wall. "Miss Rankin," I said, "you mentioned a dog that could growl and bare its teeth if it was not rewarded. Would Mr. Griggs somehow threaten you? Could he do so?"

Glenna May folded her arms across her bosom. At length she said, "John Griggs claims he has something on paper… something I wouldn't want to have known, not in public."

"A document?" Roddy asked. "Or something of a personal nature?"

A long moment passed. "Women troubles…" she said. "What a man won't get into for a woman…."

Roddy's brows lowered in confusion. "Do you mean to say that Mr. Griggs—?"

"—heavens no, not Griggs." Between a laugh and a scoff, she said, "It's not him. It's other women." She looked from

Roddy to me. "My brother never chased women until he got divorced. Then it was 'Katy, bar the door.'"

"What door?" I asked.

"It means 'look out for trouble,'" she snapped. "It's a saying. My brother kept on the straight and narrow until that wife of his sued for a divorce. She's Lewis's mamma, so I won't speak ill, but the man near worked himself to death for her, and she sued for desertion and got away with it. And Lewis has been the worse for it...a young man adrift in life."

Roddy cleared his throat. "Miss Rankin," he said, "we need not stray into such family matters." He spoke slowly, with lawyerly gravity in his voice.

But Glenna May pushed on. "You went to the memorial service," she said. "You saw that tramp...hair like brass...."

Roddy and I exchanged a sidelong glance.

"And hat feathers waving like a flag...well, I could tell her about the woman's combs I found in Leon's suite." She pointed to a far door. "His bedroom," she said, "all full of his clothes and shoes, but a woman's combs with red hair caught in the teeth."

"And may I ask," Roddy said softly, "whether John Griggs's document pertains to this matter?"

She seemed not to hear the question. "I sit here at this very table with Mr. Taggart, and it makes for a long day, and I hardly go out. A body deserves fresh air without being pestered."

"A short walk," I said, "is refreshing, even in cold weather. And Central Park is just across the street."

She pointed at the closed draperies, snatched her cane, sprang up, and pulled back the drape. Pointing to the windowpane, she said, "Yes, out there is Central Park. And the doorman says they skate on the frozen lake in the daytime. I would like to see them skate before I go back to Florida."

Roddy had halfway stood, uncertain of whether Glenna May would return to the table. She peered into the darkness, as if to see the park and the skaters. The moment turned awkward.

Roddy said, "Miss Rankin, it was good of you to invite us to dinner, and these days are unbearably difficult for you, but...."

She silenced him with a curt wave. Standing at the window, holding back the drapery, Glenna May turned to my husband. "You are about to ask why I sent a telegram to invite you here this evening, isn't that right? You want to know why you are here."

Roddy flushed. "I hope you won't find it impertinent, Miss Rankin."

She ignored Roddy's words. "Mr. Taggart," she said, "thinks I might be needing advice from a New York lawyer. "You are a lawyer, Mr. DeVere? An attorney at law?"

My husband nodded. "I am."

She let go of the drapery and punched her cane at the carpet. "Then, sir, you have your answer."

Chapter Fourteen

THE DINNER WITH GLENNA May Rankin rattled Roddy and made me anxious. The woman had no idea that her dear brother had been murdered, nor any hint of a threat to her own life or wellbeing. Or her nephew's. Roddy and I alone shared secrets that drew us toward Glenna May's orbit. The notion that my husband would be her attorney caught me like a tripwire.

We barely spoke in the hansom cab ride home. By rights, we should have turned in for the night instead of pouring a nightcap. We lacked the verve for a good talk, and our pre-dinner ardor felt beyond recapture.

We entered a hushed household near midnight, the servants in their lodgings, our dog in her kennel. With coats and hats off, we faced one another in the foyer. The staircase to our separate bed chambers beckoned after a harsh day. For me, the hours had twisted from the "dangerous" woman to Glenna May. Roddy admitted his mood had soured from trudging through rough and trashy wharfs, then squinting for an hour at railroad business ledgers in a stuffy, ill-lighted office.

"So much to talk about..." I said.

We stood close in the foyer, our breath in rhythm. "So much..." I said softly.

"But not now," my husband whispered. He caressed my cheek. "Time for talking in the morning, Val...but not now." He gently laid a finger across my lips. "Now is our time. Let's have a nightcap."

Roddy took my hand, and we tiptoed to the darkened *Crème* drawing room.

We kissed, and he opened a cabinet and reached for a bottle and liqueur glasses. "New start," Roddy whispered, drawing a cork. "Bénédictine," he said. "We salute the monks of the Bénédictine Abbey." He poured, we sipped, and kissed again. Then Roddy loosened his tie, took my liqueur glass and set it down beside his. With his waistcoat unbuttoned and cast aside, he drew me to the divan, and his kisses tasted of liqueur...and of him. His breath in my ear.... "Val," he whispered, "now is our time...."

The divan seemed to rock as we rocked, my shoes and stockings off, my skirt pulled up high above the knees, and the vents in a gentleman's clothing allowed everything my lover needed...everything I needed until, at last, came Roddy's lightning shudder and the rolling waves that surged and surged again as I bit down to muffle all vocal cries of this moment, this night. Breathing hard, we lay face to face on the divan, time halted, the moment our very own as our breath slowed and our hearts beat in time with one another.

Later, we held hands going up the stairway, grinning at our bedraggled selves, clothing awry, shoes in hand, Roddy's hair tousled, mine loose and streaming. At the top of the stairs, we kissed gently, Roddy to go down the hall toward his suite, I to my boudoir—but not before my lover whispered this secret proposal: that we agree to make love in all the rooms of this house in the months and years to come. I sealed the agreement with a closing kiss.

※

The morning dawned bright and all too soon. Calista opened my drapery, and I blinked awake. "Sunshine today, ma'am," my maid said, "cold, but lovely at 8:15 a.m." She added, "Norbert tells me that Mr. DeVere is at breakfast."

From a deep sleep, I murmured, "Already?"

"According to Norbert, ma'am. I understand the kitchen is on holiday today, but hot tea and coffee are ready."

"Right...thanks."

I washed, tied back my hair, slipped into a periwinkle sacque and slippers, and entered the breakfast room to see Velvet on my husband's lap at the table. I jumped onto his lap with the dog. We laughed, but Velvet leapt down in alarm and eyed us warily, while the footman gave a thousand-yard stare into the distance, as required by his job.

"Good morning, my dear Mr. DeVere," I said.

In lush undertones, Roddy replied, "A good morning to you, Mrs. DeVere."

He signaled the footman for my coffee and his tea refill, and I quickly sat down across from my husband, whose navy dressing gown set off his deep blue eyes, a visual treat I savored immensely.

"I hope Calista did not sound Reveille, Val, but I plan an early start today and hoped we might breakfast together." Roddy sounded strangely serious.

Still a bit drowsy, I nodded yes to cold, leftover campfire hash and heard Roddy request bread and cheese, sliced ham and jam. The footman poured our drinks, bowed and withdrew.

The morning papers lay to the side, the headlines run-of-the-mill. *"House Passes Army Bill," "Kentucky Distilleries United," "Police Come to Standstill."*

"Nothing more about the 'Coal King,' Roddy. It seems he's yesterday's news."

"—and may he stay buried in Hearst's and Pulitzer's newspaper 'morgues.'" Roddy's forehead furrowed. He looked a bit pale...winter pale. "And may we not find a bizarre end to the life of Miss Glenna May Rankin in the headlines one morning...or Lewis."

I shivered, reached for my cup, and sipped the hot liquid. Thoughts of our nocturne in the *Crème* drawing room were drifting off as this new day landed like another season. "I said, "Roddy, is that a law journal...again this morning?"

"Recent court decisions and cases, Val. And I wanted a look at corporate governance...when ownership changes."

We fell into a somber silence. The Junghans clock hit the hour, nine a.m., as our plates were set before us. Last night at the Plaza suite nudged into mind as I lifted a forkful of cold hash and Roddy sliced a wedge of cheese. "Roddy, suppose I invite Glenna May to see the skaters in the park this afternoon."

"Skaters?"

"She shouldn't be cooped up all day, not with Central Park a stone's throw from the hotel suite. She reminds me of women in the mining camps, independent and outspoken. She deserves an outing.

"However..." I said slowly and evenly, "a pleasant 'taste' of Central Park in winter must not put us under further obligation to Glenna May. Please tell me you are not planning to become her attorney."

A silent moment passed. My husband spread jam on a bread slice. "Not exactly," he said.

When baffled, my papa would ask, 'Can you cut the deck a little deeper?' "What do you mean, Roddy? Not to sound cold-hearted, but Glenna May's legal matters have nothing to do with our 'q.t.' inquiry...or my lost earring."

My husband put his knife down, narrowed his eyes, and stroked his chin. "Val, there's something else...something we ought to pursue...business documents."

"What documents?"

"The records I reviewed yesterday afternoon," he said, "are a troubling mix of bond issues and stock shares. Star Coal and the railroad are heavily encumbered…in debt."

"Oh….?"

He patted the dog and fed her a pinch of cheese. "Taggart hinted at problems, and the hour I spent with the Barret & Nitro records outlined Rankin's recent moves. To finance his Florida hotel, he let his businesses become a piggy bank…and therefore a house of cards. The coal mines and the railroad are financially shaky."

"Roddy, why should we care—?"

"—because I'm talking about homicide."

My husband laid his fork and cheese knife in a perfect parallel on the breakfast plate. "Leon Rankin was stabbed to death, and his memorial service was an unholy brew of rage by men who might have killed him.

"Or the woman…" I said. "…'no fury like a woman scorned'."

"Or the woman," Roddy repeated. "So far, we think of Griggs lurking in the lobby and threatening Miss Rankin, assuming the 'weepy' banker might stab the 'Coal King' to clear the path to his newly rich sister…a soft touch for money."

"And Jeremy Dent is still in town," I said, "dining and drinking and looking for a lawyer to wreak revenge on the railroad scheme that cheated his family…but possibly furious enough to kill Leon Rankin at the opera."

"But I fear," said Roddy, "the new president of the Star Coal Company is about to be attacked."

"Attacked?" In the West, the word meant bullets and buckshot, arrows and spears. It meant fists that broke jaws and fractured bones.

Roddy paused, his cheeks flushed, but his face pale. "Glenna May will be the victim of savage litigation."

"What 'savage litigation'?"

"A fight to the death when a lawsuit destroys the coal companies, the railroad, and the Keymont Bank...don't think that I exaggerate. Think about the Southern Pacific Railroad."

This sounded beyond loony. "The West Coast railroad? *The Great Pleasure Route of the Pacific Coast*?"

The airy motto failed to lift Roddy's mood. "The Southern Pacific," he said, "got into a dispute about fencing along its track, and the case went all the way to the Supreme Court. That court," he said, "extended the rights of a person to corporations."

"A person...? Did you say 'a person'?"

"Under the Fourteenth Amendment...all about economic liberty."

"A corporation is a person?"

"Under the law."

It took a moment to grasp the notion of a railroad transformed into a human being....Frankenstein on a railroad track. My thoughts spun. Leon Rankin murdered, but his company, or companies, were living persons?

"Roddy," I said at last, "what does this have to do with Glenna May?"

He folded his arms across his chest. "When valuable assets go up for grabs, attorneys spring to the nearest courthouse to file…in this case, against Star Coal, or the Keymont Mine, or the Barret & Nitro Railroad. Or the Keymont Bank. Or all of them…a slew of suits."

"From Jeremy Dent? Or Griggs?"

"Yes, indeed. Backed by investors, either one could file a suit, claiming numerous injuries. Dent would probably resurrect a claim against the B&N in the name of the original Barret railroad line. As for Griggs, whatever 'paper' he threatened to expose, it might involve loans to Star Coal by his former bank…or a crafty transaction that ruined the Griggs Bank."

Roddy frowned. "We don't know about Amos Suggs or the woman at the church, but Griggs and Dent are front and center. The Rankin holdings would be bought up at a fraction of their value, pennies on the dollar. It doesn't mean the mines will shut down or the railroad quit hauling coal. It means a takeover."

"But the Rankin companies would be killed?"

"Yes."

I said, "And the new Star Coal president completely cut off?"

"Highly likely, Val."

I gazed at the frosted windowpane. "So, Leon Rankin would be murdered twice…his body and this companies…and his son…and sister…."

"Penniless in her old age. Think about Glenna May, Val. You suggested inviting her to Central Park, and you'd call for her at the Plaza Hotel…."

"Of course."

"...where her suite and her meals and her hairdresser are all paid for by Star Coal...where a maid tidies her rooms and the bellmen and waiters bring whatever she needs at the press of a button."

"Roddy, why go on this way?"

My husband would not be stopped. "Imagine her homeless...sleeping at night in the police station with the vagrants...begging for nickels...destitute, shivering in the cold...pneumonia waiting to claim her."

Roddy lifted his teacup, but snapped it down, leaving me unsure of what to say. "If the axe falls, Val, the financial press will exalt, and other papers as well. And the 'minor' assets will be picked apart, including Rankin's Metropolitan Opera share and box. News hounds smell blood, and they'll lie in wait to question Glenna May, whether she's here or in Palm Beach...and don't forget Amos Suggs and the woman in Rankin's box at *Don Giovanni*."

My husband poked at his plate of cold ham. "And something else...." His frown deepened.

"What?"

He hesitated, reluctance in every feature of his face. "I wish I could spare you...."

"Spare me what?"

He jabbed at the ham. "My mother," he said. "She stopped in for a few minutes...about an hour ago."

"Oh?"

"She had heard about the kitchen staff's day off…the 'special holiday'."

"…from Mrs. Thwaite," I said, between annoyance and humor. From the housekeeper to Eleanor DeVere, a telegram couldn't be faster. "And she disapproves," I said.

Roddy nodded.

"Just like the wages we pay," I said, "…upsetting Society's 'apple cart'."

Roddy pushed his hair from his forehead. "And another thing…."

My husband's face turned from serious to grim. He reached across the table to take my hand. "How rumors begin…" he said, "is anyone's guess. But they escalate…."

"What rumors, Roddy?"

He sipped his tea, still holding my hand. "Mother says it is whispered that your earring was found in the late Leon Rankin's vest pocket when his body was examined in the morgue."

The words rushed at me like a steaming foreign language. Mute, I felt unable to say my husband's name. His hand tightened on mine, his lips moved, and I managed to ask him to repeat the next words to be sure I had grasped them when he said, very slowly, "…according to the rumors, Val, it is believed that you somehow hastened Leon Rankin's fatal hemorrhage."

Chapter Fifteen

THE PREPOSTEROUS RUMOR APPARENTLY had spread widely. I couldn't eat another bite, and Roddy pushed away his ham and cheese.

"Gossip needs oxygen," my husband said, "and the truth will stamp it out."

"Roddy, don't be naïve."

"Let's try for 'optimism,' shall we?"

I shut my mouth. The footman removed our breakfast plates, and Velvet followed him, nose twitching.

Roddy said, "I told mother the earring was lost at the opera but said nothing about the Wendells' box."

"And the Police Commissioner? My confiscated earring?"

"Not a word to mother about the police. The gossip does not involve the police."

"Not yet." My voice rose. "The rumor probably started in the opera house," I said, "...with Hoff." I clutched my throat. "Who else, but Hoff?"

Roddy frowned. "Doubtful, Val. The DeVeres are long term shareholders. Maurice Hoff would be asking for trouble."

"—unless 'Wild West' Valentine is dispensable."

"Val...."

"It's true. Divorces in Society have become run-of-the-mill, and you can marry an appropriate debutante...if I'm out of the way."

"I won't listen to this nonsense."

I blinked back angry tears, and Roddy looked stern.

"I could have a word with your parents, Roddy."

He shook his head no. "I spoke for us both, Val. Let it go for now." He sat back. "We have no idea where the rumor started, but Mother promises to tamp it down. Our best move is the fact-finding 'q.t.' inquiry. For today, I suggest the sight of rosy-cheeked ice skaters cutting figure-eights."

"With Glenna May Rankin...."

"If she'll come with you to the skating pond, you'll listen for down-home talk about her late brother. Or Lewis, his son and her nephew."

"Or their foes...."

"Friends or foes," Roddy said.

After breakfast, Sands summoned a Western Union messenger and wired Miss Glenna May Rankin at the Plaza. If I did not hear otherwise, I would meet Miss Rankin in the lobby at 12:45 p.m. I looked at our social calendar, dreading the upcoming dinner at the Stadlers…Hornby and Phillipa Stadler. The social obligations fell to lady of the house, and I must keep track. I had promised Roddy to try harder.

Mrs. Thwaite got to me first. "Ma'am, if you would, the carpet samples are ready for your selection and approval… if your day allows the time."

The housekeeper knew perfectly well that my "day" left scads of time. Her barbs never quite reached the point of belligerence, and I hoped that she would one day announce her departure from the DeVere household. Not a day too soon.

"Yes, Mrs. Thwaite," I said, "let me see the samples."

I sat in the nearest reception room, and the housekeeper brought the carpet squares, which stirred the memory… *Don Giovanni*, the blood…the corpse.

"Ma'am, are you feeling unwell?"

My throat felt tight.

"Ma'am…?"

When his breath shortened, Roddy always closed his eyes and imagined a low hum. I closed my eyes and mentally hummed.

"Ma'am, would you wish smelling salts…?"

"No." Eyes open, I shook my head just seconds before the housekeeper released a vial of ammonia from the pocket of her uniform. Ladies carried hartshorn for fainting spells, but Mrs. Thwaite kept her salts like a chemical spray.

"I'm fine," I said. "Let's spread these squares."

They ranged from pale neutrals to charcoal gray and black. Why the senior DeVeres and the Wendells had chosen pale carpeting for their opera saloons and boxes was a mystery, especially when the opera season meant boots crusted with slush and mud.

"I'll select this gray one, Mrs. Thwaite, for both boxes, numbers seventeen and eighteen. Please inform the carpet man."

"I believe Mr. Sands will so inform him, ma'am. I will tell Mr. Sands of your choice."

Another pinprick, meaning the household division of labor confused the lady of the house…the butler's domain separate from the housekeeper's, the rank and file order of servants, the coachman and groom and stable boys. So military. "Will there be anything else, Mrs. Thwaite?"

"Yes, ma'am…distressing news." She paused, looming large, holding the carpet squares and squaring off before me. "I must report damage done to the furniture."

"Oh?"

"In the *Crème* drawing room, one leg of the divan has splintered."

"Splintered, you say?"

"As if undue pressure had been applied to a most delicate antique …prized by Mrs. DeVere, as I recall."

The housekeeper's "Mrs. Devere" referred to Roddy's mother, Eleanor.

"…purchased, if I remember correctly, during the DeVeres' travels in Italy," she said. "And irreplaceable, I should think."

I tried to nod gravely. Roddy would share my amusement.

The housekeeper did not move. "If I may say so, ma'am, I suspect the temporary maid is at fault."

Once again, the housekeeper's grudge over the new maid I had hired, Mattie Sue Joiner. My failure to consult Mrs. Thwaite had become, as we said in the West, the "burr under her saddle." I waited until she spoke the maid's name aloud.

"I will speak to Mattie Joiner," I said at last. "And about an artisan to repair the damaged leg...would that be your undertaking? Or Mr. Sands's?"

She drew up sharply and huffed intentions to consult the butler, meaning that she had no idea which of them ought to seek a restorer of antique furniture legs. In retreat with the carpet samples, her heels thumped and her keyring clanked. Relief when she vanished.

Calista walked with me to the Plaza at noon. We took Velvet. Etiquette prohibited ladies from walking solo in public, though servants were assumed to be on errands, a freedom denied to the female employer in the city calling itself Gotham. Calista seemed pleased to bundle up, and we snapped the dog into her fleece coat. The booties never stayed on her paws, so we left them despite Sands's dismay at the front door.

Glenna May's broadtail mink and matching hat caught my eye in the Plaza lobby just after 12:30. The doorman helped us into a Hansom cab, and we set off for 72nd Street and the Central Park Lake that the park designers called a winter "skating pond." The bracing cold curbed conversation, but Glenna May said she was no charity case and could walk just fine with her cane, no help from me.

This was not to be an afternoon from a Currier & Ives print, but it could yield important clues if I kept my head. In moments, I found my plan blown to the winds.

"Auntie Val! Over here, Auntie Val...."

High-pitched cries and waving little arms drew my gaze to a lakeside bench.

"We're going to skate...."

Two children, a boy and small girl, waved frantically, while two women bent low to the snow. I waved back, resigned. The plan to glean information from Glenna May Rankin crumbled at the sight of my friend, Cassie Forster, her children, and their nanny.

Why hadn't I guessed they might be here? Winter afternoons meant sledding or skating in Central Park. Buckling skate blades onto the children's boots, Cassie had not yet seen me. On the lake, skaters circled as pairs linked arms, children squealed, and solitary young men skated forward and back. No way could I wave, blow kisses, and guide my companion to a distant bench.

"Looks like you got friends over there," Glenna May said, pointing her cane toward the Forster bench.

"We'll join them, shall we?" I walked slowly with Glenna May, careful about her cane and wondering how to salvage the afternoon. I would introduce Miss Rankin to Mrs. Dudley Forster. Glenna May and Cassandra could chat about the Royal Poinciana Hotel in Palm Beach, since Cassie and her husband, Dudley, had been guests of the hotel where Glenna May had been living for the past few years.

I would show polite interest in visiting Florida in the wintertime. Cassie would inquire about West Virginia and listen closely, and Glenna May would be sociable in her own way. The two young children's nanny would be on hand to help fasten skates and chafe cold little hands. Smiling at the skaters, we all would stamp our feet to keep warm.

In minutes, we joined the Forsters, and Cassie stood, smiling, her voice lyrical. "Valentine DeVere, what a sweet surprise." My friend's fashionable hourglass figure was contoured in heavy layered outerwear. Her soft brown eyes shone, and her lustrous auburn hair had been tucked into a bonnet that I recalled once sporting feathers at the crown. She smiled at me and kept the smile for Glenna May.

"Mrs. Dudley Forster, may I introduce Miss Glenna May Rankin...." Suddenly aware that my friend was not cued about the name so recently smeared in the press, I relied on Cassie's manners. Introduced to Lady Godiva, she would chat politely about the white horse.

"...and may I introduce my children, Charles and Beatrice. And our dear nanny, Cara." The young women looked up from her task and nodded pleasantly. Cassie said, "Children—?" in a voice that rose the tiniest bit. "Children—?"

The boy and small girl looked up and said, "How-do-you-do?" to Glenna May, who bent down to see their skates and express keen interest.

"I am going to skate all by myself, no holding anybody's hands," insisted the little girl whose pink head scarf wound like a turban.

"I will do a figure eight," proclaimed her brother in a Cossack cap.

In the next minutes, Cassie and I stood back as the children explained ice skating to the elderly woman who amazed them by admitting ignorance of the steel blades being fastened onto their boots. I overheard Charlie, age six, explain the physics of steel moving on ice as detailed by his scientist father, and four-year-old Bea assert her plan to fly on ice like Peter Pan's Wendy.

All the while, Glenna May bent close to them, absorbing every word. Bea asked about the cane, and Glenna May told a secret, that she had skidded on a big red flower. The children laughed. They had made a new friend.

"Auntie Val" had been sidelined, somehow demoted, and I felt peeved. Cassie gave me a smile that said "Oh, come now, Val" but also warmed my heart. Skates fastened, the children stood with nanny Cara and marched the few feet to the ice.

"Valentine," said Cassie, "why not step closer to watch the children? I'll enjoy chatting with Miss Rankin." She turned. "And may I call you Glenna May? My friends call me Cassandra...."

Dispatched to the ice, I applauded the Forster children who ventured, fell, got up, stroked forward, glided, tumbled, fell again. I cheered them on, calling aloud as at a Nevada rodeo calf-roping. "Go, Bea, you can do it…Charlie, good turn…do it again…let's see you do it, Bea…yes…."

Real cheers, but several feet away at the bench, my friend stood close to Leon Rankin's sister, both women's breath steaming in the cold air. Apart from the social palaver, what did Cassie intuit? On rare occasions, I had seen her collapse from some unseen force. I turned, however, at the sound of laughter, seeing the two women huddle, as if confiding secrets.

I retreated toward the bench and heard Glenna May say, "…best witch in West Virginia. Everybody used her."

Did I hear 'witch'? Did my friend start a conversation about witches? Or did Glenna May?

"The gift runs in families, I understand," Cassie said.

I cocked an ear to listen. How did this conversation get started?

"It does run in families," Glenna May replied. "Third generation on it now. Some favor copper, but she swears by a forked wood divining rod. 'course, the witch keeps the particular wood her secret. Some say willow."

"I heard ash and hickory," said Cassie. "My husband doesn't believe a word of it."

"…probably no faith in spirits either."

"He's a scientist," Cassie said with rueful pride.

Glenna May chuckled. "For well water in West Virginia, he'd best set aside his doubts. Where the witch's rod bends down, there's water directly below, so start digging."

I stood with them, but apart. For the moment, neither my friend nor Glenna May seemed aware of my presence. They gazed at the lake and waved to the children whose cries filled the air. A bright red cardinal flew toward the bench and veered off to the trees.

Cassie abruptly leaned forward to grasp the back of the bench in both gloved hands, as if to steady herself. She asked Glenna May something about "spirits." Did she mean high spirits, enthusiasm?

"Oh, for sure," Glenna May said. "Ghosts in the old West Virginia Penitentiary and the asylum too. And some claim they see an apparition on a river I crossed as a schoolgirl... somebody's shape in the fog, a woman that disappeared years back. Never saw 'her' myself, but those that do feel sure that's who it is. She comes during the quarter-moon."

I heard Cassie ask, "Glenna May, do you believe...? Do you...?"

Glenna May poked her cane in the snow. The cardinal chirped from a nearby branch. "Cassandra," she said at last, "I no longer disbelieve. The older I get, the more things look beyond my ken." She cocked her head "Not to get too pesky, Cassandra, but why do you ask?"

Cassie's hands gripped the bench railing tighter. Her face looked nearly as white as the snow. "Glenna May..." she said, "Glenna May Rankin...you ought to...please do take care." Cassie stood straight, as if with great effort. "You too, Valentine, my good friend. Take good care of yourselves," she said. "...very good care."

Chapter Sixteen

IN SNOWY WINTER, OUR warm conservatory gave us summertime luxury of green plants, wicker furniture, and a burbling fountain. The glass skylight etched with snow and the surrounding panes felt like a snug igloo in the city. I had loved this space from the moment I first saw it.

"Roddy, we must spend more time here in the conservatory." I had just come home in the Forsters' big brougham that had room for Glenna May and myself. Shedding a heavy cloak, gloves, hat and boots, I found Roddy and our dog amid the plantings and flowers in gardenia-scented air. Velvet licked a welcome, and my husband rose from a wicker settee to greet me, his face fretful. A thick stack of papers lay on the cushion beside him.

"What's all that?" I asked.

"Nothing good," Roddy answered. He tapped the papers. "I thought the fountain and the palm trees would cheer me up."

"And?"

"Not so far."

I sat on a chair beside the settee. The footman appeared. I asked for hot chocolate.

Would my husband prefer tea, the footman asked?

"Hot cider, Bronson."

The footman withdrew, and the dog lay under a banana tree in a terra cotta planter and began to snore softly. "Nice life," Roddy said.

"As we have remarked many times." I pointed to the papers. "Something to tell me?"

"Not yet. Not until I hear whatever Glenna May had to say about Leon or his son, Lewis...or Griggs or Jeremy Dent. Or perhaps the Suggs fellow. Or the woman with blonde coiled hair? Or is a new name in the picture? What did Glenna May have to say?"

I moved a small pillow on my chair. The greenery had not cheered my husband, and Cassie's warning to Glenna May would stir up a tiff if I told him everything now. I flashed a chipper smile. "Glenna May confirmed that a water witch with a wood divining rod is certain to find the best spot to sink a well."

Roddy blinked and bit his bottom lip.

"Roddy," I said, "Glenna May stiff-armed me all the way from the Plaza to the Lake. Then she charmed the Forster children, and they charmed her. Then I watched Bea and Charlie skate. When I rejoined Cassie and Glenna May, they were into a tête-à-tête about water witches and...."

"And what?"

I paused, relieved that the footman appeared with a tray and served the cider and chocolate and a plate of ginger cookies. One of my mother-in-law's manuals insists that two servants are necessary to serve at teatime, since one alone indicates a woeful household. The West had its codes, but no such fuss.

"Thank you, Bronson," I said. "Please thank the kitchen for us."

He bowed and was gone. We sipped the hot drinks, the fountain splashed, and a yellow leaf fell from a Ficus tree. Roddy asked, "…and what else did Glenna May have to say?"

No point in dribbles and drabs, so I blurted, "She said that a West Virginia prison is haunted, also an asylum. And a ghost…an apparition of a woman is seen near the Barret River at a certain phase of the moon." I added, "You'll be relieved to hear that Miss Rankin has not seen the ghost."

Roddy reached for a cookie. "…and Cassandra drove you home afterwards? And then took Miss Rankin to the Plaza?"

"In that order. When I left the brougham, the children were reciting rhymes about snowmen. Glenna May tapped her cane in time."

Roddy bit the cookie. "Val, are you holding out? You know my sincere regard for the Forsters, the best of friends. But when Cassandra is involved…." He broke off, but his meaning was clear. "Ghosts and apparitions…" he said. "As a lawyer, the circumstantial evidence is pointing…." He met me gaze. "Need I say more?"

"Roddy, you're already upset. Why make it worse? Whatever's in the papers stacked on that cushion.... I'll say this, Cassie felt something ominous...dangerous. She warned Glenna May to be careful...and me too. We were nearly ready to leave. The children were coming off the ice with their nanny, and Cassie suddenly clutched the bench as if struck...bodily." I added, "You know what I mean."

"I do. And I would hope Cassandra does not recommend that Miss Rankin employ the woman who reminds her of her old Nanny...or the woman who shines fingernails."

"Madam Riva," I said. "I doubt it, but let's not go further...."

We sat in silence. Cassie's Madam Riva, a manicurist-turned-medium, parlayed her daytime skills with nail files and buffers into lucrative evenings when she summoned spirits of the dearly departed. With a florid head wrap, bangles in her ears, and ballooning colorful skirts, the woman reminded Cassie of her beloved nanny, Saffira-of-the-Islands, who led little Cassie into a spirit world from childhood, a world invisible to everyone else. Madame Riva pronounced herself a Romanian countess, though the more frequent term was gypsy. I had serious doubts about her, though Society embraced its Ouija boards, and rival mediums conducted séances in the New York mansions and palatial Newport summer "cottages."

I reached for a ginger snap. "Those papers, Roddy... did they come from Mr. Taggart? Did you see him this morning?"

"I did. We had a talk. These documents came out of his office safe."

From a locked safe, the papers looked newly valuable.

"They are on loan to me," Roddy said. "Miss Rankin wired Taggart late last night to permit my examination of pertinent documents. The wire referred to 'R. DeVere, my lawyer.'"

"She wasted no time."

"None. Taggart had a satchel filled for me this morning. Val, have you heard the expression, 'watered stock?'"

I had. "Two meanings, Roddy. In western rangeland, it's cattle drinking at a stream. But in Nevada mining country...." I saw his face, grim around the mouth. "It's the second meaning, isn't it?"

Roddy nodded and sipped his cider. "My grandfather used to rail about 'Uncle' Daniel Drew's Wall Street tricks... and his clothes. Drew started as a cattle drover and dressed like one. He made sure his cows drank lots of water before he sold them, based on their weight. Drew won and lost fortunes on the Street. In the devil's dictionary of finance, his entry is 'watered stock.'"

I knew the term from the silver mines, when Papa shook his head about men who took large risks on false information. The papers stacked on the cushion beside my husband suddenly seemed "watery."

"Is that what you found in those documents? Inflated values of Star Coal? The B&N Railroad?"

"Both...and I haven't had time for the Keymont Mines or the Keymont Bank records." Roddy thumbed the papers. "Most men who handle railroad properties will water the stock by degrees."

"So it's not noticed?"

"Exactly. But Rankin ballyhooed the B&N and Star Coal in glowing terms, and buyers took the bait. The stocks boomed, and printing presses rolled out certificates. So far, the share prices have stayed high."

"But not the true values?"

"Not by a long shot."

"Roddy," I said, "Papa talked about mine stocks that boomed and went bust. I never asked how or why."

My husband's sad smile lingered as he reached to pat Velvet, who sniffed at the cookies. "Brokers' commissions, Val. The broker makes money with every sale. Rankin whispered to his broker that favored clients ought to know about a hush-hush contract in the works between the Navy and Star Coal."

"The US Navy? Our Navy?"

"For the coaling stations for our naval vessels...in the Caribbean ...Hawaii... worldwide. Our steamships run on coal...battleships, cruisers, every vessel must be refueled. A coal contract with the Navy would be worth millions... and the coal would be hauled by the B&N Railroad. Rankin passed the word, and his broker went to work."

"Nobody checked?"

"...too fearful of getting left behind, especially when the "Coal King" suddenly got the reputation as the brilliant head of several railroads and mines, a bench of judges, US senators, unlimited lawyers, an opera box, and a chorus line of dancing girls."

"But there's some truth to it, isn't there?"

The dog lay down at Roddy's feet, and my husband stroked her ears. "Let's say that Leon Rankin headed one railroad and two mining companies. And a bank. About the judges, senators, and my fellow barristers, I wouldn't be surprised. The dancing girls are a possibility, and we know something about the opera box and ought to know more right now."

Roddy reached for his cider. "Rankin's death has not affected the stocks…yet. But news of the debt will send it plunging when word gets out that he borrowed against the railroad and the mine to finance his hotel. It looks like Rankin deliberately triggered the boom with false rumors about a Navy contract."

"So the stocks would jump sky high…."

"Which they did," Roddy said. "The stocks boomed, and Rankin borrowed against them."

"The Leon Rankin house of cards," I said.

"The house of cards," my husband repeated.

Our dog snored, and the fountain splashed. I ate another cookie. Roddy said, "And one more irritant today…get ready."

"Something about the house? About us?" Another Ficus leaf fell. "What is it?" I asked.

"A query from Police Commissioner Gork. He took the liberty of paying a call this afternoon. I spoke with him."

I picked up the two fallen leaves but said nothing.

"He'd care to know about progress of our 'inquiry.'"

"Commissioner Bernard Gork is keeping track? Are we on his schedule?"

Roddy finished his cider. "He visited the opera house again at Mr. Hoff's request. Reporters have been at the building asking the employees questions...maids, custodians, stagehands...even singers. Hoff requested aid from the police. He told the Commissioner he fears the rehearsals are being disturbed and performances could suffer."

"...or is he really worried the reporters are snooping into Rankin's scandalous death in the Diamond Horseshoe?" I stood and walked in tight circles. My voice sounded choked. "And did he bring up our names, Roddy? My name?"

"Val—"

"—did Hoff spread his poison about my earring and Rankin's corpse?"

"Valentine Mackle DeVere...." Roddy sprang from his chair and wrapped me in his arms. "Shhh...." He held me tight. The dog growled softly. A moment passed as the tension slowly eased and Roddy gently sat me back down.

"Sorry, so sorry..." I said. "The vile gossip is much closer than I thought."

"Of course it is...."

We sat for a moment. Velvet settled for a nap, and the fountain plashed. The light and shadows moved until, at length, I asked what the Commissioner of Police had to say.

"Nothing much," Roddy said. "He assured me that our inquiry ought not to be rushed, but he hopes to alert the mayor and Chief Devery about our progress. His Honor is most interested, as are other parties."

"What 'parties?'"

My husband hesitated. The sunlight was fading, the conservatory light dimming. "Val, let's not start a guessing game just now. The 'party' we need to have in mind is dinner at the Stadlers'. Noland will have the Hackneys hitched and ready. The invitation is for 7:00. We ought to arrive at ten past the hour, sharp."

Chapter Seventeen

PRECISELY AT 7:10 P.M., the Stadlers' groom assisted Roddy and me from our carriage onto the carpet rolled out to cover the wintry sidewalk. Street lighting threw shadows on the French Renaissance chateau that was built after Hornby and Philippa's five children had grown up and gone. The façade struggled for elegance, but the iron balcony bulged and the window ledges looked like stone teeth.

Once inside, Roddy surrendered his overcoat and top hat to a footman, while a maid took my sable cloak and guided me to an anteroom so my hair could be tended by another maid. Calista had suggested a teal velvet gown with lace at the shoulder and a sapphire necklace and matching earrings, plus blue-green long silk gloves. I kept my fingers on both earrings as my hair was touched up, then joined Roddy, stepped toward the reception room entrance, and prepared for a dull evening.

"Valentine and Roderick, so pleased that you could join us," said Philippa Stadler in her high-pitched squeal. Her salmon taffeta dinner gown, couturier-designed, suggested window draperies on her stout frame.

"So very pleased to be here," Roddy replied. My husband spoke for himself and meant what he said.

The cavernous reception room surrounded us with pink plasterwork—*cartouche*—molded into medallions, flowers, vines, and fruit. Against a far wall, little flames flickered deep inside a fireplace overwhelmed by a massive mantelpiece of veined marble.

The room buzzed with conversation of the Goelets, the Camerons, Miss Delafield, Mr. Potter, the Rutherfords…the social set I joined as Roddy's wife. A sudden voice at my ear cheered me with familiar irony.

"Mrs. Roderick DeVere…formerly Miss Valentine Mackle, I do believe."

I turned. "Theo…Theodore Bulkeley."

"Your faithful friend and occasional escort, at your service." He turned to Roddy, who moved off when Theo said, "Roderick, I shall attend to this lovely lady, so feel free to mingle and be amused."

Theo's bow showed the slim, agile frame known to be wicked on the tennis court, while his pale blue eyes twinkled with mocking merriment. A confirmed bachelor and man about town, Theo Bulkeley regarded Society as an arena of human folly, a circus maximus for his entertainment. Deep down, he was kind and thoughtful. A Bostonian, Theo had adopted New York as his home, and Society embraced him as a favorite son. He volunteered to be my "Galahad" at events meant for couples when Roddy was summoned to hush-hush cocktail "emergencies."

"May I wish you a Happy New Year, Valentine?" Theo said, "and my apologies for failing to pay a call on the first day of January. I was visiting cousins in Boston, while you received the gentlemen of the city…and how many hours of confinement to your home 'throne'? Ten? Twelve?"

He eyed me with puckish glee. "Sentence suspended until next year, but what do I hear about the DeVere opera box being shut tight? And the Wendells' as well?"

If we were served wine before dinner, I could seize the moment to take a sip while thinking fast. "…seepage on the carpets, Theo," I said at last. "Some leakage from the Wendells' box. They're traveling, you know."

"Rented their box, didn't they? To that poor fellow that died… 'King' of coal?"

"Leon Rankin," I said. "Yes, very sad."

"Quite the ladies' man, I understand."

"Oh? I wouldn't know." Somehow, I hadn't thought to tap Theo's war chest of gossip. Theo Bulkeley often knew what Pulitzer and Hearst's reporters had missed. Membership in several men's clubs, he said, provided better and faster news.

"You're the man with inside hearsay, Theo. Maybe you have details?"

"Never met the man, Valentine. The question is, why didn't he buy himself a yacht? People ask the same question about Stanford White."

"The architect?"

My friend flashed a sly smile. "Gentlemen of Society host private parties on yachts in the harbor because apartments and hotel rooms are sure to cause trouble. Stanford White's buildings are brilliant, but the man ought to give up the secret apartment with mirrors and the red velvet swing. He's asking for trouble. About the coal man...." He shrugged. "No details, but he should have got himself a yacht. Too late now...but what about your opera box...?"

"Nothing interesting, Theo. New carpets are ordered, so you can count on an invitation to Box Seventeen very soon. Roddy has been starved for opera, and the two of you must go."

"Without you? Your favorite singer is coming up, Madame Nordica."

I said, "We'll see," hoping to fend off more questions.

My tactful friend changed the subject. "Would you guess which mementos we will take home tonight? Gold-plated playing cards? Gemstones?"

I rolled my eyes. Dinner guests' souvenirs had become competitive. So far, the votes favored a dinner memorable for little sterling silver pails filled with sand. Each guest was given a tiny silver spade to dig for buried diamonds. Roddy and I had not attended that famed dinner, but the hateful label, *Idle Rich*, rang too true.

"Here comes the butler," Theo said. "Courage...."

The butler's "Dinner is served," meant each gentleman must escort a particular lady whose name he was given on a card, but never his spouse. Theo went to find Miss Delafield, and Roddy was out of sight, when a whiff of a certain men's cologne assailed my nostrils.

"Mrs. DeVere? Perhaps we will dine together for the first time this evening. I am Chadwick Bourne."

A familiar name, Bourne? I smiled at a thickset man with blooming side whiskers and let him march me to the dining room, where the walls presented life-sized portraits of cavaliers and milkmaids. The table gleamed with crystal and silver. "Here we are...if you please." Chadwick Bourne held my chair.

That name? Did I remember Bourne? It sounded familiar. The ladies were seated, and he took his place on my right. The man reeked of Patchouli, my least favorite men's scent.

"Ah," he said, "we begin with *caviar frais en crêpes*." He leaned closer. "I understand that you are our very own Annie Oakley," he said, "so, may I offer to translate the names of this evening's dishes?"

"—starting with raw fish eggs in rolled pancakes?" I replied. His whiskers seemed to puff and retreat at once. "It is rumored, Mr. Bourne," I said, "that in Colorado we eat bear meat and wolf, but I know for a fact that Virginia City, Nevada, had chefs from Paris, so...to each his own, shall we say?"

My crack was sure to make the rounds. Blame the Patchouli.

Footmen poured wines and served the courses I knew from countless dinners like this one...the light soup, the trout mousse, the dressed cucumbers carved into clever shapes, then to *poulet* barely recognizable as chicken. Somewhere between the beef and salad, just before the dessert, Chadwick Bourne restarted a conversation.

"I believe you recently met my wife at a meeting far downtown. Paulina as spoken of you."

Paulina? Yes, the stately, gray-eyed woman who reported the dismal wages of Lord & Taylor salesclerks—and eyed my earrings. A glance far down the table showed the silhouette of the tight-lipped Paulina. "What a coincidence," I said. "From Henry Street to the Stadlers' dining table in just a few days." I added, "I look forward to our next meeting so Mrs. Bourne and I can become better acquainted."

"Oh, as to that...very doubtful," he said. "You see, my Paulina's sister has married into a New England family of do-gooders, and my wife has felt she must keep up with her sister." He sipped his wine. "But one foray into the secrets of the department store was quite enough for her, and this 'dangerous' woman coming to the Consumers Club—"

"—League," I said. "The Consumers League."

Driving toward his point, he did not hear me. "...and when I learned these meetings take place in the Lower East Side, I put my foot down...down. Perhaps Mr. DeVere has spoken similarly?" He stroked his side whiskers. "Or perhaps the DeVere household is caught up in certain other matters...."

I should have kept quiet to block Chadwick Bourne's "other matters" from tempting me on, but I bit, asking what "matters" he might have in mind.

"Far be it for me to speak out of turn," he said, "but Mrs. Bourne has heard something about a fatality at the opera and…and really, I should say no more…."

He left off, but stared at my right ear lobe, a hard fixed stare at the sapphire earring as footmen removed our plates. I felt my cheeks flush but kept my lips closed. The desserts were coming, little cakes *au caramel*, followed by coffee and liqueurs. It appeared that mementoes of the dinner would not be presented, which was a relief.

Then cigarettes…. Customarily, the gentlemen left the table to enjoy cigars, the ladies to smoke cigarettes. Roddy would join the men but forego the cigar. With the ladies, I would try not to choke. Cassie, an accomplished smoker, had offered to teach me, but so far, I only hoped not to cough out loud.

At that moment, a chime sounded. "If you please, dear ladies and gentlemen…."

Hornby Stadler, a wraith of a man, had risen from his seat at the foot of the table to address his guests. "May I request that everyone remain seated at the table while our footmen serve each of you a delicacy of the House of Stadler?"

The Stadlers, Roddy told me, had headed a drug and wine importing firm since colonial days, and someone nearby whispered about after-dinner drugs as the liveried footmen dispensed cigarettes from gold trays, each guest to take one in hand and await another footman with a lighted taper.

Were we all to sit at the table smoking cigarettes? I took mine, as did Chadwick Bourne, holding it in the "V" of two fingers. The cigarettes, I saw, had been rolled in yellowish, mottled papers that burned but seemed thick. In moments, clouds of tobacco smoke rose...as did laughter... peals of laughter.

"Bravo, Hornby!" a man called out, and others laughed loudly, ladies and men in chorus. Trying not to choke, I looked at Chadwick Bourne's cigarette, then peered at my own. The memento of the evening was being consumed by fire. I now had good reason to choke. The cigarettes had been rolled in hundred-dollar bills.

Chapter Eighteen

"UNFORGIVEABLE," I SAID. "I am furious."

Seated across from me in our carriage, Roddy reached for my hand, but I would not be soothed. We had just left the Stadlers' to find refuge in our brougham. Noland held the reins, and the carriage felt like a bunker.

"They all puffed away, Roddy. You heard them, gay and cheering. Did you cheer?"

"Of course not."

"No one else at the table stubbed out their cigarette," I said. "Not one soul."

"But you did."

In my gloved hand, I held the charred cigarette, tucked out of sight from the table to the cloak and the farewell at the door when the Stadlers' groom announced, "Carriage for Mr. and Mrs. DeVere." Escape at long last.

"How many at that table, Roddy? Thirty?"

"Thirty-six, I believe."

"Three thousand, six hundred dollars up in smoke."

"Not quite. Your banknote might be salvageable," he said. "And someone else did not light up."

"Who?"

Roddy reached into his topcoat, felt deep into his formal wear, and brought up the rolled cigarette. "Intact," he said. "On any such occasion, I must preserve a discriminating taste for liquors, wines…bitters…."

My husband's calm felt annoying. "Was it only about your palate, Roddy? What about morality? My disagreeable dinner partner called Hornby Stadler a 'genius.' He thinks the hundred-dollar cigarettes take first place over the silver sand pails."

"Chadwick Bourne is no one's favorite. His application to the Union Club was hotly contested."

"But he got in?"

"He did."

"Of course he did. They always do. The idle rich…. And he hinted about my earring and Rankin's death—"

"—what?"

"Not in so many words, Roddy, but his wife stared at my earring at a Consumers League meeting a few days ago, and her husband mentioned death at the opera and peered long and hard at my ear lobe until dessert…."

I broke off. Here I sat, swathed in ermine, snug inside a closed carriage pulled by purebred horses and driven by a uniformed coachman. In the Colorado mountains, Papa had wrapped me in bearskin and warmed my itchy wool Union suit by the fire so I could go to sleep in comfort. An hour from now, thanks to my maid, Calista, I would find a silk nightgown laid out for me, and I would glide into a featherbed with softest sheets and angora blankets. In the mining camps, I had never heard of angora. Neither had Papa. My mama did not live to sleep even one night in such comfort.

"Val, are you all right?"

The horse's hooves drummed softly.

"Why Val, you're weeping," Roddy said. I felt his handkerchief dab at my wet cheeks.

"I didn't stand up, Roddy," I said. "I could have stood up at the table and called out the wrong of it. I could have, but I didn't. I put out the cigarette and hid it."

"It's all right, Val. It's all right."

But it was not "right." And I knew it.

I declined the chamomile tea Roddy suggested when we got home. He shepherded me upstairs as though his wife had taken ill. I was too riled to argue, too sad to talk.

Came morning, and once again, the day started in the breakfast nook with the dreadful Junghans clock, but also Velvet, who jumped and licked her welcome. The clock clanged the half-hour, 7:30 a.m. Roddy was not yet downstairs.

"Coffee, ma'am?"

"Good morning, Bronson," I said. The word, "coffee," was on my tongue tip, but a glance at the frosty window changed my mind. "Not yet," I said. "I will walk Velvet first."

"Ma'am?" The footman eyed my peignoir, my slippers.

"Right now," I said. "Please see about Velvet's coat and leash and meet me at the front entrance."

The footman's face, somewhere between wonder and horror, began what I later called a palace revolt. In moments, Sands was at the front door, and Mrs. Thwaite at his heels. The new maid, Mattie Sue Joiner, had been at work in a room off the foyer, and she too appeared, feather duster in hand. The three stared.

"The ermine cloak will do, Sands," I said. "And the hat and boots from last evening."

"But if I may say so, ma'am—"

"—not at this time, Sands. My cloak, if you please."

Between the butler and me, the fur cloak looked ready for a tug-of-war. My "If you please" gave him no choice. Mrs. Thwaite stood frozen, but Mattie knelt to help with my heavy boots. Her nose, I saw, had a decided bump from the episode that brought her here last fall. "Thank you, Mattie," I said. "And now gloves…?"

"Gloves…" said Mrs. Thwaite in a choked voice. "Gloves…."

The cloak covered my nightclothes, the hat already warmed my head, and the boots were laced. Somehow, my gloves were not to be found. Bronson stood with Velvet, leashed and snuggled in her fleece coat. A shuffle continued for the missing gloves.

"I regret, ma'am," said Sands at last, "the only gloves available at the moment are Mr. Devere's." He held up Roddy's lambskin gloves as if they spelled doom for my walk, as if the gloves were tokens of a battle the butler had won.

"Excellent, Sands," I said. "I shall wear Mr. DeVere's gloves...the door, if you please...."

An open-and-shut case, literally, as the front door closed behind me and I led our dog down the front steps. "Velvet, here we go." I walked toward 63rd Street, and the cold air on my face, the crunch of hard-packed snow, the silence of the early winter morning felt like a tonic. I walked fast, the dog keeping pace, and we crossed the street and went toward 64th Street. In front of each house, footmen had spread cinders on the sidewalk, so footing felt secure.

They say that dogs do not understand human language, but we talked to them anyway. "Velvet," I said, "Roddy's gloves fit well enough...a bit roomy...we'll go a few blocks further..." I looked up at the tree branches, tufted with snow. "Just look at those birds, Velvet...listen to them...and see that squirrel? The squirrel lives in that tree.... In the Rocky Mountains, the squirrels have black tails."

A carriage passed beside us on the avenue, and I waved to the coachman, a breach of etiquette. He tipped his hat. "See that, Velvet?" I said. "Feels good, doesn't it?"

Was I outdoors by myself for half an hour? Forty-five minutes? The household seemed in shock when I returned. Mrs. Thwaite lurked behind a massive Chinese cloisonné vase, and Sands looked stricken, his face bloodless. Mattie Sue was nowhere in sight, but the two footmen, Bronson and Chalmers, looked braced for whatever might happen. I took off my hat and unclipped the leash. "Please, gently warm Velvet's paws," I said to the footmen.

Chalmers stepped forward in evident relief. "Yes, ma'am. And I'll take off her coat."

I quickly thrust the ermine cloak, my hat, and Roddy's gloves into the butler's arms. "Mrs. Thwaite," I said, "perhaps a hand with these boot laces…?" She had no choice but to leave the vase, help with the boots, and bring my slippers. "And now," I said to Bronson, "I'll have that cup of coffee… and if Mr. DeVere has not yet come down to breakfast, please send word to his valet that I hope he will join me soon."

Roddy was not in the breakfast nook, so I sipped coffee and scanned the papers. *"Warehouse Destroyed by Fire," "Mother Kidnaps Her Own Child," "'Princely' Sum for Carnation."*

I began with the "princely sum" of thirty thousand dollars for Mrs. Lawson's flower, when my husband appeared, his hair tousled and not yet shaved.

"My dear…." He sat, peered at me, and rubbed his eyes. "Here you are," he said.

"Where else would I be?"

"I don't know…. Funny thing, I woke up and rubbed the frost from the front window in my suite to have a look outside…. I glimpsed a woman alone with a dog…much like Velvet. Where is Velvet?"

"Warming her paws," I said. "Tell me, who was the woman?"

He tightened the belt of his dressing gown. "I got just a glimpse of her fur cloak…probably a maid, but the fur looked…like it might belong to…a lady."

I cocked my head but stayed silent. Bronson brought Roddy's tea, poured, gave each of us a glance, and retreated in haste.

My husband looked closely at me, squeezed his eyes shut, opened them, and narrowed his gaze. "Val," he said slowly, "don't tell me...."

I nodded.

He poured milk into his tea. "Why on earth...?"

"Why not?" I said. "Velvet needs her daily walk, and so do I. Why can Calista go outside by herself, but I need a chaperone?"

"—because serious crime threatens a lady who is clearly well-to-do."

"Easy to solve that problem, Roddy. From now on, I will go outdoors in shoddy wool instead of ermine...or mink, or sable, or Persian lamb. Name the fur, and I have at least one...raccoon, rabbit, sealskin...." I reached for my coffee. The cup rattled, and coffee spilled on the tablecloth.

"Val, your hand is shaking."

I hid both hands on my lap. "...ridiculous, Roddy...the money thrown away.... Look at the *Journal*...thirty-thousand dollars for Mrs. Thomas H. Lawson's carnation...a single carnation."

"I believe," Roddy said quietly, "that Lawson has honored his wife with a carnation named for her."

"For thirty thousand dollars."

"Tom Lawson has made money in copper, Val. There's plenty to spare. He loves his wife."

"That's not the point. Little children in this city need clothes and food and school and decent places to live and...."

I stopped just as Bronson came for our breakfast order. Roddy asked for poached eggs. I could barely speak, and my husband requested porridge for me, as if I were ill.

"Now Val...." Roddy nearly whispered. "You're upset, and every right to be...but the Stadlers' dinner was difficult in more ways than one." He rubbed his bristly cheeks. "Before dinner, Hornby cornered me with questions about the opera. He'd heard the 'outrageous' rumor that a coal company could be a new shareholder, and he pressed questions that no one can answer right now...."

"Such as...?"

"Such as, what about the share values and the property? Is the whole thing 'sound?' What would happen if box holders sold out, and the property fell into 'excessive decline'? And would certain business interests be saddled with losses they could ill afford and touch off another downturn?"

Roddy sighed. "I fended him off as best I could, I was never so happy to hear 'Dinner is served.'"

He sipped his tea. A silent moment passed, and the sound of approaching paws eased us both.

We called out at once, "Velvet!"

"Feel her paws, Roddy."

He pulled her into his lap. "Toasty," he said. The footman approached with breakfast, and he put her down. "No poached eggs for you, Velvet, and no porridge. She's been fed, Bronson?"

"Yes, sir, we fed her before Mrs. DeVere went...." He blushed bright red. "I mean, she has been fed, sir."

The footman fled. "I rattled the household this morning," I said.

Roddy nodded. "I passed Sands in the hall...looked as though he'd seen a ghost."

"And now you know why," I said.

My husband smiled, and we dutifully turned to our food. Velvet settled under the table.

"You'll review the rest of the Rankin documents today?" I asked.

Roddy nodded. "The Keymont mines and the bank too." He glanced at the wall clock. "Then the Dewey Committee again this afternoon," he said. "We're deciding whether to show an Edison film about the war, *Shooting Insurgents, Spanish-American War*. Will the audience stay seated or run riot in the streets?"

"And is it suitable for ladies? I bet that's the other question, isn't it? But no lady will be asked to preview the film and have a say about it. Am I right?"

He gave me a fishy stare. "Val, let's not go into that right now. Tell me about your day."

I cringed despite myself. I, too, was expected at a meeting this afternoon. The looming "dangerous" woman had cast a pall, and Chadwick Bourne's self-righteous decree that he'd put his foot down to protect Paulina from the Lower East Side and the "dangerous" woman.

"Roddy," I said, "when you hear of a 'dangerous' woman, who comes to mind? It's not a trick question," I said. "Who comes to mind?"

"I don't know...maybe Lady Macbeth? Lucrezia Borgia? Or in the Bible...Delilah? Salome? How about Salome?"

"Somebody in the present," I said.

He raked fingers though his hair. "Hard to say...the papers report a furious Temperance woman said to be sharpening an axe to smash saloons' liquor kegs to terrify customers into denouncing 'demon rum.' She could be dangerous, and my associates are alerted for news of her."

"Not her," I said. "I doubt it's her."

"And Lizzie Borden, the axe murderer...." He leaned forward and gazed directly at me. "Val, what's this about?"

"—about a meeting at the Consumers League," I said. I'm supposed to meet a woman they call Mother Jones, and she's called 'the most dangerous woman in America.'"

Chapter Nineteen

I DAWDLED. THE PROSPECT of the "dangerous" woman drove me into household tasks that guaranteed late arrival for the 1:00 p.m. meeting in Henry Street. The etiquette books forbade prying into the "why" of a lady's delay, so, for once, etiquette would be an ally.

What to do? A review of my wardrobe could take an hour, and Calista agreed to work alongside. She and I had a late-morning bite and went upstairs to a closet the size of a sitting room. "Too much..." I said, peering at the volume of gowns. "Too much, too many...."

"Ma'am?" My maid stood beside me, her dark hair pulled back against her head and her dress in cleanest lines. Beside me stood a living rebuke to these flounces and pleats.

"I'm thinking about excess," I said. "...surplus is on my mind."

Calista kept quiet. Years on the coastal steamers had taught her to "read" moods. At length she said, "Ma'am, shall we postpone the review of the gowns?"

"Yes, and skip the furs. Let's look at the recent deliveries of springtime clothing...the croquet outfits...and the tennis...."

We moved to a different closet, where the red, white, and blue outfits hung neatly on a rod, and the shirtwaists folded on a shelf beside the bowties printed with red and blue stars.

"Calista," I said, "would you like to have these things? I don't play croquet...."

My tactful maid did not reply that croquet lawns were not in her sightline. Nor were tennis courts.

"Thank you, ma'am," she said, "but no thank you.... though patriotic colors are in fashion just now, the war won and the soldiers and sailors home again." She paused. "Unless you plan to wear the bowties...the next Independence Day when the servants have our picnic, I might consider—"

"—take them, Calista. Help yourself."

"Ma'am, do you feel well?"

I flushed, embarrassed. The servants' picnic...in another life, it would have been my picnic. "Calista," I said, "I have a meeting downtown. We'll deal with the spring clothes when...when it's spring."

We agreed.

The Consumers League meeting was adjourning when I arrived at Henry Street, driven in the phaeton by our clumsy groom, who guaranteed a slow, jerky ride to the Lower East Side.

The flow of departing members showed faces scrunched and brows furrowed. A few ladies raised a hand in greeting, and I waved to Felicia Ordway and her daughter, but they moved on briskly. Was it the cold weather, or did the rumors about Rankin's death and my earring keep them at a distance?

Like a tardy schoolgirl seeking credit for attendance, I wanted my effort to be known. I needn't have worried. Here came Daisy Harriman.

"Valentine DeVere, we almost gave up on you."

"Daisy, good afternoon."

"...a truant, Valentine, and you missed the most enthralling speech. Mother Jones held us spellbound. In her own way, she's as powerful as Mrs. Kelley."

I shuddered. Florence Kelley, the head of the new Consumers League, was already proving herself a "force of nature." Admired and feared, she was earning her nickname, "Niagara Falls."

Daisy took my arm. "Fortunately, Valentine," she said, "you're just in time. I'll introduce you to our guest speaker. Remember what I said, you'll find that she's your—"

"—I know, my cup of tea." Daisy led me through the main room tinctured with odors of wax and medicine and into the small meeting room. In the chair where Paulina Bourne had perched just days ago, a plump, grandmotherly woman sat as though the plain bentwood seat were a plush wing chair with arms.

"Mother Jones, let me introduce Mrs. Roderick DeVere, the lady I mentioned from the West." Daisy smiled. "I would love to stay on, but my train to Mount Kisco leaves on the dot." She was gone.

I sat across from this notorious figure, a study in black and white, except for bright blue eyes and rosy cheeks. This full-faced woman had fashioned herself in a tailored costume of midnight black, too stylish for mourning. A ruffled, snow-white shirtwaist and flowing neck piece highlighted the snowy curls that framed her face.

Her leather handbag lay on the table. Did a stick of dynamite lie inside? A firearm?

"My bag," she said, "is full of bank cheques from the ladies this afternoon." Her soft, strong voice rang with a disarming lilt. "The Consumers League ladies listened with open minds and open hearts," she said. "The difference between a charity and a cause...all the difference in the world." She flashed a trace of a smile and folded her hands on the table, as did I. Her short, rounded fingernails had been filed, like mine. She wore no jewelry, and my diamond ring looked terribly large.

"I'll be honest," I said, "I have been reluctant to make your acquaintance."

She laughed, a surprising, full-throated laugh. "You fear for your life, is that it? The 'most dangerous woman' might send you to an early grave?"

Her eyes twinkled as I both cringed and joined in her laughter. I said, "Is there a kernel of truth—"

"—in the 'most dangerous woman in America'? I hope so, but not the way you fear." A trace of a smile played at her resolute mouth. "I was arrested for violating an injunction against public speaking. So, off to jail with me. In a courtroom in Parkersburg, West Virginia, the prosecuting attorney pointed his finger at me and roared, 'Your Honor, there is the most dangerous woman in the country today.'"

"And?"

"And the judge summoned me to his chambers, and we discussed constitutional rights. His honor dismissed the case against me, but reporters lapped up the prosecutor's words, and the newspapers spread it far and wide." She tapped a finger on the table. "The attorney's 'pet name' serves the cause…and I do believe you know our cause."

The constant lilt in her voice was distracting. "Mrs. Harriman told us that your name is Mary Harris," I said, "and you rally the coal miners."

Her jawline tightened. "Missus," she said, "I rally for life and liberty for men who have been robbed for years by masters who made them into industrial slaves." The steel in her voice matched the sparks flashing in those eyes.

"So you would like a contribution from me," I said.

"For the cause, not for me…for the lawyers and the bail and the families that nearly starve when a strike is called…a strike of necessity."

Her lilt had tapped something deep in my memory. "Apologies for asking," I said, "but are you Irish?"

"County Cork," she said.

"My parents both came from Ireland," I said.

"Thousands upon thousands in the starving time," she said, "some here, some to Canada, even Australia." She narrowed her blue eyes and looked closely, as if appraising me. "Why offer 'apologies' for the simple question, am I Irish? You look like a sprightly lass, so speak up. You've got a tongue in your head, so use it. I learned that lesson long ago. You want to know why Mary Harris is 'Mother Jones,' don't you? Speak up."

"Yes," I said.

"Louder," she said.

"Yes," I nearly bellowed.

"Your folks," she said, "are they here on earth or in Heaven?"

"Heaven," I said. "Both in Heaven."

"...like my dear husband and our four little ones," she said, "swept off by yellow fever. I washed their bodies and readied them for burial. This was the year 1867 in Memphis, Tennessee, the whole city ravaged by that plague. And so, alone and grieving, I went to Chicago. I had the schooling to be a teacher, but dressmaking suited me, so I sewed...sewed for the lords and barons who lived on Lake Shore Drive in magnificent houses. And I would look outside the plate glass windows and see poor, shivering wretches walking along the frozen lakefront, jobless and hungry. My employers seemed not to notice or to care. Do you hear me?"

"I do." I said it clearly.

"In those days," she said, "the Knights of Labor was the union, and I went to their meetings in the evenings. My husband, George Jones...may he rest in peace...he was a member of the iron moulders' union, so I knew something about organized workers."

Her mouth tightened. There's fear of working men... they've died in strikes... steel workers in Homestead...the rail car workers in Pullman's plant when he slashed their wages. And the strikers get blamed for the hoodlums that set fires and riot. The owners hate the working man...."

"Or woman?"

She raised an eyebrow. "A good point. You might yet be worthwhile. You're young enough to work for the vote."

Somehow, I felt delegated.

"But my remaining time on earth is committed to the United Mine Workers of America. The miners that enrich the Consolidated Coal Company and Fairmont Coal—"

"—and Star Coal? And Keymont?"

"Them too, all of them. I am mother for the miners and their families, Mother Jones." She paused to hear her name. "I pondered 'Sister,' but the power is the 'Mother,' so I am Mother Jones. Mother Jones am I."

She reached across the table and took my hands in hers. "I have a warning for you," she said. "By nightfall, I'll be on my way to West Virginia, where the coal barons' pet poodle dogs are warm and have a comfortable breakfast...and where the 'slave' miners that move the world's commerce are out on the highways without shelter, thrown out of the company shacks to face the blasts of winter weather." She stared hard at my face. "But you have work to do here."

I nodded, my fingers caught in hers.

"A judge in a courtroom called my actions 'unworthy of a good woman.' That man sat high on the bench in his robe and held up his gavel, and he made a speech. Prissy man, he called me 'she' as if I was nowhere in sight."

Her voice turned high and nasal. "'**She** ought to follow the paths which the Almighty intended her sex should pursue.' And '**she** should engage in conduct shown to be the true sphere of womanhood.'" I heard him declare it 'unworthy' of me to be 'used as an instrument of reckless agitators.'"

My hands began to cramp, but she held tight, her gaze locked on mine.

"Here's my warning," she said. "A woman can be free, but a lady is at risk. I saw it in Chicago...Lake Shore ladies that longed to escape tea party life...but couldn't manage it. They disappeared... became shadows of themselves. Do you understand?"

"I think so."

"That's the risk," she said, "You must speak up. You have work to do. I hope you hear me. You must do it."

Chapter Twenty

"A WOMAN PREACHER?" RODDY asked. "She sounds like a missionary."

"Exactly," I replied. "Mother Jones is a woman on a mission."

Upstairs in the Bergere chairs, my husband and I talked about our day. We were late. Roddy had been delayed by a carriage crash that brought traffic to a standstill, and our groom's clumsy driving gave me an anxious hour to mull over Mother Jones's message—and her warning.

The room felt cool despite the glowing fire. "Shall I mix a cocktail?" Roddy asked.

"I think sherry this evening," I said.

My husband spoke Spanish to the footman about a certain *jerez* label and year, and in moments we sat before the fire with a decanter of amber sherry, glasses, and a bowl of nuts, which somehow were not calming. The tall clock's throaty chime would harken to a town crier's "six o'clock, and all's well." The closed drapes did, at least, spare us the drear of pitchblack windowpanes. The new moon seemed like no moon at all.

We touched glasses and sipped. Our dog would cheer us, but she was downstairs at her feed bowl. "So, you plan to contribute money to the miners' union," Roddy said in a dry voice.

"I do."

"You know what our friends will think…what the newspapers will say if they get wind—"

"—that Mrs. Roderick DeVere is a Wild West Socialist," I said.

"Probably."

"For certain," I said. "So what? In Virginia City, Papa started out in the Miners' Union, and I treasure his old membership papers…two dollars to join, twenty-five cents monthly dues. He had to resign when he went out on his own and struck the Big Lode, but he always believed in the union. The contracts were holy writ, and the union took care of families when a man was hurt…or worse."

I reached for a walnut. "You went down into a silver mine in Virginia City, Roddy. You remember how horribly hot…."

"I remember who I saw in that deep, dark shaft." He reached for my hand, and his voice warmed.

We held hands across the chairs, both quiet. The scene of Roddy and his parents in the Nevada silver mine would forever shine in my mental album. Inspecting a mine with Papa, I had heard the elevator clanking down into the ink-dark mineshaft, where a foreman alighted to guide visitors. Rufus and Eleanor DeVere had frozen, petrified, but the young man with them had looked about, plainly curious. Candle flames on miners' helmets gave just enough light for the young man to see me, while my eye caught sight of his firm jaw, his deep-set eyes.

We found ourselves at neighboring dinner tables that night at the Silver Queen Hotel and Saloon, talking together while Papa warned Rufus not to invest in certain mines. Rufus DeVere turned a deaf ear to Patrick Mackle's warnings, but Roddy enchanted me with his demonstration of a flaming Blue Blazer whisky drink at the bar, and now I sat with the love of my life, Roderick Windham DeVere, on Fifth Avenue, New York City, in January, 1899.

"Val," Roddy said, "I ask only that your donation to the coal miners be kept quiet at present. The Leon Rankin murder is quite enough...." Roddy sipped his wine. "Something came up today."

"The Dewey celebration film, *Captured Insurgents*?"

"We decided on *Raising Old Glory*."

"No offence to anybody," I said.

My husband gave me a fishy glance and reached for almonds. "Before the Dewey meeting," he said, "I took a satchel of files back to the Star Coal office, and Taggart promptly locked them in the safe. I'll need a few more days to review the bank papers and the B&N Railroad records, but the picture looks dismal. Taggart agrees. He fears he could be liable when Rankin's empire collapses."

"Could he? Is a comptroller at risk?"

"A hothead prosecutor might go after him to make political points, but a criminal defense attorney could make a strong case. Elmer Taggart saw storm clouds gather when Rankin got fixated on the hotel in Florida, and he tried to warn the 'Coal King' but felt helpless. Rankin called the shots. Now Taggart feels he's up against something new…a 'situation,' but it sounds like a threat."

"A real threat? Should I shiver?"

Sipping sherry, Roddy paused. "The apartment on 26th Street," he said, "…rented to Star Coal month-to-month."

"For Rankin's dalliances…." I said.

"Taggart guessed as much, but the 'Coal King' bluffed about the apartment used for company business, so the comptroller played along until Rankin's death. A few days ago, he notified the building owner that Star Coal would cease payments at the end of the month. But the apartment has become a problem. Taggart turned red as a beet when he told me it's occupied…."

"A 'lady friend' has moved in?"

Roddy frowned. "One particular 'lady friend' has lived there for quite some time, over two years. The owner said something about eviction, and Taggart went to the apartment to slip a letter under the apartment door."

"A personal letter?"

"Official, typed on company letterhead. But the door popped open, and Taggart found himself face to face with a woman in *dishabille*. He called it 'night clothing.'"

My smile faded at my husband's gravity.

"They didn't speak. She reached down to pick up the letter, and Taggart fled. He remembers her pink robe and blonde hair, which caught my attention, and so I asked…."

"And?"

"Hair like vines, Taggart said….like coiled yellow vines."

My heart skipped a beat. "Roddy, the woman at the memorial service with the ostrich hat and blonde coils…"

My husband plucked an almond, then spoke the words already forming in my thoughts. "…the woman in the opera box the night Leon Rankin was murdered." The tall clock chimed the half-hour. Roddy put the almond on the table.

"There's more, Val. Taggart got a sob-sister letter pleading for more time, but he held firm…on behalf of the company."

My husband shifted in his chair and faced me. "He got another letter yesterday, this one very different. He showed it to me. On pink paper that smelled perfumed, Miss Gloria Bates wrote that she has information of great interest to certain parties, and she offers to discuss the matter with Mr. Taggart before going any further. She hopes not to 'go any further unless forced to do so.'"

"Blackmail," I said.

Roddy nodded. "Taggart is at wit's end. He feels bewildered. The man rues the day he came to the big city…wishes he'd stayed near the Canadian border where he belongs."

"Roddy," I said, "this will sound cynical, but for the sake of our 'inquiry,' shouldn't Miss…Bates, is it?"

"Gloria Bates."

"Shouldn't she live in the apartment? If she moves, she might vanish into the city...or wherever. Suppose we find that she conspired with Jeremy Dent? Or John Griggs? Or—"

"—or acted alone? Found out about other women and took revenge?'"

I stood to poke the fire, and Roddy reached for his sherry.

"So...," I said, "we want Gloria Bates in place on 26th Street for the time being. We want her in the apartment feeling free of any suspicion."

"And we need to know what 'information' she might have." Roddy capped the decanter. "Val, I have taken a liberty...."

"What 'liberty'?"

"I suggested that Taggart take Miss Bates to dinner... that he invite her to a fine restaurant to talk things over. I suggested the Astoria Hotel dining room."

"And...?"

"And Taggart was reluctant. He does not dine in such establishments but finally saw my point. Even so, the man could be too anxious to hear whatever the Bates woman tells him in the dining room. Her words might be lost, unless...."

"Unless what?"

"Unless we are seated at adjoining tables...our party of two in earshot of Elmer Taggart and Gloria Bates."

⁂

Two nights later, at seven forty-five o'clock, Roddy and I entered the dining room of the Astoria Hotel on 34th

Street, a "veritable palace," said the *New York Times*. By agreement, the maitre d'hotel led us to one of two tables, quite close but not crowded together. The silver, the crystal, the snowy napery, the gleaming candelabra on the walls and Rococo mirror frames—all of it struck me as a stage set, and the two of us the actors. Roddy had donned a false mustache and goatee he retrieved from an old costume party set, fearful that Miss Bates might recognize him from the opera box *entr'acte* when he scolded the Coal King's group for noise. I doubted the woman had noticed me at the church service, but a swooping hat brim shaded my face. Taggart expected us to be seated nearby, like recording secretaries. He agreed not to look our way, nor acknowledge our presence.

The Astoria dining room was Roddy's choice, and his chat with the manager guaranteed custom service. Mr. George Boldt, the Svengali of hotel managers, did not bat an eye when informed that Mr. Elmer Taggart and his lady companion must receive "kid glove" treatment because Mr. Taggart haled from a remote farming village in the far north and must be spared the embarrassment of unfamiliar menu items or service. Mr. Taggart's beverage preference was not known, but neither he nor his guest ought to mistake the Astoria for a lobster palace. Mr. Boldt assured Mr. DeVere that nothing of the kind would mar the evening.

Seated, our napkins unfolded, Roddy nodded to the waiter who poured champagne. "One glass, Val, but no oyster cocktail tonight, and no *hors d'oeuvres*. Nothing but plain fare for us. If Taggart should glance at our table, he must see no exotic dishes to make him uneasy."

By agreement, Roddy and I would discuss the weather or another neutral topic. We would take no interest in the couple that was expected at the adjoining table. It seemed simple, but my eyelid twitched...perhaps the annoying hat brim.

Or was it the evening to be spent just a few feet from a possible murderess?

My husband requested bread and butter. I lifted a small bread slice when, at the next table, a waiter's "Madam" and "Sir" cued our spying. The couple was seated. From the corner of my eye, a vaguely familiar Elmer Taggart showed a fringe of hair circling a shiny bald head. His high forehead seemed to push his cheeks and broad nose to a shortened lip and narrow mouth. Eyeglasses slid down his nose, and his evening suit looked shiny from too much pressing...perhaps a rental.

"Butter, my dear?"

"Thank you," I said, unnerved by the bearded, mustached man with Roddy's voice.

Spreading butter and ready for the sight of ostrich plumes, I shifted my hat brim just enough to see a woman with a china-doll face, cupid lips, a porcelain complexion and rouged cheeks. Her gentian purple collarette matched a gown with deep décolletage. A sequined aigrette crowned the many rolls of brassy blonde hair.

"Your first time here..." I heard her say in a surprisingly firm voice.

Elmer Taggart pushed his eyeglasses up. I heard her say, "Then you must let me...."

Our waiter placed the dinner menu cards before us. At the other table, a different waiter bowed to Taggart, but his companion leaned forward and crooked her finger for attention. She queried the waiter in a sing-song voice, seeming to recognize him, a slim man with a soft voice who nodded...and nodded again.

"My dear," Roddy said, "your dining pleasure this evening?"

A glance at the menu. "Chicken," I said, "...and rice... and boiled peas."

At the other table, the waiter stood back and the woman resumed in a firm voice, "Mayonnaise, Elmer? You do? Then let's start with *homard en mayonnaise*" and "artichokes. Such fun...I'll show you...and yes, of course, champagne, but first, the special Astoria cocktail. Shall we? Oh, let's do...."

Elmer Taggart murmured, but the firm voice of Miss Bates trilled, "...yes, we must." The waiter withdrew, and Gloria Bates lowered her voice to confide in her companion. I leaned to hear, "...named for John Jacob Astor the Third... or is he the Fourth? He built the hotel, you know. His mother is *the* Mrs. Astor, the 'Queen' of Society...."

Elmer Taggart shook his head and asked something I couldn't hear. Roddy placed our order, my chicken and his roast beef with boiled potatoes. Roddy requested water without ice, and we spoke about the promise of snow in the days ahead. "If the air stays moist," Roddy said, "the snowfall will be heavy and wet."

Laughter at the next table, hers brittle, his a short heh-heh. Their cocktails had arrived, a risqué drink for a woman in a public place. She raised her glass. "To our evening...." He pushed up his eyeglasses and clutched the cocktail glass. I heard her say, "...just gin and vermouth... and a dash of orange bitters. See if you taste the orange, Elmer. The orange is the tang."

The cocktail glass touched his lips and was quickly set down. She sipped and licked the rim. "No," I heard her say, "but I have met Mr. William Astor...at parties on his yacht in the harbor...the most fascinating yacht name...it means 'light of the dawn,' like the light when the party is over, but there's a naughty meaning...shall I tell you?"

Elmer Taggart's words were lost, but Gloria Bates twice repeated, "Harem." She batted her eyes. I could not see his expression. Across from me, Roddy began to stroke his chin, touched the phony beard, and promptly reached for the bread platter. With our water glasses refilled, he passed the bread, just as the lobster *hors d'oeuvres* and artichokes arrived at the next table.

"...one petal at a time," I heard from Miss Bates. "See, Elmer, just nip it at the tip.... No? But the mayonnaise lobster? You do? I thought you would...no, let's not talk 'business' just yet. The evening is young. Let's see about the entrées, shall we?"

Our dinners arrived, and we proceeded very slowly to the perfectly roasted chicken and perfectly roasted beef. And boiled peas and potatoes, both beautifully served on

Hotel Astoria china. I said, "But powdery snow if the air is dry, and so much easier to clear away."

At the neighboring table, Miss Bates named the dishes she felt would be "just topping" for their dinner. I heard the soups, veal à la several sauces, fish and fowl every which way, side dishes and creamed vegetables, all of which arrived in due course, one after the other, until their table had no room for one more plate, saucer, or gravy boat.

Miss Bates had sampled each dish but signaled *no more* after a taste. Elmer Taggart dutifully forked bite after bite, nodded, and finally took off his glasses, wiped his mouth and face, and managed to request water. I heard him say, "...not another bite" and I heard the word, "apartment," but Miss Bates smiled and said, "Desserts first, Elmer...delicious desserts and liqueurs...do you enjoy cognac...?"

Roddy gave me a narrow-eyed glance. I had heard nothing about Leon Rankin or Star Coal and doubted that my bearded husband had heard more than I had. Between courses, Taggart tried to bring up the apartment, but Gloria Bates sloughed off his words to inquire about Broadway shows he might have seen...*The Belle of New York*? *The Telephone Girl*? *Fancy and Free*? She described the plays. A menu for dessert and after-dinner drinks was put before them.

"My dear, shall we have dessert?" Roddy asked. "I recommend the apple cake. And a cup of coffee."

"Apple cake and coffee," I echoed. By now, it seemed clear that if the perfumed letter had a veiled threat, Gloria

Bates had second thoughts about lifting the veil. Instead of blackmail, she worked to win over the comptroller by fogging the man's mind with alcohol and stuffing him with rich food…seasoned with her wiles.

I was wrong. With our cake before us, and a crystal snifter of cognac in front of Taggart, Gloria Bates leaned toward the Star Coal comptroller and spoke slowly in a voice that scratched like a diamond on glass. "Many times," she said, "I have dined in this room with Leon…rest his soul."

Her cleavage deepened as she leaned closer. "We sometimes met for dinner after he staked fortunes in the bar… the mahogany bar in this hotel. His day on Wall Street came first, and then the bar, and then our dinner…" She wet her lips. "So very many evenings…."

Taggart murmured that Mr. Rankin did not drink alcohol.

She snickered. "So much the better for a Wall Street man. The bar has a ticker tape machine, you see, and Leon talked to me about market men willing to bet on anything, in any amount. He talked to me about Star Coal and the railroad in West Virginia…and his bank too. He said some men played chess with the bulls and the bears, and how a stock could rise or come crashing down."

Elmer Taggart's mouth sagged. His eyeglasses had slipped down, apparently unnoticed.

"…and sometimes Leon brought friends from the bar to dine with us. I made their acquaintance, and I listened to what they had to say. Any day now, I could have a word with them…present my card and be received."

She reached across the table and pushed Elmer Taggart's glasses up the bridge of his nose.

"About the apartment," she said, "it would be ever so inconvenient to move just now. It could be so unfortunate for what we might see coming."

She paused, then tweaked his nose. "And it would be ever so helpful to continue my monthly benefit…in memory of my dear Leon."

Chapter Twenty-one

"WHAT 'MONTHLY BENEFIT?" I asked. "Did you find out from Taggart this morning?"

Roddy held off while we buckled Velvet into her coat, clipped the leash, and left the house. The cold, crisp afternoon drew us for a walk in the park. A perfect afternoon for a sleigh ride, but we agreed the exercise would do us good.

Impatient to hear Roddy's news, I fell into stride on the snow-packed pathway. In the distance, children sledded on gentle slopes, and a pair of "White Wing" city workers widened the path with shovels.

Roddy had spent the morning with the remaining financial documents, then took the satchel to the Star Coal office, hoping to see Elmer Taggart. "If the man wasn't stricken with indigestion..." Roddy had said as he had left the house this morning. "The food and—"

"—and Gloria Bates too."

We had laughed uneasily. I spent the morning wiring money from the Mackle Trust to an account held for the United Mine Workers. The transaction took several certifications, and I hoped no reporter from *Town Topics* lurked in the telegraph office. Society's scandal sheet would relish nothing more than an "exclusive" on Mrs. Roderick DeVere and her coal miners. I could imagine the headline.

By the park path, Roddy scooped snow into his gloved fingers and patted his chin and upper lip. "That damnable goatee and mustache," he said, "I forgot about the rash after the costume party…the glue. Elmer Taggart took one look and asked, was I feeling well? He offered me Bromo-Seltzer, said it helps when he faces thorny problems."

"Like Gloria Bates's 'monthly benefit?'"

"For a start." Roddy shifted Velvet's leash. The dog trotted nicely. "The so-called 'benefit' was for upkeep of the Star Coal apartment. Taggart did not question the payments as long as Rankin's companies stayed well in the black."

"But now…?"

Roddy tightened his collar. "The man does not know which way to turn. He admitted the woman terrified him last night…."

"He said 'terrified?'"

"He said 'alarming.' He agrees that it's best, for now, to keep up the monthly payments and the rental. The wasp's nest will be stirred soon enough…and yes, he said 'wasp's nest.'"

"A comptroller with a literary slant."

"A comptroller sipping Bromo-Seltzer and eyeing the mechanical adding machine on his desktop. He has the usual bills from the Royal Poinciana Hotel...."

"For Glenna May...."

"Of course. And Leon's son."

"Lewis...the heir."

Roddy nodded. "And he mentioned alimony payments for Lewis's mother...Rankin's former wife. Taggart said the alimony was to stop if she remarried."

"And?"

Roddy shrugged. "Her second marriage is in question. Was it legal? Until the facts are known, the payments are 'uneven.'"

"What does that mean, 'uneven?'"

"Probably when the woman duns Star Coal for money. I didn't press. Meanwhile, Taggart has new invoices for Rankin's hotel in Palm Beach...lumber, stone, lime, roof tiles. And the salary for the construction manager."

"Suggs, isn't it?" I asked. "Amos Suggs...the man we heard in the church...the third man in the opera box that night?"

Roddy locked his gaze on mine. "The fellow who rescued Leon Rankin from the coal mine...."

"And became his sidekick. In the church he sounded so bitter...."

"...and at Rector's," Roddy added, "we heard that Rankin has wronged Amos Suggs."

"...although Jeremy Dent was drunk when he said it, Roddy. So, is it *in vino veritas*? Or was he shifting the blame?"

I tightened my coat collar. "It's a good thing Gloria Bates will stay put for the time being...but then, where is Jeremy Dent...?"

Roddy paused. "He seemed in no hurry to return to West Virginia. I suspect we could locate him at Rector's or another lobster palace...or at a Bowery stage show...or coaxing a shyster lawyer to take his case against the B&N Railroad."

"And the banker?"

"Griggs," Roddy said. "He's banished from the Plaza lobby, but he'll try to reach Glenna May some other way. I'd bet on it."

The sharp air stung my nostrils. "It's too much, Roddy.... We say 'for now,' but the fact is, our 'q.t.' inquiry is going nowhere. Glenna May Rankin bides her time in the Plaza suite while Taggart tutors her about the business...but he hides the awful truth from her, doesn't he?"

"I believe Taggart tries not to distress Miss Rankin. She plans to return to Florida soon and hopes her nephew might visit her."

"...so, she does not know the Rankin 'empire' is on the verge of collapse. And nephew Lewis...Lewis Rankin? All we know is that he's past his eighteenth birthday and hunting wild pigs in Alabama—"

"—Louisiana. I believe Miss Rankin said Lou—l"

"—Louisiana, Arkansas, Idaho, what's the difference? Nothing is clear, and the Police Commissioner will come knocking on our front door for a report, and you will warn me that business deals in New York will blow up if the opera shares hit rock bottom because of the 'murder box.' And all the while, I am suspected of complicity in Rankin's death."

I kicked at a clump of snow. "Roddy, in these warm wools and furs...I feel a chill."

My husband nodded, his face stoic, his chest heaving. I took his arm. We paused while Velvet nosed into a snowbank, and we watched her paws scratch and dig, her 'bat' ears back as she sniffed. We said no more, distracted by sleighs passing on the nearby wide drive, each coachman and grooms wearing the livery of their household. Mrs. Vanderbilt's blazing red carriage swished past, the gold bells on the horses jingling. "Horse jewelry," it's called in the West. We had not once gone sleighing this month, though the high-stepping Hackneys seemed bred for just such outings.

Instead, the murder in the opera box.

⁂

We needed the comic relief we brought on ourselves by a fluke in the next hour. Back inside with our coats off, we oversaw Velvet's evening feeding and fretted over her expanding girth as she smacked and lapped every bite. Her ideal canine hour-glass figure had filled out. Her veterinarian had warned about her weight. An extra pound was not healthy.

"Let's weigh her," I said.

"Let's ask Bronson to do it," Roddy replied.

The footman fetched a kitchen scale and put it down in the Corinthian reception room. The dog ogled it, backed off, looked at us, growled softly at the foreign object, and planted her paws, bulldog-style.

"Here, Velvet...."

"Come, girl...."

Nothing doing.

I could not say she 'turned tail' because French bull dogs have no tails, but Velvet ran, and Roddy and I gave chase. Around sofas and chairs, round and round the Corinthian columns, her paws clicked on the marble and my skirt flapped against the furniture.

"...head her off at that table...."

"...at that chair...."

Under tables, circling a plant stand, the airborne dog sailed over a hassock and finally hunkered down under a Louis settee.

"Here, girl...come on out."

"Good girl...."

We waited, breathing hard.

"Sir...ma'am, I have a dog treat," said Bronson, who had stood by with a thousand-yard stare. From his pocket, the cookie-like snack was set on the pan of the scale, and three "big dogs" backed away and waited.

It took a good minute, but Velvet crept toward the scale, put up one paw, sniffed, climbed aboard and chewed as the dial swung past twenty-four pounds. She looked annoyed that another snack did not appear.

"She's gained another pound," Roddy said.

"Bronson," I asked, "does Velvet enjoy treats in the household during the day?" At his sheepish nod, I added, "...with some frequency?"

"Ma'am," he said, "we are all of us guilty...except Mrs. Thwaite."

"I would imagine not," I said.

Roddy shot me a glance from a household rule book: never be familiar with your servants. He seldom slipped up. "And Mr. Sands?" he asked.

"Sir...." The footman swallowed hard. "...on occasion, sir."

"I shall speak to Mr. Sands," Roddy said.

On cue, here came Sands, who murmured about "commotion," saw Roddy's arch gaze, and adjusted his "butler" face. At my husband's nod, Bronson returned the scale to the kitchen, and Sands assured us that dinner would be served at the usual eight o'clock.

We prepared for the sherry hour, first scanning the afternoon mail to find, among letters and cards, the notification that carpeting had been installed in opera boxes number 17 and 18 at the Metropolitan Opera House.

"I think we're due for an inspection of the boxes," Roddy said. "I also want to speak to Hoff. I'll send a message." He spoke softly. "Val, if you think the interiors would be too taxing...."

Eyes wide open, I said, "We will go together."

Chapter Twenty-two

THE OVERCAST MORNING THREATENED snow, but Noland drove us to the 40th Street *porte cochere*, where the opera house door was opened by a swarthy, curly-haired young man whose front teeth gaped as he smiled.

"Mr. and Mrs. DeVere," he said with a short bow.

"Antony," I said, "good of you to greet us."

"Madame…sir," he said, "Mr. Hoff requested that I first escort you to the parterre level for inspection of your box… and box number 18 as well."

Was his short cardigan jacket and black leather bowtie for our benefit? Work gloves were tucked unto the jacket pocket, and underneath, overalls with the name badge of Antony Dessey.

We followed him up the gallery stairs and along the corridor toward Box 17. A piano sounded, and men's voices from the stage…German?

Roddy murmured. "Wagner...."

"Sir," said Antony, "Richard Wagner's *Tristan and Isolde* will be presented tomorrow evening. The steersman and the shepherd are small parts, but the maestro requested a rehearsal. The steersman is a baritone. When you hear the tenor, that's the shepherd."

The voices swelled, and Antony's broad face became childlike. His eyes closed, as if the usher were miles from this corridor. Roddy cleared his throat with a sharp *a-hem*.

"Sorry sir...." The young man's dark caramel skin flushed. "So sorry...the music, you see...."

Roddy could surely "see," but annoyance flickered in my husband's eyes. "The keys...Antony, is it?"

"Antony, sir." We walked quickly to the newly polished *DeVere* nameplate, and the usher keyed us into the box.

The saloon, I should say, the silk-paneled coat room that led into the curtained box, but the curtain had been left open, and new gray wool carpet looked like paint poured from the saloon door to the furthest edge of the box. Our six chairs faced the stage below, where a pianist and two men huddled at the keyboard.

Antony waited behind us. "Sir...madam, if you wish more light to see the box...a lantern? I believe your chairs are in place...."

"They are," Roddy said, "all six. We'll step out. Do lock up. We'll inspect box number Eighteen."

The usher promptly turned our box key, moved next door, and turned the *Wendell* key. I held my breath and stepped into the saloon with a memory of Leon Rankin's death flooding my mind's eye. Underfoot, the slate gray carpet, the same scent of new wool, and the "death" box only steps away. Roddy pushed the curtain open, and I prepared to face the chair where he had sat, had struggled, and had bled to death.

In the dim light, with breath held, I forced my gaze to the spot where the dead man sat...to his chair.

There was no chair...no chairs. The box was empty.

"Completely new carpet, as you see," Antony said.

Roddy's hand clamped tight on my arm. He was frowning.

"I opened up the boxes for the rug workers myself," Antony said. "Mr. Hoff inspected the result...oh, do you hear that piano chord, that tenor? A high 'C,' I believe... no, a 'D'...."

"The chairs for this box," Roddy said. "Where are they?"

"Sir...apologies." As if wrested from a faraway place, Antony tugged the leather bowtie. "Mr. Hoff will have that information. If you are ready, I can take you to his office."

"One moment, please..." I said. "Antony, do you recall telling me that Mr. Rankin asked you for a favor the night he...passed away." He nodded. "And you helped him." He nodded again and raked a hand through his curls. "I wonder," I said, "whether you might have done favors for Mr. Rankin at other times...?"

The young man's shoulders scrunched. "Madam," he said, "we are under strict orders not to discuss any such thing. Strictest orders. I could lose my job…lose the music." He blinked rapidly. "I am not permitted…."

"We understand," I said, though Roddy looked dubious.

The usher locked the Wendells' box and led us silently to a back stairwell, where we climbed down, turned corners, and walked along a hallway where a voice spoke in Italian, then French, then in English, "…twenty apiece, not one dollar more…contraltos, not worth another nickel…my final word."

The snap of a telephone earpiece, and the bearded Maurice Hoff, elegant in a bespoke chocolate brown suit, stood at the open door of an office suite, bowed to kiss my hand, shook hands with Roddy, and dismissed Antony with a flick of his fingers.

"Madame DeVere…Mr. DeVere, so good of you to call. Do be seated."

He gestured toward velvet sofas and plush chairs overlaid with tasseled scarves beneath walls festooned with opera programs in heavy gilt frames. Ten feet away, an open rolltop desk burst with papers and folders, an inkstand, a cuspidor, a blotter, a telephone, and two office chairs. On the wall above the desk, framed in heaviest gold Baroque, a huge oil painting of the opera house seen from 40th Street.

"So you see," Hoff said, "the impresario's two worlds, a *fin de siècle* boudoir and a clerk's cubicle from a Charles Dickens story." He chuckled.

We had sunk into purple velvet chairs. "This 'royal velvet,'" he said, "persuades opera's great ones that the

Metropolitan is their home stage." He smiled at me. "Madame DeVere, your most admired soprano is...?"

Quizzed, I managed, "Nordica...Madame Nordica."

"Madame," he said, "Lillian Nordica has graced the very chair that you grace at this moment. But numbers tell unpleasant truths." He pointed to the desk. "Much of my time is spent wrestling with costs. The state support the opera enjoys in Berlin, in Milan...nothing of the kind in New York. We are beholden to shareholders' goodwill."

He touched his wing collar. "This very morning, we narrowly averted a labor strike by the chorus...imagine, if you will, the Metropolitan Opera chorus marching outdoors on Broadway, holding up signs, catching their death in the winter...a disgrace to the profession."

He "shot" his French cuffs and fingered his lapels. "Every member of the chorus secretly believes that he or she deserves a role, at least a maid's or servant's part. And the house employees...take that young man this morning, Antony...."

"Our usher on performance nights," Roddy said.

"And a custodian otherwise...new this winter, a decent worker unless a rehearsal is underway, when he's under a spell, hypnotized. We have our foreigners, like Janko. You remember...?"

Roddy nodded. I shuddered.

"Gone, vanished. The first chance to earn a few more pennies, the foreigners disappear. I manage the opera company, not the janitors...but it's all one *ménage*, if you see my point."

"Mr. Hoff," Roddy said, "we are pleased that the two *parterre* boxes have been carpeted, but the chairs in the Wendells' box—"

"—those chairs are being refinished." Hoff paused. "I would imagine that you know why…certain stains on a particular chair…perhaps damage to others."

Shortsighted, I had not thought of bloodstains on Rankin's chair. And damage? What damage?

"The stained carpeting," Roddy said, "…it was appropriately disposed of?"

"A junkman took it off our hands."

"You sold it," I said.

Hoff stiffened. "Every penny counts, Madame DeVere."

The silence gathered around us.

"Mr. Hoff," my husband said, "I understand that a lady's earring was found in *parterre* Box 18, the Wendells' box."

"Indeed, yes."

"And no attempt was made to find the owner?"

Hoff smoothed his sideburns. "Mr. DeVere, my calendar fills day and night, and no task too small for my attention." He looked pained. "But fortune smiles from time to time. By chance, the janitor, Janko, brought the item to me…late in the day of the cleaning, just when a police official visited…the Commissioner. He offered assistance finding the owner, and I gladly accepted. One task off my shoulders. We have our lost-and-found on the auditorium floor. Perhaps we ought to consider the *parterre* level…."

Hoff leaned forward. "Commissioner Bernard Gork leads me to believe that you are assisting…and your help is of greatest concern. Newspaper reporters have appeared lately. They hover about the doors to harass our employees, the stage hands, even the musicians and singers."

His voice deepened. "That young man, Antony, came to me, as did several others, and I issued strict orders. Any employee who speaks to a newspaper reporter concerning any event whatsoever will be dismissed…even if I must open *parterre* box doors myself…." He added, "Of course, one hopes it will not come to such a pass."

Roddy said, "Indeed not."

"Understand, Mr. DeVere, that the offer of a dollar is a temptation. Hearst and Pulitzer are equally unscrupulous, and their reporters offer cash for gossip, so let me say this—"

At that instant, his telephone rang, and Hoff rose to answer it, asked for a moment's delay, and turned to us. "…apologizes, madame…monsieur…an important call…I must…."

He hurried us out, led us down the hall and upstairs to the door and the *porte cochere*, where Nolan waited on the coachman's box.

"The chairs will be returned," Hoff said. "The next chapter of our saga, however, will be yours to write…if you understand me."

We nodded that we understood. Silently, Roddy and I settled into our carriage, and Apollo and Atlas trotted in rhythm. We were about ten minutes from home when Roddy turned to me. "Val," he said, "I think the time has come for a trip to Florida."

Chapter Twenty-three

"CALISTA, WOULD YOU LIKE to go to Florida?"

My maid's eyes darkened. "No, ma'am. I have heard of alligators ...panthers...swamps...."

"No, no, " I said, "we will go to a hotel...near the ocean. Let's get the atlas." In minutes, we sat side by side on a settee in my boudoir and peered at the East Coast map of the United States.

I ran a finger from New York to Palm Beach. "Mr. Henry Flagler has built a railroad all the way down Florida to Palm Beach," I said, "and a hotel too. And another hotel is being constructed. Mr. DeVere and I have a...business interest in the new hotel."

Calista looked dubious, but dutiful. "When would we go, ma'am?"

"As soon as the *Louisa* is stocked with fresh groceries and ice," I said.

"And who is Louisa, ma'am?"

"Our rail car," I said.

She blinked. "You own a railroad car?" Eyes like saucers, she sat straight, then blushed.

"It belonged to Mr. DeVere's parents." I also blushed. From mining camps to a private railroad car…and to my Roddy. At times, the distance caught me in life's vise. From the pine-clad mountain ranges with Papa, the vast canyons steeped in purple gloom, the dry streams and rocky hollows…his calloused hands at work in blazing sun and icy cold, his eyes always in search of ores that eluded him for so many years before the Big Bonanza Lode.

The riches didn't change my papa. He worked all the harder in Virginia City, where he insisted I go to school and polish my voice and my manners. I sometimes thought Papa prepared me for Roddy, gave his hand in marriage to a young man whose parents had owned a railroad car. I doubted that my husband would have yearned for a railroad car. Nor would I. We just…had it, registered on the New York Central Railroad to Mr. and Mrs. Roderick Windham DeVere.

"It has staterooms for guests," I said to Calista, "and also…." I hated the word, servants. "…and compartments for you and perhaps Mr. Devere's valet."

"Norbert," she said.

I nodded. "And a chef and butler."

"Mr. Sands?"

"No," I said, "someone arranged by Mr. DeVere…by the railroad."

We sat in silence.

Calista stood. "Short notice, but we'll see to it, ma'am. I'll look into your warm weather wardrobe. We'll be ready. Count on it."

We dashed about in the few next days. Roddy told his parents we sought relief from winter, and I held my breath in case Rufus and Eleanor proposed going with us. Fortunately, Mrs. Astor's annual ball, the most prized social event of the year, took place on the last Monday night in January. The invitation to the ball topped everything. Thank you, Mrs. Astor.

My husband arranged with the Florida East Coast Railway to hitch the *Louisa* to a train bound for Palm Beach. ("...we will be more than glad to haul your car over the line, Mr. and Mrs. DeVere...."). I tuned out the specifics of switching the car from New York Central track at St. Augustine.

My own "homework" demanded hours of "regrets" to invitations for upcoming social events, plus an afternoon in our coach on the Upper East Side, leaving calling cards that must be delivered to households in our social set, each card bent at certain corners to signal that Mr. and Mrs. Roderick DeVere will be out of town. (Etiquette manuals taught the correct corners to dog-ear.)

Our coachman, Noland, would make certain that Atlas and Apollo were exercised in our absence, and Sands began to strut like a generalissimo in charge of battalions, while Mrs. Thwaite became the maids' "Mother Superior." Ought the furnishings to be draped with muslin coverings during our holiday? she asked.

The furniture did not need shrouding, I assured her.

Mrs. Thwaite "presumed" that the recently damaged antique divan leg could undergo repair during our absence and "trusted" my approval of her oversight. She also promised to keep a close eye on the newest maid, "Joiner."

"Mattie Sue..." I said.

Her mouth puckered. Hiring the young woman without her say-so offended the housekeeper no end. She smirked to learn that our dog would come with us.

I visited the Forster household to tell Cassie our plans, expecting my friend's surprise to mix with a skeptical gaze. "You and Roderick to Palm Beach? So very abruptly?"

"To the Royal Poinciana Hotel," I said too fast. "You and Dudley have been its guests. Remember the railroad's motto, 'Every day a June day, full of sunshine—'"

"—'where winter exists only in memory.' But Val, you and I don't mince words. I won't pry, but it doesn't feel right. No...no excuses. You'll tell me when you're ready."

Cassie offered tea, but I was rushing off.

"I recall," she said as I left, "that the Royal Poinciana Hotel is Miss Glenna May Rankin's home at present, is it not?"

"It is."

"Is she going with you? I hope so. I've thought about her, Val. That afternoon in Central Park while the children skated.... My forebodings about you and Miss Rankin were intense, and I hope you take her with you and you both take good care. Look out for her...and for yourself.

Cassie's idea about Glenna May took root. Two or three days at close quarters might give us valuable information. The journey would provide leisured hours in the *Louisa*'s comfortable "parlor lounge" as would meals together at the cozy dining table. We would be likable hosts, and Miss Rankin would detail her brother's history with the men and the woman in his party when *Don Giovanni* marked Leon Rankin's murder. One day in the future, Roddy and I promised ourselves a venture for a "honeymoon" on the *Louisa*, but this trip meant purpose. Glenna May could yield a trove of clues.

Her resistance startled us. Surrounded by her brother's belongings in the Plaza suite and tutored by Elmer Taggart, she felt "snug as a bug in a rug" for the time being, she told us at tea at the Plaza when we presented the Florida East Coast Railway time-table schedule and invited her to be our guest.

Roddy had brought photographs of the *Louisa* interior, the high vaulted maple ceilings, the electrical lights in frosted glass shades, the tie-back curtains on the big windows, the floral carpeting and ample seating arrangements, the observation room and dining area. He pointed out the stateroom reserved for Miss Rankin, the private bath.

She brushed the photos aside. "You brought evidence like a good lawyer," she said. "But New York winter reminds me of West Virginia. It's cold both places, and I Iike it. Trees in Central Park remind me of trees in Suggs Run. Seems to me, the winter trees ought to be bare. That's a fact."

"Stiffed," Roddy said when we left the Plaza. "We'll go without her. We'll take the 6:56 p.m. from Grand Central. We'll be in Florida by the end of the week."

We did board the 6:56 evening train, but delayed departure for one more day. By a lucky break, Glenna May changed her mind. Her nephew, Lewis, wired from the Royal Poinciana Hotel to say he had suddenly come from New Orleans and must see her as soon as possible. When would she be back in Palm Beach? The trains to Florida were fully reserved, so she would come with us.

"...a strong-willed woman at her nephew's beck and call," Roddy said.

"...a caring aunt who feels responsible for a grieving nephew who has recently lost his father," I replied.

Whichever, Glenna May accepted our invitation, and I took credit for a sly, bright idea: that Miss Rankin ought to have the services of a personal maid. I had never seen the faces of women freed from the Riker's Island prison, but Mattie Sue Joiner's face glowed when I proposed that she accompany us to Florida as the personal maid of the elderly Glenna May Rankin. Never in her twenty-three years had Mattie Sue worked as a personal maid, but she vowed to "work fingers to the bone."

I shuddered at the image, but the words reminded me to notify the Consumers League of my plans. The telephone was answered by Mrs. Florence Kelley, the League's formidable executive secretary. "—a unique opportunity, Mrs. DeVere," she blared. "You must take notes on the conditions of women's labor in Florida. We will expect your report."

At 4:30 p.m. on Saturday, January 21, under a darkening sky and light snowfall, Noland drove Roddy and me—and Glenna May—to the Grand Central depot. Velvet hunkered down in a carrier at my feet, and we fell silent when my chit-chat went nowhere. On track number 8, the varnished nameboard on the car announced **LOUISA**, and Roddy helped our guest into the car. I hitched up my skirts and mounted the steps. Roddy followed with Velvet, snug in the carrier.

Our baggage had been delivered that noon by the footmen, Bronson and Chalmers, who wished us bon voyage. The bellmen at the Plaza had taken care of Glenna May's single suitcase, packed in haste when she learned of her brother's death three weeks ago.

Calista and Mattie Sue had boarded the car in mid-afternoon, unpacked our things and Glenna May's, making certain of fresh flowers in the vases and toiletries in the bathrooms. An onboard chef and butler had seen to the pantry, icebox, and beverages. Roddy had decided on the hotel's valet, so Norbert stayed in New York.

The locomotive left the Grand Central depot promptly at 6:56 p.m., pulling the *Louisa* at the rear of a half-dozen passenger cars, a club car, dining car, barber shop, writing room, and library.

"We're off," Roddy said. "We're underway."

Miss Rankin stayed fretful even now when we sat in the warm, comfortable *Louisa*. "I'll just keep this on," she said about her coat, the broadtail mink that hugged her like a child's blanket.

The train wheels "clicked" softly, and the gentle sway of the car invited calm, though the air felt tense. Glenna May gripped her cane, and I asked,

"Would you like an ottoman?"

"A what?"

"A footstool."

Roddy slid a stool in front of her chair, but she kept both feet planted on the floor. The butler appeared with menu cards and inquired about refreshments.

"Miss Rankin," Roddy said, "would you like something to drink?"

"I'm not thirsty."

Roddy requested sherry, and I chose mineral water in deference to our guest. The menu listed the usual beef and chicken, in French.

Glenna May plucked spectacles from her coat pocket. "Everything's à la," she said, "just like the hotels. The Royal Poinciana knows I like plain English, and the Plaza finally got used to me. Maybe I'm not hungry…."

Her hand trembled, and it dawned on me, the woman felt anxious, trapped in our car. "Miss Rankin," I said, "I'm looking at veal cutlets and grilled chicken…and fried eggs too…."

"Fried eggs," she said.

On white linen with heavy silver, Roddy enjoyed *filet de boeuf, sauce béarnaise*, and Miss Rankin and I dined on fried eggs and ham. We did not bond over eggs-over-easy, as I hoped. After dinner, Roddy excused himself to "take the air" in the observation room, leaving Miss Rankin and me on the blue frieze plush chairs in the parlor.

If my husband thought two women would relax together, he was wrong. The electric lights glowed in frosted glass shades, but a frosty feeling continued, Glenna May wrapped tight in her fur coat. The evening felt like railroad tracks to nowhere. If we did not connect over the next two days on the *Louisa*, the odds would worsen in Florida. If I habitually bit my fingernails, as many do, I would bite them now.

When humans don't connect, however, count on a dog.

"Velvet…here, Velvet…come, girl…come back…come…..." Thumping down the aisle, Calista sounded frantic.

Our dog streaked into the parlor, chased by the maid, who apologized in English…and in Greek. Arms out, she grabbed for the dog.

And missed.

Across from Glenna May, I opened my arms, but Velvet ran to the older woman, paws up and licking.

I jumped. "Velvet, no…."

But Glenna May scooped the dog and let her lick at her cheeks and nose, laughing all the while.

Calista stood at attention, and I perched on the edge of the chair. Face to face with Glenna May, our French bulldog sniffed and wriggled. Her little growls matched Glenna May's soft gruntings.

"Ma'am?" said Calista. "Shall I...."

The elderly woman and the little dog looked like a picture on a greeting card. "Calista," I said, "please bring her water bowl, and let Velvet stay here with us."

The icy atmosphere did not melt right away but leaving Velvet in Glenna May's arms was my best move in recent memory. I kept quiet while the two became fast friends.

"She's our first dog," I said at last, "a purebred French bulldog...but a rescue. I grew up in mining camps in the far West. We moved around. We couldn't have a pet dog."

Glenna May stroked Velvet's ears. The dog purred like a cat.

"I remember you had a hound dog," I said. "You mentioned a coon hound...."

She settled Velvet on her lap. "Blackie," she said. "Sweetest dog, spoiled rotten...a useless hunter."

"...a pet," I said.

She scoffed. "Where I come from, no man or boy wants a dog that won't hunt. But Leon wouldn't let them tease about Blackie. He stuck up for me. Long as I could feed her, I could keep her."

The plush chairs wouldn't move, but I leaned closer.

"...the dog takes me back in time," she said, "...to high school." Her coat had opened.

"Across the Barret River," I said.

A moment passed. "On school days," she said, "me on the mule, and that dog went as far as the riverbank with me. She'd wait for me till school was out." "You can love an animal...."

I paused. She wiped her eyes. "...and you can love a brother that helps you keep her, I said."

The train wheels grumbled. Had we crossed into Maryland? Northern Virginia? The train had not stopped at any station after Philadelphia.

"Folks didn't understand Leon," she said. "They got him wrong."

Her coat had slipped off her shoulders, but she seemed not to notice. Velvet slept in her lap. Calista brought the water bowl, set it on the floor at the side, and tiptoed off.

I said, "The men in the church...we got an earful at the memorial service."

"Grudges..." she said. "Some folks can't let go. Or else, they won't."

"The storekeeper, Mr. Dent..." I said, "...he seemed very upset about the railroad. And Mr. Griggs...it sounds like he lost his bank."

"Those two...." Her voice hardened. "They wanted handouts, something for nothing. The Dents' general store... they'd sell you flour with weevils, and claim it was your own doing. And Griggs Bank...my brother said he might as well throw money in a ditch." She touched her silver hair. "Leon allowed as how he got rough now and again. But he'd say to me, 'Glenna May, business is not charity.'"

She cuddled Velvet. "Leon's favorite Bible verse is in Ecclesiastes, 'For there is not a just man upon earth that doeth good, and sinneth not.'"

"Nobody's perfect," I said, quiet for the moment. "It can take a while to appreciate a person," I said. "I'd guess you see a good deal of Mr. Suggs in Palm Beach…Amos?"

"Not so much," she said. "He's busy where the new hotel is going up, and he keeps to himself. Just as well. I always thought Amos had a hungry look about him. He still does. He makes me nervous. Last Christmas, he scared my nephew."

"Lewis?" She nodded. "Scared like…Hallowe'en?"

"More like a threat. Something to do with Lewis's mother and her friend. That woman…."

Her voice trailed. How much longer before Glenna May suspected that I "pumped" her? And yet I felt for her too, alone in the world except for the nephew who came and went.

"…difficult for a child without both parents…" I said, "a girl…or a boy."

"—hard for a man without a good woman," she snapped. "Leon was not the same man after Lewis's mother. The judge in New Orleans said Leon left her, but she left him, left him flat. Left him and Lewis both. The boy was just a tyke. As far as women were concerned, Leon was never the same man after Doreen."

"Doreen," I said.

"Doreen Benoire Rankin, Lewis's mother. I try to keep my nephew away from Amos. And I worry why he's back in Palm Beach so soon, calling after me to come down there in a big hurry."

Glenna May swallowed and laid both hands on Velvet's back. "Mrs. DeVere," she said, "you and the mister kindly let me come on your train car. Could I ask a big favor? I'd sleep a whole lot better tonight if I could have your little dog with me. Nothing like a sweet dog to soothe jangled nerves. Nothing like a dog to quiet fears."

Chapter Twenty-four

AT MIDMORNING ON MONDAY, January 21, the *Louisa* crossed the Flagler Trestle, the spur line that ferried private rail cars across tidal Lake Worth to a lemon yellow clapboard fortress glowing with white trim and dark green shutters that flanked hundreds of windows—the Royal Poinciana Hotel.

"Exactly on time," Roddy said.

"...and arriving backwards," I added. The locomotive slowly backed us onto the rail siding beside the hotel, stopped with a shudder, uncoupled from the *Louisa*, and puffed ahead to await the next private car.

"There's enough track here for fifty cars," Roddy said, "including Henry Flagler's *Rambler*."

I frowned at the troublesome number. The railyard of the rich boded ill for Miss Rankin...and maybe for me. She risked everything in this place. Her brother's empire neared collapse, and she hadn't a clue. Amid palm trees and balmy breezes, Glenna May and her nephew were on thin ice.

As for me, gossip about the Coal King's body and my earring could travel south on any number of the private cars. Speculation about me would deepen if rumors leapt from apoplexy to homicide.

This Florida jaunt might be a blunder, too quickly dreamed up, too easily arranged, the "q.t." inquiry a sinkhole.

Too late now.

Near the train car door, we readied for summer-in-winter in the linens that replaced our wools early this morning. Glenna May chose lightweight black, though the mink coat was off. Calista and Mattie Sue tended last-minute details in the rear compartments.

"Is Velvet too much to handle, Miss Glenna?" I asked. "With your cane....?"

"Not one bit, Valentine. Her leash is a big help."

The door opened, and we stepped into Palm Beach... perfumed air, restless palms, and fierce sun chafing every cheek. An army of bellboys and baggage men sprang for trunks, valises, and what-have-you, leading our maids to a back entrance and service elevator to the upstairs suites. A middle-aged man in a dark suit with palm tree medallions on the lapels stood ready to welcome us, most likely a manager.

I saw no one who might be Lewis Rankin.

Roddy spoke to the manager, who had bowed to Miss Rankin, while a porter stepped up to tip his cap, a lithe man with ebony skin and a welcoming smile. "Miz Glenna May, welcome back."

"Why Horace, very good of you to remember."

"Looks like you got yourself a puppy dog, ma'am. And so sorry to hear about Mr. Leon."

"Thank you, Horace."

Still, no one who might be Lewis Rankin, despite Roddy's wire specifying our arrival. We had crossed the trestle exactly on the dot. Where was he?

Glenna May craned her neck to scan the platform, tapped her cane on the concrete, and searched in vain for her nephew. The porter, Horace, stood in for her welcoming committee. Lewis Rankin had not met the train.

"Got your wheel chair right here for you," Horace said. "And wheel chairs for you friends, ma'am...."

Wheel chairs?

I blinked to see a lineup of wide wicker chairs mounted on bicycle frames, each to be pedaled from the rear by a uniformed Black man in a visored cap. I recalled that no horse-drawn carriages were permitted in Palm Beach. A chair ride to the hotel entrance appeared to be required. Glenna May sat with Velvet in Horace's chair. "Sweet Velvet," she said as Roddy and I seated ourselves in the next wheel chair and followed close behind.

The hotel stretched for a half-mile along a waterway edged with yachts and houseboats. I counted six stories high, plus gardens, lawns, and pathways. No construction site from the *Louisa* windows or this wicker wheel chair was visible, and Glenna May had said nothing about the exact location of her late brother's hotel.

At the grand entrance, an American flag flew from a rooftop bell tower rising over classical columns and porticos. Dozens of palm trees waved on this spit of land boasting the architecture of ancient Greece and Rome, plus our own Gilded Age, which was Mark Twain's label for the wild excess of these days.

Bellmen flocked to Glenna May and Velvet at the entrance, and my husband eyed the scene before us at the registration desk —the desk clerks, the elderly woman with a cane, the dog, and me. Extravagantly welcomed, Miss Rankin was assured her suite was ready. Her dog, of course, was also welcome. A bellman would bring a dish and water bowl to her suite right away. Whatever the little dog liked to eat, the Royal Poinciana would oblige. Mr. Flagler's own snow-white dog, Delos, often spent winter weeks here, often seen on the colonnade.

Glenna May turned to me, her face a mixture of embarrassment, resolve, and entreaty.

Maybe the woman needed warm, living fur in this time of grief and mourning. If not her mink, our dog. If not her nephew to greet her, Velvet's canine warmth.

Roddy winked a signal to me. "Miss Glenna," I said, "would you like to have Velvet in your suite for a while?"

"Oh, could I, Valentine?" She sounded plaintive, the strict schoolmarm almost girlish.

I said, "For now, we will entrust Velvet to your care."

"On the second floor," she said. "Near the north parlor."

Which meant nothing to me, or to Roddy.

"Where it's quiet," she said.

We agreed to meet later for tea in the "Coconut Grove" and watched a bellman escort Glenna May and our dog to the elevator.

Minutes later, it was our turn in the elevator to a third-floor suite that struck me as a tropical version of the Plaza Hotel—figured green wallpaper, green rush mat flooring, and mahogany furniture. Framed watercolor scenes of boats, quaint fishermen, and gentle seas adorned the walls of the sitting room and bedroom. Our windows looked out on Lake Worth, where fishing boats motored, and a few sails caught the breeze. On the opposite shore, West Palm Beach showed a few low buildings amid palm trees.

Calista had already arranged my things from the trunk, and Roddy's hotel valet tended to his clothes.

"Shall we take a short stroll, Mrs. DeVere?"

"We shall."

Calista found my broad-brimmed sun hat, and Roddy's summer straw "skimmer" slanted rakishly across his forehead.

The entrance below took us to the "Palm Walk," reserved for pedestrians and free of bicycle bells that warned guests of oncoming wicker. We walked in privacy, just after noon.

"Roddy," I said, "I fear we're on a fool's errand."

"Val, we just arrived...."

"I don't like it. It feels stuffy...like a 'Lotus Land.' The air feels wet and smells like fish."

"Sea air...."

"And the sun, fierce." Far up ahead, a woman sauntered with a parasol. "And I will not walk with an umbrella unless it rains. Does it rain in Palm Beach? Or does wealth keep everyone dry all winter long?"

"Valentine, my dear...."

"And we're caught up in Glenna May Rankin's sad life, Roddy. The porters and other servants work for wages and tips. When Rankin's 'empire' collapses, she will be ousted without a fare-thee-well. And where is her nephew? Lewis Rankin summoned her here and couldn't be bothered to meet her train.

"Val, please...." Roddy pressed my arm and slowed our pace. "Let's remember why we're here. Our purpose—"

"—is to nose around the hotel construction site...to size up Amos Suggs and decide whether he might have killed Leon Rankin."

Roddy slowed us to a standstill. "Yes, but the larger purpose is...is...."

"What?"

My husband cleared his throat and gazed steadily into my eyes. "...is clearing you, my love, of all suspicion...all of it." He touched his throat. "The hours I spent on the *Louisa* observation deck let you befriend Miss Rankin, but I thought about our life, yours and mine...ours."

He held his gaze on mine. "I am responsible, Val, for the life I promised you when we wed. 'Honor' is a cliché in these times, but all the more important to me.... You left your beloved West behind and put faith in me. I will not let you down."

"The mix-up over my earring..." I said, "...material evidence."

My husband gripped my arm. "High-minded words could come into play, Val, and legal terms too...but I commit to 'honor.' Everything we do here and in New York... it's no longer about the opera or the collapse of Rankin's businesses...it's clearing you...absolving you."

"Finding me 'innocent' of all charges?"

"Please do not trifle with me, Val. I am deadly serious. The 'q.t. inquiry' is urgent. This is no longer about the police commissioner or New York's mayor or financier J.P. Morgan in his favorite box at the opera...or the opera. This is about us...our own life ahead...." He gazed closer. "Just that," he said, "our life ahead...our love."

Roddy's grip on my arm felt like a brace. "We'll do our best," I said, but the gravity of my husband's feelings struck deep as we slowly strolled on a path of seashells that were smashed to bits.

The aptly-named Coconut Grove drew hotel guests with white-cloth tables that promoted the notion of exclusive membership in a space circled by coconut palm trees. Couples and small groups chatted amiably, a string orchestra played teatime music, and a maître d'hotel led us to a table for four, where Glenna May sat alone. Velvet lay in the shade at her feet, jumped to greet us, and sat up in hope of a snack.

"Miss Glenna, good afternoon," I said. "Velvet…is behaving herself?"

"Take her anywhere…" she said. "Perfect pooch."

Roddy and I sat down, smiling at the dog to keep our eyes off the empty chair that broadcast Glenna May's nephew's absence. Itching to ask about Lewis, we knew better. If she had she seen him, she gave no sign. The waiter took our order, and I was ready for small talk about the weather, when a young man in a seersucker suit and white shoes bent over Glenna May's shoulders from behind and brushed his waxed moustache against her cheek.

"Auntie…."

She turned, startled. "Lewis…where have you been?"

"…been eager to meet you for tea in the Grove," he said in cool, crooning tones that streamlined from one word to the next. Not quite tall, Lewis Rankin struck a loose-jointed, nonchalant pose until a waiter seated him. He then swept off his wide-brimmed planter's hat to reveal a thick head of hair that was cut to accent dark, rippling waves. His features somewhat echoed his father's newspaper photos—a narrow face with dark eyes, but smoother cheeks, a fuller mouth, and a short goatee. I had thought that moustache wax was out of fashion, but apparently not.

Roddy introduced us, and Lewis's soft bow to me, handshake with Roddy, and peck on his aunt's cheek met the dutiful moment before he ordered a glass of champagne and sat back, unapologetic. I guessed him to be in his mid-twenties.

"Resort hotels," Roddy said, "tempt guests to fill the days with entertainments...day-long fishing trips, sight-seeing.... Perhaps you've taken today's opportunity?"

"Actually, Mr. DeVere," he said, "I spent the day in West Palm Beach."

"Across Lake Worth," I said.

"Promising terrain," he replied. "They call West Palm the servants' quarters, but it holds great promise for the farsighted among us ...." He broke off as our tea and his wine arrived.

"We understand that you have been traveling in New Orleans," I said.

"Traveling, Mrs. DeVere?" He sipped his wine. "I have been visiting my mama." He looked sideways at Glenna May, paused, and took another sip. "Mama no longer lives in the *Vieux Carré*...the French Quarter...doesn't want to live with the Creoles anymore. She wants everyone to know she's moved on up."

Glenna May's eyes darted from her nephew to Roddy and me. She said nothing.

"So," he said, "the former Mrs. Doreen Benoire Rankin... is nowadays known as Missus Augustus Pierce. She's in the Garden District now with plantation friends...cotton merchants. Her friend gave me this planter's style hat," he added, touching the hat as if to goad his aunt, whose jaw clamped shut.

Velvet sniffed at his trouser cuff, and he leaned down to touch her ear.

"Auntie Glenna," he asked, "what sort of dog have you got here?"

Glenna May's flush could be mistaken for too much sun.

I said, "Velvet is a French bulldog."

"So it is," said Lewis, "but if you had asked me, Auntie, I would have advised a pug or a dachshund…the breeds favored by our sort…and I understand that John Jacob Astor keeps an Airedale terrier."

I said, "Mr. Rankin, your aunt has kindly agreed to tend our little dog, Velvet, for a few days here at the Royal Poinciana."

"The 'Ponce' as we call it, Mrs. DeVere. And may I apologize for any offence. I'm sure the French bulldog will come into favor in due course." He gestured for another glass of champagne. I began to understand why Glenna May stewed at the mention of his name.

"So you three journeyed on a private rail car," he said.

"We did indeed," said Roddy.

"A real treat," added Glenna May.

"Travel as it ought to be," said Lewis. "Countless times, I urged Father…rest his soul…to outfit us with a car of our own. Why he refused a yacht or a rail car, I never understood."

Glenna May sipped her tea, drew herself up, and said, "Lewis, your father got seasick every time he boarded anything floating on the water. You know that. And he rented private rail cars…as you might recall."

"Ah, Auntie Glenna…let us not revive unpleasant times…my days of boyish pranks are best forgotten." He turned to Roddy. "So, the car that brought you here is named *Louise*—"

"—*Louisa*," Roddy snapped before I could open my lips.

"Perhaps the owner's sentimental choice," the young man said.

I realized that Lewis thought we had rented the car. His aunt's brows knit in dismay. She put her hand on his wrist, probably to quiet him.

"…though do consider," Lewis continued, "that Mr. Collis Huntington's *Oneonta* and Mr. Charles Crocker's *Mishawaka* are both on the hotel siding for the winter weeks."

The names, Huntington and Crocker, were two of the "Big Four" who built the Central Pacific Railroad that unified the country by rail a generation ago. Papa met with them when he struck his Big Lode and became a Silver King. He lunched with them in San Francisco.

"And of course Mr. Flagler's *Rambler*," the young Rankin went on, "You will see their parties in the dining room or on the colonnade."

"You must be quite the railroad hobbyist," Roddy said, his voice tight.

Lewis faced him. "I care to know who is in my midst."

"The DeVeres are here to see about the hotel," Glenna May said, abruptly businesslike.

The young man's face suddenly turned chalk white. "Father's hotel? The 'Ocean Grande?'"

Glenna May nodded.

"What for? What on earth for?" Before any of us could utter a word, Lewis blurted, "I hope you haven't promised my help, Auntie. I am not available on that score…not after what happened at Christmastime. You don't talk about it, do you? Nobody needs to know. Nobody needs to be the wiser."

Chapter Twenty-five

"'THE WISER ABOUT WHAT?"

"No idea," Roddy said.

Upstairs in our suite, we sat in deep, palm-patterned armchairs, as the sinking sun beamed through open windows overlooking Lake Worth. We had lingered at the Coconut Grove tea table after Lewis hustled Glenna May and our dog inside, suddenly insisting that he and his Auntie must discuss private family matters.

"Two words for that young man," Roddy said, "'insufferable' and 'snob.'"

"No wonder Glenna May looks like she's sucking lemons at the mention of his name. Still, she feels responsible.... you saw his face at the mention of Rankin's hotel...bloodless."

Roddy nodded. "What knocked him, I couldn't guess. He has no access to the business records that Taggart shared with me."

"So, it's personal…connected to Amos Suggs and whatever happened here in Palm Beach this past Christmas season…." I gazed at the lake. "Glenna May said that Suggs frightened her nephew, something to do with his mother."

"But not the hotel?"

"I don't think so." I pushed at my hair, which went limp in the sea air. "I'm curious about the New Orleans visit. Lewis's mother is no longer in the French quarter. What does that mean?"

Roddy raised the windows a few more inches. "It means she now lives in the part of the city favored by the planters, the Anglo class…the whites. She's left the French Quarter 'gumbo'… people from all over the globe…from Europe, Africa, Haiti…you name it." He sat back down. "As for Lewis hunting wild pigs…."

"I picture him in a custom-tailored hunting jacket," I said, "ordering his valet to fire the gun."

We chuckled. The setting sun brought us to the awkward hour between afternoon and evening. The fishing boats on Lake Worth had docked, and the sailboats moored. Not a breeze stirred.

"I suppose Glenna May is with Lewis…" I said. "And of course, Velvet…."

Roddy took my hand. "My dear, our dog will be pampered, and Miss Rankin can take care of herself. The hotel staff fawns over her, and the young maid we brought along helps too."

"For now, yes. Calista praised Mattie Sue's efforts in the *Louisa*, and Glenna May seems grateful, especially with her ankle and the cane."

The two maids would "bunk" together in the servants' dormitory above the topmost floor and have their meals in the hotel servants' dining room. I had asked Calista to take notes on the food, the dormitory situation, the washrooms, and, if possible, to find out about the wages. The Consumers League, Mrs. Kelley insists, must survey women's work everywhere, and Calista will be my "eyes" and "ears" behind the scenes at the Royal Poinciana.

"We'll get an early start to the hotel site tomorrow morning," Roddy said. "Taggart showed me a sketch…about a mile south, between Lake Worth and the ocean. He said we can't miss it. So, shall we dine early here at 'The Ponce'?"

I stood and smiled. "'The Ponce' it is."

※

On hotel bicycles, we set out by 8:00 a.m. as the sun rose over the palm trees. "Keep to the path," the attendant advised, "or your wheels will sink in sand." At Calista's urging, I brought a cotton duck bicycle suit "just in case." Roddy's linen crash jacket and trousers let him move freely, though pedaling on crushed shell made a cyclist appreciate asphalt. Roddy doubted that Amos Suggs would recognize him as the man who hushed the party in Box 18 during the *entr'acte* but refused a facial disguise in this tropical heat.

The narrow path by the Lake Worth shoreline seemed hacked from a dense jungle of scrub foliage, strangled trees, and bulbous roots. On our right, the broad waterway sparkled, and I nearly veered into the sand.

"Eyes front, Val," Roddy called behind me.

Ready to call, "aye aye, sir," I listened, instead, to voices and hammering that echoed from a vast clearing just ahead. In moments, I saw tents and mules, bare-backed men…a vast foundation and rising beams, wood framework… scaffolds, and piles of brick and lumber. A wide lakeside ramp cut across the path into the water and ended at a dock floating about fifty feet offshore. The scene expanded for acres upon acres, a monumental enterprise. The Royal Poinciana boasted one thousand rooms. Did Rankin plan to outdo Henry Flagler?

"The Ocean Grande…" Roddy said.

We stopped. No one looked our way.

"Do you see Amos Suggs?" I asked. "Would we recognize him?"

We stood by the bicycles, two winter tourists watching men cement concrete blocks into a wall, tread the high beams, load bricks into wagons pulled by mules. I tried to count the tents…a tent city and, in its midst, one large shed roofed with tarpaper. I saw no women.

Roddy waved, and a workman jogged our way, pulling on a shirt as he called, "Morning, folks, you lost?" Thickset with a handlebar moustache, he drawled, but his dark eyes flashed.

Roddy said. "We're looking for the Ocean Grande Hotel construction site."

"You done found it, mister…ma'am. If you're thinking to get a room, you're a year ahead of yourself. If you're selling something, nobody here's buying." He peered behind us at the water. "Nobody here's got the beans."

"Beans?" I asked.

He grinned. "The moola…the wages, ma'am."

Roddy said, "We are looking for Mr. Amos Suggs."

"The big boss." His jaw clenched, and I thought he muttered "speak of the devil" but wasn't sure. "You're early," he said. "Ain't here yet. He's due from Juno. Barges load up with gravel and lumber in Juno." He sucked a tooth. "Better be two-by-eights this time. We got enough useless lumber as it is."

Roddy said, "You expect Mr. Suggs today?"

"Any time." He pointed to the ramp that led into the lake and dock. "Tugboat tows the barges in, and Mr. Suggs rides the tug. He'll come ashore, get on a mule, and watch us bust our guts unloading…." He broke off with a short apologetic bow to me, the lady with delicate ears.

Roddy said, "A race against time, is it?"

"…to get the whole thing up before the hurricanes." He glanced skyward. "And a prize for the best crew…masons against carpenters …against pipefitters…."

I said, "Friendly rivals?"

"No, ma'am…more like cutthroats. Mr. Suggs was a coal miner a long time ago…says it's like the coal mines, shift against shift. Me, I'm a Cajun from Louisiana, never wanted to go down in a mine. Wished I stayed in bayou country... better off hunting 'gators. This job...big promises, but we're all stuck...no pay till it's done...winners 'ginst losers." He wiped a sleeve across his forehead. "Better get back," he said. "They'll skin me alive. Wait if you want. Don't get croton juice on you...raises blisters."

"Your name..." Roddy called. "What's your name?"

He had already walked away. "Never mind," he called back, "never talked to you."

We propped the bicycles against a palm tree and watched the "Cajun" disappear behind stacked lumber. Insects buzzed, mosquitos whined, and thistles grabbed my stocking. My skin felt sticky in the battering sun.

"How long should we wait, Roddy? And why call it a lake? It's more like a branch of the ocean...but the 'Ocean Grande' won't face the ocean, will it?"

"Not unless...." Roddy broke off. "Val, look...."

A tugboat towing two barges came into view, and squads of workmen sprang into action with ropes, pulleys, and huge hooks that swung like pendulums. Seagulls circled and cried.

"What's that thing being wheeled on planks?" I asked. "...like a gallows."

"A crane, Val...to raise the cargo from the barges."

A wiry man in a dark suit and cap stepped out of the tugboat wheelhouse, angled his way on foot along the barges, and jumped into the water to wade the last few feet ashore.

He mounted a mule being held for him, surveyed the scene, and began pointing at the men.

"Suggs," Roddy said. "That's him."

For over an hour, we watched pallets of lumber and bulging canvas sacks hoisted from the barges, lowered into wagons and driven off, while the wiry man on the mule sat stiff with his back arched and head held high, pointing occasionally with two fingers. He never opened his mouth or waved his arms yet seemed in strictest command.

"Like a plantation overseer, except for the whip," I said.

"Or the prison 'captain' with a shotgun," Roddy murmured.

By high noon, the barges emptied, the tugboat whistled and steamed off, and men gathered at a cook tent, where odors of fried fish wafted. Amos Suggs had dismounted, handed the mule's reins to a worker, and tramped to the shed.

"Let's go, Val."

We crossed hot sand, knowing we had traveled a thousand miles for this moment, quite possibly a fool's errand.

Inside the shed, a man's voice cursed what my papa called "a blue streak."

Roddy tapped on the door. "Mr. Suggs?"

The foul cursing got louder, and a *thuck-thuck* sound. Whoever was being lambasted inside did not speak.

"Mr. Suggs...sir...."

The shed door opened. "What?"

The figure familiar from the Calvary Church service filled the doorframe, the same off-center features, the narrow chin, wide mouth, thin nose—and piercing blue eyes. His coat was off, and his shirt stuck to his shoulders and chest from the heat. His trouser legs had crusted with dried salt from the water, and his left hand held a pencil...no, a dart.

"You're on private property." He spoke through his teeth, his jaw barely moving.

"Mr. Suggs," Roddy said, "if we may have a few minutes of your time? It's about Mr. Rankin...the late Mr. Rankin...the man you rescued from the mine many years ago."

He blinked without moving a muscle.

"My wife and I attended the service for Mr. Rankin," Roddy said. "We heard your testament."

Without a word, he let us into space that he alone occupied. One hand yanked cardboard cartons off a pine bench and flung open a folding chair, pointing Roddy to the bench and me to the chair. Seated, I eyed a worktable and stool, a safe, a cot, a steel file cabinet, and last year's calendar drooping from a nail. Lanterns hung from brackets, and a tripod at the back wall supported a target—a dartboard stuck with darts. Amos Suggs pitched the dart with his free hand and hit the bullseye with a *thuck*.

He faced us on the stool. "What's on your mind?"

Roddy introduced us. "...from New York," he said, "and we're here because Mrs. DeVere and I attended the memorial service, but also the Metropolitan Opera... on the second night of this month."

Suggs jiggled one knee.

"...the night that Mr. Rankin passed away," I said, "...from apoplexy...a hemorrhage."

Suggs sucked his cheek and looked from me to Roddy. "You in business with him?"

Roddy said, "No."

"Then why the church?"

"A friend owns the opera box Mr. Rankin rented for the season," Roddy said, "and I agreed to keep an eye on it."

"Damages from the mess, is that what you're after?"

"The mess..." I said. "Mess?"

"Champagne wine slopped on the chairs and floor," he said. "There's a man name of Taggart at Star Coal in New York. He pays the damages...if you can get it out of him."

"Actually," Roddy said, "I have spoken to Mr. Taggart."

"Then I got nothing to say. Plenty on my mind...kegs of nails, paint...window glass...shingles...half a million feet of lumber...lead pipe by the mile...and another barge full of the wrong lumber today, this morning....can't they read an order?" He glared. "Try to find carpenters that know a chisel from a claw hammer...plumbers that can solder an elbow joint...Hunkies, Wops, Crackers...."

"Skills..." Roddy said.

"Sign them up wherever...Tampa, the Glades, New Orleans—"

"—New Orleans?" Roddy said. "So far away?"

Suggs seemed not to listen. "Best carpenters in New Orleans...plumbers too. Leon's idea about the hotel was, get the workers from the French Quarter." He scratched his neck. "...spent time down there, off and on. Learned a little French. *Parlez-vous francais*?" He spoofed the words.

"Didn't Mr. Rankin consider business in New Orleans?" I asked. "Was it ice?" My question intended to hold a place in this talk.

Suggs glared. "Where'd you hear that?"

To say Glenna May Rankin's name might send us cursed from the shed. "The newspapers," I said, "after Mr. Rankin's death…his business ideas, besides coal…."

"Coal…railroads, a bank…." He snorted. "Maybe I wouldn't be stuck in the sand with coconuts in this god-forsaken place if Leon went for ice. Big business, ice. New Orleans got it going good…Louisiana Ice Manufacturing Company, biggest in the world. Tons of ice, and ten men to freeze it…payroll of ten men, no hordes of 'coconuts' whining for pay and running like rabbits."

He swiped at his trouser legs. "Runaways," he hissed, "thieving no-goods…scatter like palmetto bugs at night. They'll get their money, and I'll get mine…when it's done. You run off, I tell them, you get nothing. Nothing. Stick it out, it's money in your pocket."

A message, I thought, likely meant for him. "Mr. Suggs," I said, "the loss of Mr. Rankin—"

"—and now that sister of his, and Sonny Boy."

"Lewis," Roddy said.

"Big for his britches…wet behind the ears…came at me at Christmas, all hot and bothered. 'Shut down the hotel, Suggs. Shut it down right now.' 'Who says so?' I asked. 'If your daddy changed his mind, I'd hear it first…from him.'"

"But you didn't…?" Roddy said.

"Some scuttlebutt in New Orleans about Leon in hot water…money troubles. Scared the pants off the kid. 'Why tell me?' I said. 'Talk to your Old Man.'"

"And did he?" Roddy asked softly.

"Not a chance. Too scared Leon would cut him off. The kid moaned and groaned at me to shut down the Ocean Grande. I told him, 'Shut up, or I'll tell a few things about your daddy…your daddy and your mama's companion, Celeste.' 'Might just be, I said, some money won't come your way.' That shut him up good."

I glanced at Roddy. We'd heard of Doreen, but who was Celeste? How could we ask this furious man?

Veins stood out on his forehead. "Salt air…" he said, "everything rusts."

He slapped a mosquito on his cheek. "Them too…whine all night when you try to catch a little shut eye. Clouds of them, drove Leon out of his mind…got me spraying kerosene in every puddle…. 'Spray them good, Amos. Kill every last one.'"

Spittle flew from his lips. "Not him, just me. Not Leon Rankin to lift a kerosene can…him in the fancy Poinciana hotel, me bushwacking down here. Blood brother, my eye…."

"It must be very difficult…." Roddy said.

Suggs glowered. "I got no time for chit-chat. You go back to New York, tell Taggart this hotel will get finished one way or another before the hurricanes…if it don't burn to the ground first."

Chapter Twenty-six

"SUCH RAGE, RODDY...EVERY WORD he spoke."

"Incensed at Rankin," my husband replied. "Probably wishing he'd left him trapped in the West Virginia coal mine."

We had bicycled back to the hotel, washed up, changed, and now sat together for a few moments on the edge of the bed. Lunchtime had passed, but I didn't care. Nearly two o'clock, and my face felt hot. Roddy's forehead had turned a bright pink. Too much sun, even with our hats, but Suggs scorched us.

"Total discipline on the mule in front of the construction workers..." Roddy said.

"But he explodes in private in the shed, cursing and pitching darts," I said, "but not for fun."

"No...not for fun," Roddy said slowly. "He fires from anger...at the workers, at his life, but mostly at Rankin. The man is dead and buried...."

"...but the rage lives on."

We sat in silence, and Roddy posed the question that drummed in my mind: did Suggs's rage explode in a New York opera box three weeks ago? On the night of January second, did he return to the box by himself to have it out with Leon, lose control of himself and commit murder?

"We came to Florida to see about Suggs," I said, "and we'll probably depart with one big, fat 'maybe.'"

"He has a motive, Val." Roddy tightened a shoelace. "Too many years at Rankin's beck and call, waiting for the promised 'brotherhood'—"

"—to be achieved by the Ocean Grande...or so he hoped?" I shifted on the bed. "Suppose that Rankin promised a big reward when the hotel opened but waffled when Suggs tried to pin him down. You saw no contract in the business papers from Taggart?"

"No, nor letter of agreement. Any promise Rankin made without a document is hearsay, invalid in a court of law." Roddy rubbed his cheek. "I'm thinking the New York holiday was the last straw...a few days in the lap of luxury while Rankin dodged hard talk about the 'reward.'"

"And Suggs in bondage to the hotel...on a tight schedule."

Roddy nodded. "With crews of inept, unreliable workers, barges filled with the wrong supplies...and of course, the shed."

"But far from the murder scene," I said. "He rushed back here just a day or two after the memorial service."

"Perhaps to get back to work right away," Roddy said. "A court might be persuaded that Suggs's construction work entitles him to a share of Rankin's estate…or a share of the hotel's value. And 'Sonny Boy' sent him a signal at Christmastime about the Coal King's money troubles."

"But Suggs brushed him off. Either way," I went on, "Amos Suggs is one more "maybe' murderer. So, we add him to Jeremy Dent and John Griggs…and Rankin's girlfriend with blonde coils."

"Gloria Bates," Roddy said. "…all four of them…greed, misery, vengeance…." He rubbed his cheek once again, sighed, and stood. "I need a shave, Val. And we both need to pause and catch a breath. I'm going down to the barber shop. And you…?"

"I'll see how Glenna May is doing…and Velvet."

"In that order?"

I tried to think up a clever crack as I reached for the telephone, but Roddy had gone. The switchboard connected me to Glenna May, who said Velvet was fine, and I could visit her suite, if I must.

Must? Did the phone wires distort her voice, or was she distressed? I skipped down the stairs to face an elderly woman who had aged a half-dozen years. Glenna May looked stooped, her shoulders slouched, her uncombed hair pushed behind her ears, and her eyes bloodshot. Had she been crying?

"Velvet," she said in a tremulous voice, "look who's here…."

The dog pawed my ankles in play. Before me, a cheerful dog and a distraught woman without her cane. If the ankle had healed, surely she would celebrate. Perhaps Glenna May feared that I had come for Velvet.

"Miss Glenna, may I sit down?" I asked.

"…plumb forgot my manners." She sounded hoarse. "Sit yourself down…I ought to fill Velvet's water…won't take a minute."

Behind her, a dog bed printed with a Royal Poinciana crest lay on the floor beside two bowls and a bone. Bowl in hand, Glenna May limped to the bathroom, closed the door, and the sounds of gushing faucets wide open.

I perched on a loveseat by the window, and Velvet jumped beside me. The suite's furniture had personal touches—an earthenware jug in the corner, a homemade straw broom propped at the side, and colorful speckled quilts draping all four chairs. Western women saved remnants and sewed "crazy quilts" for cold nights. Maybe the West Virginia quilts cheered Glenna May in this hot, tropical foreign land she now called home.

The bathroom door opened, and Glenna May limped to put the dog's water bowl beside the bone. Velvet showed no interest.

"Miss Glenna," I said, "you have given up your cane."

"Might as well…." She sank into a chair.

"I saw quilts like these in Colorado," I said, "and Nevada too…sewn with love."

She fixed me with a straight stare. "Call it love if you want, Valentine," she said, "but need came first. Every scrap…use it…use it up. Same with food."

Her words mixed pride with truth, the same tone as in New York and the *Louisa*. In the next instant, however, she wilted.

"My mama and aunts pieced the scraps together…" she whispered. "West Virginia winters…not like here. They say 'cold snap' in Florida,' but the mountains get real winter." She pulled the quilt around her knees. "Before the diphtheria…" she said. "Hard times, but good times…not like nowadays."

In the quiet moment, I noticed she had combed her hair and patted cool water on her eyes. If I spoke her nephew's name, would she shut down, or open up? Lewis had summoned his aunt to Palm Beach, and "Sonny Boy" clearly aggravated and distressed her. "Miss Glenna," I asked, "are you feeling well? Perhaps Velvet is too much…?"

"Valentine, turn your head toward that wall." She pointed to a cluster of framed photographs across the room, where Leon Rankin glowered at us, the "Coal King" in a top hat, a bowler, a golfing outfit…and one with a young boy in knickers at his side. A father-son photo with Lewis? Hard to tell, the boy looked blurry. Several hooks fastened to the wall meant pictures to be hung…or pictures removed. I shivered.

Glenna May's gaze lingered at the photographs of her late brother. "If he was here…" she began.

"Leon," I said, "…so much in your thoughts."

"He would straighten everything out," she said at last. "My brother was too smart to get behind."

"Behind...?"

"In money," she said, "or business. Same thing, money and business." She traced a finger on a quilt edge. "I don't believe a word Lewis tells me...trash. All trash."

"Something he said to you?" I asked quietly.

"From New Orleans...rotten place...that mama of his...."

"Doreen, if I remember..." I said.

"...supposed to be the one-and-only, but the others...."

"...perhaps a Celeste....?"

She turned so fast her hair came loose. "Where'd you hear that name?" She wrung her hands. "—from Amos, wasn't it? You heard it from Amos Suggs...."

"This morning," I said, "Mr. DeVere and I visited the Ocean Grande construction."

"...way too much time in New Orleans years back," she said, "Leon and Amos both. My brother ought never to have gone down there. Chasing ice, he got caught." She swallowed. "Shoots off his mouth, Amos does. You take what he says as blowing smoke."

She pressed her knuckles to her lips. "And Lewis ought to stayed at the tea table yesterday so Mr. DeVere could set him straight."

"Straight about what, Miss Glenna?"

"To tell him Leon's business is solid as a rock. New Orleans stuffed his ears with lies...that everything Leon Lee Rankin touched is near to failing."

I swallowed hard.

"If Mr. Taggart was here, he could talk sense too. All those days at the Plaza Hotel, Mr. Taggart guided my hand. My brother put trust in that man. 'Not much for gabbing,' Leon said, 'but Elmer Taggart can run numbers to the penny in his sleep.'"

Beside me, the dog yelped as she felt me stiffen. I stroked her back. "Rumors," I said, "fly like the wind. "Your nephew... is naturally concerned for his future."

"He better be, with what he did...be the death of me... what he's done."

"I hope he's not a gambler," I said.

"Not with cards or dice," she said, "but the boy...no knack for business, not like my brother. They tangled about it. Leon called him harebrained, and Lewis swore he'd show his father one of these days." She sniffled. "Leon's gone, but the boy acts like he's got something to prove. He went to West Palm Beach again yesterday."

"Again?"

"Like at Christmas, when Leon went with him to look at sea turtles in a tank.... Owner calls himself 'Alligator Joe,' keeps turtles and sells off land on the side. Leon and Lewis came for the turtles, and he beat their ear selling land."

"A Realtor," I said.

"...wrestles alligators too. Leon said that land was everglades...worthless swamp. But my nephew took the bait. You heard him yesterday, all about 'farsighted' folks buying up West Palm Beach."

"Lewis is considering investing...?"

"Considering...." Glenna May huffed and clutched fistfuls of quilted cloth. Her eyes beseeched me. "You come to tea again, you and Mr. DeVere. A New York lawyer can talk sense to my nephew and get him out of the Alligator man's jaws." She sat up straight and pressed her lips into a thin line. "My nephew has signed a promissory note, Valentine. He owes this 'Alligator Joe' every cent we've got till kingdom come."

Chapter Twenty-seven

TRAILING GLENNA MAY'S ANGUISH, I found Roddy poring over a sheet of thin paper in our suite. "Western Union," he said, "...a telegram from Hoff."

Brooding over Glenna May, I wrenched my mind to the opera impresario. "Hoff, "I said, "what does he want?"

"Not exactly clear...." Roddy handed me the paper.

PROGRESS MUTUAL ISSUE. WENDELL BOX APPLICANT.
SEE ME ON RETURN NEW YORK
MAURICE HOFF

The capital letters signaled urgency, as telegrams always did. I reread the words. "What 'Wendell Box Applicant?'"

"Perhaps a rental for the rest of the season."

"But the 'Mutual Issue,'" I said, "is surely our 'q.t.' inquiry or...could it be my earring? Roddy, tell me this is not about my earring...material evidence...." I fought panic. My throat closed.

My husband spread his hands on my shoulders. "Doubtful, my dear."

"What else could it mean? When did you get it?"

"...from a bellboy as I left the barber shop." Roddy's steady grip, warm to the touch, sat us down on a sofa. I managed to swallow. My face felt hot from the sun.

I read the message a third time. Nowhere did 'EARRING' appear, but the handful of words brought Leon Rankin's murder into our suite once again today.

And the rumors that swirled about me.

Roddy took the telegram from my fingers and laid it aside. "Val, I've been mulling over something. Can you listen? Can you hear me?"

He meant, was I too upset to pay attention? "Try me, Roddy."

My husband closed his eyes for moment. Roddy's forehead was turning from pink to tan. "Ready, Val?"

"Ready."

"I've batted this back and forth since we inspected the new carpets and visited Hoff's office. It doesn't square with me that he junked the blood-stained carpet and sent all the chairs out for refinishing...evidence gone from Box Eighteen."

I nodded. My face felt fiery.

"Star Coal was about to become an official shareholder of the Metropolitan Opera and Real Estate Company," Roddy said. "And Leon Rankin charged every possible dollar to the coal company."

"So..." I said, "the engraved brass plaques outside the boxes would soon read, Vanderbilt, Astor, and ***Star Coal Company***?"

"Most likely," Roddy said.

"...and *Town Topics* would spew out something like... 'Coal Shoveled in Diamond Horseshoe.'"

Roddy nodded.

So, then..." I said, "...are you thinking Hoff might have killed Leon Rankin to keep the Horseshoe pure and his reputation high? Is that it? We now add Hoff to the list of possible killers? Amos Suggs, John Griggs, Jeremy Dent... Goldilocks...and Maurice Hoff too?" My throat felt tight, my cheeks on fire. "Grimy coal at the opera would be enough for murder? Surely not."

"People have been killed for less, Val." Roddy bit his lower lip. "

The moment grew quiet. "You think he planned...it?"

My husband shook his head. "Very doubtful. I'd guess weeks of brooding, and then the chance to slip into Box 18 when Rankin's party left. Maybe Hoff planned to discourage Rankin, downplay an opera box...but then saw champagne bottles and glasses...."

"And lunged in rage? Stabbed Rankin in the neck?" I swallowed. "...with a knife? An icepick?"

"Val, we needn't imagine weapons. Something sharp and pointed. Let it go at that."

I could not "let it go." Squeezing Roddy's hand tight, I relived the sight of Rankin's body halfway rising from his chair, bloodied, stiffened in death. "Hoff could have slipped out, couldn't he?" I said, "...tidied up in his basement office and got ready for whoever found the body...a maid, an usher, a janitor. But not Mr. Roderick DeVere in Box Seventeen."

"No," Roddy said. "He wouldn't have thought about blood seeping into our box...but he'd welcome us as confidantes...." Roddy paused. "And he'd expect a finding of death by hemorrhage from a major artery."

"But why this telegram?"

"...to assure the DeVeres that Maurice Hoff, their ally, is in touch...and concerned about the Wendells."

I touched my sun-seared cheek and my nose too. "So, we add Maurice Hoff to our list," I said at last. "Though we're no closer to the truth, are we?" I touched my ear lobes to make sure two garnet earrings were secure.

"We ought to go back to New York," I said. "What more would we learn from Amos Suggs, except that he might have flown into a rage and killed Leon Rankin?"

"Val...." Roddy massaged my neck. "I'll see about the FEC Railway schedule, but another day with Glenna May and her odious nephew might yield a few new facts about Suggs, or Jeremy Dent, or—"

"—or Griggs with his threatening document and failed bank. Or 'Blondie' Bates...and now Maurice Hoff...the whole rollcall."

Did I sound as sick-and-tired as I felt? The slanting sunlight meant that Glenna May was kept waiting in the Coconut Grove for Mr. DeVere to free her nephew—and herself—from financial ruin.

She would soon know that nephew Lewis Rankin's foolish impulse was just one part of the looming catastrophe. "Roddy," I said, "Glenna May is waiting for us, but before we go, I have something to tell you about Sonny Boy's latest…. And when we talk to Glenna May, try to find out about a woman named 'Celeste'…the name that Amos Suggs used to shoo away Lewis."

"…something about the young whelp's money," Roddy said.

"Auntie Glenna got rattled when I asked, Roddy," I said. "And I asked nicely."

The teatime scene had shifted toward dusk when we entered the Grove, where colored lights twinkled in the palm trees and a band played dance music. The center tables were cleared to make way for a dance floor, where couples two-stepped and guests lingered at tea tables arranged in a ring around the dancers.

The maître d' approached, but Lewis Rankin shot forward.

"Mr. and Mrs. DeVere, at long last. Won't you join us? Auntie Glenna feared you might have forgotten all about us Rankins."

He led us to a table where Glenna May sat stiff as a board, her cane nowhere in view. She said, "Lordy, you're here…."

"Good afternoon," said Roddy. He took the wrought iron chair next to Glenna May, while Lewis held a woven rattan chair for me.

"Comfort for you, Mrs. DeVere," Lewis said. "The Coconut Grove is not your ice cream parlor with chairs of bent wire." The young man's chair, also woven rattan, left his aunt and my husband seated on wrought iron metal.

"Supper here's not till eight o'clock at night," said Glenna May. "In West Virginia, that's bedtime in the winter...dark as one of Lewis's daddy's mines."

"Auntie Glenna, let us enjoy the Ponce without dismal thoughts."

His aunt's eyes narrowed. "Every lump of your late daddy's coal keeps us in comfort, Lewis Rankin."

No one spoke, but I thought of "the most dangerous woman in America" devoting her life to the miners. What would Mother Jones think of the Royal Poinciana Hotel? What would she say about the Coconut Grove?

This was no time to bring up labor unions, not when my husband needed to be a counsellor, financial adviser, lawyer, and inquisitor too. "Miss Glenna," I said cheerily, "Is Velvet treating you right?"

"Not only Velvet, Valentine, but also Mattie Sue. She's upstairs brushing Velvet, and that young maid gets a prize for knowing just what to do...helpful every which way. Did you know she grew up on a tobacco farm in Massachusetts? Never knew they raised tobacco way up there."

Lewis fidgeted in his pearl-gray suit that caught the soft light...silk, for sure. Ignoring his aunt, he leaned my way and spoke softly. "Your very first visit to the Ponce, Mrs. DeVere?"

"Very first," I said.

"An excellent start to the New Year," he said, "and I hope you might allow me to introduce the 'custom of the country,' so to speak."

Across the table, Roddy had begun a conversation with Glenna May. "And what custom would that be?" I asked.

"Our evenings," he said, "are brightened by amusing musical shows in the ballroom...the Marlow Minstrels... with singing worthy of the New York opera. Perhaps you and Mr. DeVere like the opera?"

When I did not answer, he leaned as if to confide a secret. "Have you heard of Mrs. Winter's 'famous' coconut cake? Guests ask, 'Is 'Mrs. Winter available?' Her seasonal name so droll at the Ponce...'Winter,' you see?"

I saw.

The waiter had approached, and the young man ordered a vintage champagne and a coconut cake. His eyes looked like the soulful paintings of martyrs. "Mrs. DeVere," he said, "I owe you an apology."

"Oh?"

"A most sincere apology...you see, I have learned that you so kindly brought Auntie Glenna here in your very own private car."

"The *Louisa*," I said, "named in honor of—"

"—and you are Valentine Louise Mackle, are you not? Your late father was a 'Silver King,' if I am correct...."

I nodded.

"So, I am correct...and humbly apologize."

"No need, Mr. Rankin."

"Do call me Lewis...here comes our wine and our 'Mrs. Winter.'" The waiter set out plates and glasses and sliced the cake as Lewis directed. Etiquette dictated the first slice to the eldest lady, but a wedge of the famous cake came to me first, delivered by Lewis Rankin's soft, white hand. The waiter popped the cork and began to pour. Glenna May turned her glass upside down and asked for orange juice.

"A toast to the DeVeres!" Lewis held his glass aloft. Roddy looked puzzled, and Glenna May irked. My wine bubbled, untouched like the cake.

"To Mr. Roderick Windham DeVere and his lady, the lovely Valentine Louise Mackle DeVere."

Lewis tapped his glass against mine and took a sip. The band began a waltz, and couples changed partners. "I hope the 1884 Mumms pleases you, Mrs. DeVere...a rare year. I have studied the matter."

Roddy once again spoke quietly to Glenna May, who was drinking every word as if my husband were an oasis in the Sahara.

Lewis angled himself toward me. "I do believe," he said, "that I have the company of a western lady who knows her own mind...and rejects the alabaster white complexion of today's fashion."

The fool. Complimenting my sunburn.

"Our splendid Palm Beach sunshine," he said, "is so often shunned by ladies who spend their days on the shaded colonnade. We gentlemen stand by, not intending to listen, but conversation in the rocking chairs can rock the boat, if you follow my drift."

I raised a permissive eyebrow, and he said, "Your earring gemstones, Mrs. DeVere…garnets, are they not?"

"They are, Mr. Rankin. It seems that wines are not your only interest."

"I try to keep abreast…a point of pride. Diamonds are for evenings, are they not? And we gentlemen delight in the star shine of ladies' diamonds in the Ponce ballroom or elsewhere…a formal dinner, the theatre…or at the grand opera."

"The opera…." I murmured.

"The opera in our cities…especially the Metropolitan Opera in New York."

He leered. Was he saying that I already stirred gossip at the Royal Poinciana Hotel? ("Haven't you heard…? Her earring was found in Leon Rankin's clothing the night he died at the opera….")

Or was I too suspicious? The band struck up a familiar tune.

"'On the Banks of the Wabash'," Lewis said, "a favorite of mine. Mrs. DeVere, may I have the honor of this dance?"

One glance at my husband and the elderly woman held rapt by his words, and I could not refuse without making a scene.

"Four quarter time, Mrs. DeVere…'Oh, the moonlight's fair tonight along the Waaa-bash….'" Lewis danced me to the edge of the floor, holding us there with a box step. "A few words," Mrs. DeVere," he said, "in this playground where past and future should meet…and join together."

The saxophones swooned, and he leaned toward my ear. "The great silver fortunes," he said, "came from the century that is closing fast, but the new century, Mrs. DeVere, will be known for fortunes from Real Estate…right here in Florida. I saw the future, and I have taken hold of it…our dance is a dance of the past and the future together…no, don't pull away. Consider my message. Come to the ballroom for tonight's show. Between the acts, we can have a talk while the time is on our side."

Chapter Twenty-eight

"THE NERVE...GREEDY BRAT...HOW dare he....?"

"Ma'am?"

At the dressing table in our suite, Calista dabbed cool lotion on my face. Roddy had gone to see about northbound trains.

"Furious at him...," I said.

My maid wisely kept quiet. A rule chiseled into etiquette books had become second nature to Calista Adrianakis: confiding in servants...*under no circumstances!*

"Ridiculous man...."

Calista's alarmed expression meant she thought me enraged at my husband, and my sudden laughter startled her.

"Nothing to do with Mr. DeVere," I said. "...a so-called 'gentlemen...but the coconut cake in that box is for you and Mattie Sue." I pointed to the bakery box on a table. "I hear it's delicious."

"Thank you, ma'am, and Mattie Sue will thank you, I am sure."

"Calista," I said, "we'll very soon return to New York. Mr. DeVere is seeing about the schedule. Our business here is nearly finished…and you have hardly seen Florida."

"I've seen enough, ma'am. I took an afternoon walk to see the sights. Give me rock over sand every time. The Lord did much better creating the Aegean Sea and the Greek Islands." She patted lotion on my cheeks. "And I have notes about the hotel jobs, like you asked." She reached for a new cotton ball. "If I may inquire, ma'am, will Miss Rankin come back to New York?"

"Doubtful, Calista."

"…because Mattie Sue says the work with Miss Rankin is most satisfactory."

"You think she might prefer to stay here?"

My maid soaked a new cotton ball, patted my face, and said, "Nothing against Mrs. Thwaite, ma'am. Your housekeeper knows her place, and I know mine. But Mrs. Thwaite and Mattie Sue …let's say, it suits her to work with Miss Rankin."

"Sleeping in the hotel servants' dormitory? And meals in the food hall?"

"So far, ma'am, Mattie Sue says she'll settle for the starchy meals and a barracks bed upstairs. When it comes to Mrs. Thwaite, she'd rather swat mosquitos."

We giggled at the trade-off. "Calista," I said, "please find me a gown for dinner and tonight's entertainment…it's something like a minstrel show in the ballroom, something with opera that Mr. DeVere might enjoy."

At 8:15, Roddy and I dined at a table for two in the vaulted hotel dining room decorated with *papier-mâché* parrots and bird cages dangling from the ceiling. "Just us two for dinner, Roddy…please, no Glenna May or Lewis."

"Just us." We sipped chilled punch.

"What did you tell her this afternoon?" I asked. "You both looked intense. And when will the *Louisa* start for New York? And what must we do about Hoff? Contact the police… Chief Devery? Should we try to recover the blood-stained carpets?"

"First things first," my husband said. "We're not quite through with Florida…and Glenna May might be caught in her brother's death—and his life—in more ways than she's willing to reveal. I told her Leon's affairs are complex and we won't know the facts until the records are examined, which will take some time."

"So, you hedged."

My husband frowned. "Val, it would not help Miss Rankin to be told right now that her brother's holdings are near collapse. She is terrified about her nephew's promissory note."

"Lewis Rankin's land grab," I said. "He couldn't stop bragging on the dance floor. What did you find out?"

"There's a man named Frazier," Roddy said. "'Alligator' Joe Frazier sold the land to Lewis. Or 'sold' the land."

"...so, it might not be his to sell?"

"Let's hope not. Miss Rankin said Lewis waved the promissory note and a rough map of Florida to 'prove' his investment skill. If her memory serves, the note bore no mark of a witness by a notary."

Roddy sipped his punch. "I'll research Florida's laws, but a promissory note without a notary witness can pit the lender against the borrower in court...and take time."

"...but if the Rankin empire soon falls, it's moot, right?"

My husband smiled his rueful, barrister smile. "'Soon,' Val, is a concept seldom applicable to the law."

He sipped again. "Another legal matter seems to trouble Miss Rankin...another claimant to Rankin's estate who might appear to muddy the waters."

"Oh?"

"You asked me to find out about Celeste...." Roddy gazed up at a *papier-mâché* parrot. "You think you know what makes a person 'tick,' but a new wrinkle alters the case as you know it."

He put his glass down. "Miss Rankin turned cagey. She sidestepped my question about a woman who might complicate her late brother's estate. I asked her, was the first Mrs. Rankin—Doreen—perhaps followed by Leon's remarriage? I used women's French names as examples, Dominique, Suzette, Georgette...but 'Celeste' stunned her. She froze and called me a tricky 'Shylock' lawyer. She said Celeste is dead, so it doesn't matter."

"Yikes."

"She clammed up, not another word. My guess is, 'Celeste' was Leon's mistress in his New Orleans days and might file a claim against Rankin's estate. The laws of Louisiana date from its years as a French colony, and the state's Napoleonic Code is a different kettle of fish.

"So, whatever Glenna May knows about Celeste, her lips are sealed?"

"For the present. Shall we see about dinner? The show starts at ten o'clock, so we needn't be rushed."

Exactly at 10:05, we made our way to the middle of a row in the ballroom, just as the master of ceremonies began, "Ladies and gentlemen of the Royal Poinciana...for your entertainment, the magic and the mirth...and the teardrops too, direct from New Orleans, the Marlow Minstrels!"

Applause crackled as we sat down. I did not see Glenna May or Lewis.

Minstrels in Uncle Sam costumes struck up "Suwanee River," and a Sambo traded jokes with his partner, Bones. The minstrels broke into "Dixie" and quieted for a skit involving Betsy Ross sewing a flag for George Washington while reciting a poem of many verses.

A drum roll began at last, and low chords from the orchestra. "Ladies and gentlemen, the Marlow Minstrels pièce de resistance...the talented Clyde Flabée, tenor *extraodinaire* who will bring tears to your eyes, dear ladies...so, handkerchiefs at the ready, and Monsieur Flabée, if you please, from *Pagliacci*...."

The lights surrounded a thin young man whose white clown suit nearly swallowed his frame. His hands trembled as the orchestral strings and deep brass rose to a *forte*.

"*Vesti la giubba, E la faccia infarina....*"

Roddy stiffened at my side. I made no claim to perfect pitch, but young Clyde sounded flat.

"*La gente paga, e rider vuole qua....*"

Around us, muffled groans stirred. My many evenings at Piper's Opera House with Papa had taught the difference between approval and an outright veto. Roddy's jaw clamped tight as the young singer clasped his trembling hands together and kept going to the finale. "*E ridi del duol che t'avvelena il cor....*"

"Torment," Roddy muttered. Someone behind us said, "Miserable...Flagler ought to hear about this...."

The ballroom rose for its exodus, and we waited to file out. A couple who waited in our row struck up a conversation. "...saw you in the barber shop, sir."

We two ladies merely smiled.

"Big loss for Marlow, the young fellow that left for the big White Way," the man said. "A real corker...could have rivaled the man they all rave about, Caruso...if he got the chance."

"Quite a tribute," Roddy said.

"Antoine," he said. "Antoine D'Cee...good-looking fellow...so dark they turned the lights up to give us a good look, and that head of hair...so curly the clown hat fell off." The man chortled, "They say his old man's a big shot that's putting up a hotel down here…had no truck with him or his singing…wouldn't send him to Italy to study…nothing doing."

"…a shame," Roddy said.

"For sure…. They say he went to the big city, bound to sing opera, no matter what it takes…."

Our row was clearing. "His name," Roddy said, now vigilant. "Antoine—"

"—D'Cee," the man said. "Sounds to me like Antoine disowned his old man and plans to show him a thing or two."

Chapter Twenty-nine

OUR TRAIN STARTED NORTH at the ungodly hour of 3:10 a.m., the wheels clicking on rails in the darkness… to Titusville, Ormond, St. Augustine…each scheduled stop torturous until the conductor's "All Aboard" got us underway once again, a passenger train with the *Louisa* hitched at the rear and bound for New York City. A telegram to Mr. Sands alerted the household to our arrival at Grand Central at 6:20 p.m., the twenty-sixth of January.

Roddy and I had barely slept for the last twenty-four hours and had not yet sorted out new, fractured thoughts. The casual remarks about the absent Antoine raised questions we would face after our hasty departure.

If only we could have sprinted to the *Louisa* and sped off, but arrangements for the *Louisa* tied up Roddy, while I faced the touchy matter of Glenna May, our departure, and our dog returned as if surrendered at war's end. I dodged the craven Lewis Rankin and urged Mattie Sue Joiner to stay in Palm Beach as Miss Rankin's personal maid while scouting for other opportunities. The young woman's gushing thanks showed that freedom from Mrs. Thwaite was the zenith of her life.

Calista packed gowns and hats and retrieved our wools. The baggage was loaded, and my maid appeared doubly relieved when the *Louisa* crossed the Flagler Trestle. The car's ceiling fans spun, and my husband quipped that the whirling blades were metaphors for our spinning minds.

"I'm too mixed up for metaphors, Roddy, and too jittery to sleep."

Heading north, we kept the curtains drawn, but the night passed in cat naps, while Velvet curled up, snoring until Roddy peeled back a curtain to have a look outside. "Not quite dawn, Val."

"Feels like we've been underway forever," I said. "What would we see, if we could see?"

"Bare branches," he said, "and pine trees."

I stared at the black window glass. "We ought to talk."

Roddy nodded.

Slowly I said the two names, "Antoine D'Cee...and Antony, the usher." Back and forth, the names merged. "Roddy," I said, "the day Calista and I went to the opera house, Antony was polishing railings. His apron badge read 'Antony Dessey.' I'm certain it said 'Dessey'...dark skin and curly hair...Dessey...and the badge was pinned on his coveralls the day we saw the box...and Hoff."

Roddy shrugged "Suppose he is D'Cee...people change names, get fresh starts. Suppose Antoine did leave the minstrel show to take his chances in the 'Great White Way.'"

"...to work at the Metropolitan Opera...by chance?"

"If he's serious about grand opera, Val, the man would avoid musical theatre and Vaudeville. Believe me, *Pagliacci* is a far cry from Gilbert and Sullivan."

"Why not audition for the chorus?"

"A soloist, Val, will not sing in a chorus."

"I did not know that." The train seemed to slow down, then speed up. "Roddy," I said, "we need to face a likely fact. Antoine's father refused to support his schooling and is building a hotel in Florida. Who else could it be? Let's say that Antoine is Antony, and his father was Leon Rankin, and...."

"And his mother is Celeste...capital 'C'...the son of Celeste would be D'Cee."

"But not Rankin," I said, "because Antoine was Leon Rankin's son...because Antony Dessey is his bastard son." I swallowed. "The question is, why is that young man working as a janitor and usher at the opera house...opening the box for the father who wouldn't help him? Bringing him champagne....? Does he know his father is Leon Rankin? Did he know? And if he did....?"

Roddy pressed his finger across my lips. "And Hoff...," he murmured, "what might Maurice Hoff have to do with... with the situation?"

The question hung as we listened to the train wheels. Factories appeared from the windows. The *Louisa* had entered the northeast corridor of cities. "A few hours," Roddy said, "and we'll be home."

I repeated, "Home," and my husband squeezed my hand. "Roddy," I said, "we've given the police a huge head start. Our 'q.t. inquiry' ends now, yes?"

"Winding down, Val."

"And I get my earring back...." The train slowed. "Baltimore depot...," I said. "Should we wire Mr. Gork to schedule a meeting?"

"Not until we see Hoff. Remember the telegram. Hoff wants to see us, and for our 'q.t.' finale, we ought to pay him a visit."

Chapter Thirty

WINTRY NEW YORK SMACKED our cheeks with a no-nonsense fourteen degrees Fahrenheit. Noland ushered us and our dog into our landau outside Grand Central, snapped the reins, and the blanketed Apollo and Atlas high-stepped for 62nd Street at a good clip over new-fallen snow. The groom drove a second carriage for Calista and a few light bags. A railway express wagon would bring trunks and bulky baggage, and our footmen would tote them upstairs to be unpacked in the morning.

Sands greeted us, as did a pinch-faced Mrs. Thwaite and the footmen who took Velvet to her meal. The kitchen offered a "welcome home" dinner. After coffee and desert, we sorted the past few days' mail, and Roddy lifted an envelope with embossed gold letters of the *Metropolitan Opera.*

"It's Hoff, isn't it?" I said.

"It is." Roddy unfolded the letter. "Mr. Maurice Hoff hopes we might do him 'the honor' of calling upon him at the opera house upon our return 'at our earliest opportunity.'" My husband read on. "'A meritorious proposal for immediate rental of *parterre* Box Eighteen for remainder of 1899 season…your assistance as emissaries of Mr. and Mrs. Charles Wendell… chairs newly installed and available for your perusal….'"

Roddy looked up. "It must be the 'box applicant' in Hoff's telegram. We are asked to inspect and sign the contract…and something about a 'diamond' of the Diamond Horseshoe.'"

"Roddy, I dread going near that man."

"Of course you do, and so do I, but the impresario of the Metropolitan Opera has no inkling of our suspicions…."

"…and neither do the others," I said. "The West Virginians…Grace Bates…the banker. Do we scour the city for them too? Traipse downtown…? Go back to Florida to the tarpaper shack to see Suggs?"

"Val…stop…."

I flooded my cold, weak coffee with cream and stirred so fast the whirlpool spilled into the saucer.

"Let's agree," Roddy continued, "that Hoff might incriminate himself if we keep our wits about us. And Antony D'Cee too. If that happens, we can go to Chief Devery and Detective Finlay—and Gork. The case would reopen…widen. The others would come in for new scrutiny too. The innocent absolved…the guilty…."

My attorney husband's idealistic self, grounded in possibility, pressed the case and drew me toward his side. Roddy's courtroom cases against the Temperance zealots hinged on justice, and their fight to shut down every barroom in the city became his personal cause. I reluctantly agreed to meet with Hoff. Roddy penned a note to say we would arrive at the 40th Street entrance at two p.m. this afternoon.

Noland drove us after lunch, and we stared at our gloved hands the entire way down Broadway until I nudged my husband in surprise at the sight of Maurice Hoff acting as our doorman at the opera house entrance.

"Mr. and Mrs. DeVere, how good of you…and welcome home."

The impresario assisted me from the carriage, a touch I endured. Roddy and I agreed to appear as though nothing was amiss and to follow Hoff's lead. We had both dressed "down," my husband in charcoal grays, me in a brown walking suit.

"…to my office, if you will…and you hear the rehearsal now underway…."

A chorus of male voices and a piano filled the warm foyer. "*Faust…*" my husband said. "If I'm not mistaken, the drinking song."

"Right you are, Mr. DeVere, "*Veau d'Or*, the song about the Golden Calf…a song for our time, as some would say. The orchestra would cost the earth, so all rehearsals are piano only. Our chorus now understands they must sing for their supper, and labor strikes are banished from the Metropolitan Opera. The chorus, you will be pleased to know, is cleansed of its troublemakers."

The malice in his smile sent shivers up my spine. I saw no sign of Antony as Maurice Hoff led us down carpeted stairs and into the private space split between a cluttered clerical office and a *fin de siècle* boudoir, as the impresario termed the armchairs and sofa overlaid with tasseled scarves.

He took our coats and led me to the purple velvet chair once occupied by the soprano, Nordica, as he reminded me. Roddy sank into the small sofa kitty corner to my royal purple "throne." Hoff pulled up a wood Windsor chair with tall spindly legs and took a seat so close I could see the buttons on his sleeves and the laces of his boots.

"I hope that my wire to you in Palm Beach did not hasten your return."

"Not at all," Roddy said, "although the 'progress' on our 'mutual interest' was somewhat mystifying."

"...as telegrams often are, though costs mount by the word, and I am accountable to the shareholders, as you well know, Mr. DeVere. Every penny counts."

Cocking his head, Hoff "shot" snowy French cuffs that shone with antique coin cufflinks. Ancient Rome? Byzantium?

"Our mutual interest in a certain *parterre* box," he said, "brings us together this wintry afternoon...and I cannot thank you enough." The impresario's navy blue suit gave his complexion a bluish pallor.

"By a stroke of fortune," he said, "a British patron of the opera wishes to rent Box 18 for the remainder of the season...a titled gentleman." He paused to let us to savor "titled."

Roddy said, "So, I represent Mr. and Mrs. Wendell's interest?"

"Quite. And the newly refinished chairs have been installed, so the box awaits final review...and a contract to be signed on behalf of Mr. Wendell. The new occupant can enjoy the season...starting with *Faust*."

"Next Tuesday," Roddy said. Already my husband knew the schedule.

I asked, "Shall we go see the Wendells' box?"

"Not just yet."

Roddy's shoulders stiffened at Hoff's sharp "yet." The impresario's chair raised him inches above our deep cushions, and he abruptly sat forward, planted his black boots at a wide angle, and flexed his fingers as if holding a quirt to lash at the air...or us.

"I have been visited by Mr. Bernard Gork," he said, "and learned of great progress made by the police in the case of Mr. Rankin's death."

"Oh?" said Roddy.

I said nothing.

"The Commissioner imparted the news...for my ears only." Hoff's glance zig-zagged from my husband to me. "In strictest confidence," he said, "Commissioner Gork alerted me that the banker, a man named Griggs, is their prime suspect in the case."

"Really?" I said.

"A revenge motive," Hoff said. "It seems the late Mr. Rankin withdrew his investments from Mr. Griggs's bank in order to fund a bank of his own. Mr. Griggs's bank then failed, and the police are confident that the man sought revenge on the very night when we three joined together… the three of us in the box of the deceased."

He touched a palm to his cheek, as if in pain. "Such a blow.… Never such a thing in my long career in theatrical production."

He loomed over Roddy in the Windsor chair. "Hearing the Commissioner's words, I could only hope that Florida offered you respite while the true facts unfolded in regard to Mr. Rankin's death. The New York police will soon 'crack' the case with the arrest of Mr. Griggs."

Somewhere a steam radiator hissed. A new expression on my husband's face reminded me of Papa's bold poker bids when I was allowed to watch the games in Virginia City.

Roddy said, "Our Florida travel was not in vain, Mr. Hoff." He spoke slowly. "We have reason to believe that a Metropolitan Opera usher is the son of the deceased Mr. Rankin."

Hoff blinked fast, squinted, and waved a dismissive palm. "Wherever such outlandish reasoning arises…."

"An embittered young man," Roddy continued in a steady voice. "…a man who might have intended great harm to his father. A young man with an ulterior motive."

"Oh, please do not speak of ulterior motives, Mr. DeVere." He dabbed his eyes with a Cambric linen handkerchief, though I saw no tears.

I said, "Perhaps we might now inspect the chairs in Box Eighteen?"

"Dear lady," Hoff said, "the chairs will wait. Just now, I wish to show good faith…and apologies for sending you on this lamentable escapade, you and Mr. DeVere searching in vain for a criminal malefactor."

He slowly reached into an inside suit pocket, gradually extended his arm in front of me, very slowly opened his hand, and watched my face as I gaped at the diamond hoop earring glittering in his palm.

"Your jewelry, Madame DeVere, I do believe."

I nodded, dumbstruck.

"Yours to take home…to adorn you, beautiful lady, as you wish."

Had my mouth not gone dry, I might have spit. "The earring…" I said, "is my own, and it came from…."

"From Commissioner Gork," he said, "because the police no longer need to secure it…although it was found in the box where a gentleman died, as we know."

"Mr. Hoff," I said, "surely you are not insinuating that I—"

"—nothing of the kind, dear lady. I merely state a fact. No need to explain. Do take your jewel." A smile slithered across his face as I lifted the earring as if touching a hornet. Roddy slipped it into his watch pocket.

"And now, in the matter of the chairs…I have arranged for an attendant to accompany you to Box Eighteen."

Hoff rose, pressed a button on his messy desk, and stood behind the Windsor chair. "Mr. DeVere," he said, "if I could have a few minutes of your time while Madame DeVere looks over the *parterre* box...."

"Mrs. DeVere alone?" Roddy's alarm rang like a bell.

"...to economize on our time," Hoff said. "The new rental contract to be reviewed, of course, and a matter of some delicacy...a word about the opera's support of the celebration honoring Admiral Dewey. Are you not a member of a steering committee for the Dewey honors, Mr. DeVere? I have seen your name."

Roddy's gaze locked on mine to say he would not let me alone with the 'attendant' that I dreaded...Antony.

Hoff pressed the button again, and we waited, my heart pounding...and suddenly weak with relief at the sight of the elderly woman in a housemaid's uniform.

"Sylvia," I blurted.

Askew on her uniform, Sylvia Liley's name badge flashed like sunshine. "Perhaps you remember me," I said. "We spoke in the *parterre* corridor.... You worked for the Wendells... for so many years...."

She did not recall me. "Many the nights," she said. Her eyes looked filmed, her shoulders frail. A key dangled from a ribbon on her pinafore sash.

"Liley will take you up, Madame DeVere. The key to Box Eighteen, Liley?"

Her bone-thin fingers touched the key. I winked at Roddy, turned, and began to follow the maid into the gloomy labyrinth of stairs and hallways.

We quickly climbed three flights in silence. Despite Sylvia Liley's frailty, she stepped fast. The operatic voices and piano rose and fell in the stairwells.

"*Faust*," Sylvia said. "By now, I've heard every last one over and again ....eyesight's not what it was, but my ears are good...and here we are."

"The *parterre* level," I said. We walked past each box, slowing at number sixteen...then our box, *DeVere*, and finally.... "This is it," I said, "Box Eighteen... *Wendell*."

Sylvia slid the key into the keyhole lock. I rehearsed my purpose, to view the set of refinished chairs and count all six on the new gray carpet. I would not let the body of the dead man enter my mind. I would not.

"Ma'am, do you want me to go in with you?"

"No need, I'll just be a few minutes."

I stepped in. The Wendells' saloon panels and curtain featured green Chinese pagodas, which I had not noticed when viewing the new carpet two weeks ago, nor seen on the unspeakable night when the janitor swung his kerosene lantern in the darkness. Come next fall, Anne Wendell would find her pagodas intact when she and her husband arrived at the fashionably late hour for the opera. Charles Wendell would push back the curtain, and the couple would step into the box with their guests.

As I would do at this moment.

Sweeping back the curtain, I stepped down into the box. Choral music swelled from the stage as I quickly counted six chairs, three and three, glinting with new lacquer in the dusky light. I touched one to make certain the finish had hardened. At that instant, the curtain rattled closed behind me.

"Sylvia...."

She didn't answer.

I turned. "I think the lacquer hasn't quite...."

The same gap-toothed smile, the thick curly hair and dark caramel complexion. I did not need to read the name on the butler's apron.

"Antony..." I said.

"Mrs. DeVere...."

I craned to look behind him.

"Sylvia," he said, "has stepped out for a bit. I will take her place."

"But Mr. Hoff...."

He grinned. "Mr. Hoff understands."

"...understands what?" I stepped sideways, but so did he, facing me, blocking my way.

"I believe I have finished here," I said.

The chorus broke off abruptly, resumed, and halted again. A deep voice scolded the singers.

"If you'll excuse me..." I said.

His answer, a sneering grin.

"Antony...please...."

The chorus sang again.... *Veau d'Or, Veau d'Or*....

I stepped back between the two rows of chairs. In my fiercest voice, I said, "Antony Dessey...."

"You mean Antoine, don't you? Say it, Antoine."

"And suppose if I do...?"

"Antoine D'Cee," he said, "...almost like Dessey."

"I wouldn't know."

He sneered. "Do not play with me, Mrs. DeVere. You went south to Palm Beach."

How could he know this? My thoughts scrambled. "Mr. Hoff told you...." I said.

The chorus halted and was scolded once again. Piano chords hammered.

"The Marlow Minstrels," he said. "I believe you do know... the sad clown song...and Negro melodies too. 'Old Black Joe'...did you hear that one?"

I did not speak. He moved one step closer.

"The sad clown at the Tampa Bay Hotel...the Royal Poinciana...the Alcazar in St. Augustine...they loved 'Old Black Joe' at the Alcazar. No need for black greasepaint."

I stepped behind the front row of chairs. Between Antoine and me, two double rows of lightweight but sturdy chairs, a barrier. The backs of my legs brushed against the wall of the waist-high box.

"Did you hear the name 'Celeste'? Did you, Mrs. DeVere?"

I did not answer. Cold air struck the back of my neck.

"...heard it from old lady Rankin, didn't you? Or was it from Suggs?"

I shook my head and shrugged.

"Or from 'brother' Lewis? Did you meet Lewis? Did 'brother' Lewis Rankin ever rub tarnish off a brass rail... ever sing *Pagliacci*?"

I stared at his name badge and kept quiet.

"The old man...what would it cost him, third class to Naples, Italy? Caruso's teacher would teach me...Vincenzo Lombardi. I showed the old man the letter from Lombardi...showed it right where you stand at this minute, Mrs. DeVere."

His dark eyes flashed. "He crumpled it, threw it down right here...the night after Christmas, *Romeo et Juliette* with a Polish tenor...I could be a better *Romeo*...I could. And I begged him...my own father...."

"...who would not support you," I said. Trying for sympathy, I heard tension in my voice.

"Not once," he said. "...like New Orleans never happened in his whole life." He reached behind to untie the apron from his workman's overalls.

Why was he telling me all this?

"...the old man at *Don Giovanni*...sat right there. Coal is too dirty for the Diamond Horseshoe, Mrs. DeVere. I cleaned out the box...on orders from on high."

"From Hoff...." I gasped, my voice like rust. "...the two of you planned the death."

He pointed to a chair. "Old King Coal thought a pal came back to the box...at the trio...*Ah taci, ingiusto core*.... 'Ah, be quiet unjust heart'...the 'unjust heart' quiet forever. I jammed it deep, no sword needed."

He leaned toward me across the chairs and wet his lips. "A sharp piece of glass will do. I'll go to Naples very soon... maybe first class. It is promised."

He slung the apron over a chair and flexed thick fingers.

"Antony..." I said, "...Antoine...." The chorus stopped singing. He started to push the chairs aside, opening space between us. "What do you want?" I asked, my voice taut.

He muscled in beside me, his face close to mine as he pointed to the stage below and whispered in my ear with a gust of wet breath. "I want to sing...down there...solo...."

I tried to step sideways, but he clutched my shoulders and spun me against him. "Too much Florida, both of you...."

"My husband..." I said but could not pull away. His grip tightened.

"An accident befalls you...," he whispered, "and maybe your suicide...."

His leg caught the back of my knee, and I slammed down against the box railing. Pinned...I was pinned down. His eyes bulged, and he grinned. "You're going overboard, Mrs. DeVere."

"No...." He pressed my chest, and my scream died in a short screech. At that instant, the chorus erupted... *Veau d'Or, Veau d'Or....* The piano pounded.

My skirt and his pantlegs...both tangled. He pushed, and my head banged against the rail.

"Overboard..." he whispered.

Was the next instant a memory...from Piper's Opera House? Or chance...? Wrestling...his pantleg, my skirt....

My head lifted up, and hands up too.

Veau d'Or!, Veau d'Or!

I grabbed his neck and hooked my left leg around his right...and pulled with all my strength.

Flipped...I was atop him, riding his chest on the railing. His arms flailed, clawed my hair, my back.... I rolled, pushing off...pushing him off the rail...pushing....

The memory would stamp itself forever. I fell face down in the box, my ears filled with a hideous long howl never heard in this opera house, a sickening slam, and men's voices that stopped at one last *Veau d'Or*.

Chapter Thirty-one

ON THIS COLD, WINDY Monday morning on the thirtieth of January, Roddy and I were driven downtown to Police Headquarters, the square, squat building whose marble façade had yellowed with smoke and grime. Promptly at 11:15, at Commissioner Gork's request, we entered the infamous Mulberry Street arena of patrolmen, derelicts, reporters, grifters, and shellacked patrol-wagons.

We climbed the granite steps, and a patrolman led us to the second-floor office of the Commissioner, who leaned across his bulky oak desk to greet us. The shield on Bernard Gork's tweed lapel shone with a crest of stars, a medallion reading "City of New York Police," and "COMMISSIONER" in swooping letters. The desk featured a "candlestick" upright telephone, a stack of books, and a baseball.

"Do sit down," he said. "...please."

We took two latticed wood chairs in front of the official's massive desk. A high window behind his armchair rattled from the wind, and the coal burning in a fireplace grate barely warmed the room. Roddy took off his hat. We kept our coats on.

"To start off," said Gork, "we will review your previous statements…but I promise not to spar with you, Mrs. DeVere."

"Spar?"

"Or throw a curve ball…." He flushed. "I mean, I'll ask the same questions as last Friday night at your home."

"I will answer directly, Commissioner Gork." The man looked barricaded behind his desk. I had barely slept or eaten for the last two days. Over and over, my weekend flashed with night terrors…on my hands and knees on the *parterre* box floor, clutching my ripped skirt to stumble into the corridor and find Sylvia Lilely. Her bony hand led me down, down, and down to Hoff's office, where Roddy stood by himself. "Hoff…" he said, "called away, accident of some sort…. Val, your face…."

I had seized my husband's arm and screamed to get us out. Sylvia patted my face with a handkerchief. The red smears meant my nose bled. "I fell on my face," I said. "Get us out…Roddy, get us out of here."

He did. Noland had been waiting at the curb with Atlas and Apollo, but the carriage rocked with my wracking sobs. Even now, the scene could replay in my brain in the Mulberry Street police headquarters.

"I mean to say," said Commissioner Gork, tapping his desktop, "that questions we asked at your home last Friday evening, myself and Detective Sergeant Finlay.... I will go over them again this morning. Detective Finlay is at work on a new case. Otherwise, he would be here."

I wished the trusty Detective Colin Finlay were with us today. His lightning-fast response to Roddy's call for help on Friday evening had lent sanity to the scene in our Corinthian room after the opera box mayhem. Calista had dabbed a poultice on my swollen face while Roddy and the detective listened to my broken account of the fatal wrangle. Our dog had frisked around the columns and footmen brought hot broth, while Detective Finlay took notes furiously. He apologized for having "nominated" Roddy and me to undertake the "q.t." inquiry. ("I should never have put you in such a fix, Mrs. DeVere...Mr. DeVere.")

The detective had used our telephone to call the Chief, who summoned Commissioner Gork from his ringside seat at the prizefights downtown. When he arrived, I repeated everything I already had told the detective. I said that Sylvia Lilely might have information and warned about Maurice Hoff, whose name set the Commissioner yanking at his whiskers and twisting his signet ring.

Bernard Gork implied that my accusations against the impresario indicated female hysterics. I bristled, but Roddy backed me up, every word. Detective Finlay had nodded solemnly, but the Commissioner turned a pasty pale. The two police officials finally left when our hallway grandfather clock struck midnight.

Whatever the police did the next day, Saturday, to pursue the investigation was not known to us, nor whether Sunday church bells had halted their work on the case. Roddy stayed with me every minute, kept me in his sight the entire weekend. We walked and talked and stayed quiet for long hours at home.

The Commissioner now took a file from a desk drawer and peered inside as windowpanes drummed from the wind and coal smoke puffed into the room. "Mrs. DeVere," he said, "on the Friday afternoon of the...near miss...."

"My near miss," I said. "Mine."

"Yes, ma'am." He swallowed. "You say that the usher—Antoine D'Cee, alias Antony Dessey—attempted deliberately to push you over the railing of the opera box...deliberately... with homicidal intent."

"yes."

"And the attempt was premeditated?"

"Planned," I said.

He cleared his throat. "His motive for such a crime...?"

"To prevent a further probe...investigation...into the murder of Leon Rankin. As I explained to you and to Detective Finlay on Friday night, Mr. DeVere and I had learned about his identity, who he is...was."

Roddy laced his fingers in mine. A two-inch column in the newspapers had reported the "unfortunate" fatal mishap of a young custodian who had slipped and broken his neck while carrying out his duties in the auditorium of the Metropolitan Opera house. His next-of-kin was sought.

"Mr. DeVere and I learned," I continued, "that Antoine was the son of the late Leon Rankin who refused to acknowledge his paternity or support him in other ways."

"—a natural son? Is that your understanding?" The Commissioner tugged at his whiskers.

If I said "bastard," the man would blanch. "...illegitimate son," I said. I wet my lips, still swollen from the fall in the box. "Mr. DeVere and I already suspected," I said, "that Antony D'Cee murdered his father in vengeance."

The Commissioner peered at Roddy, at his file, and then at me. "You stated that Antoine D'Cee, deliberately stabbed Leon Rankin with sharp glass...and admitted doing so, to you."

"Yes."

"Deliberate homicide."

"Yes."

"But you willingly put yourself at his mercy in the opera box."

Roddy spoke up before I lost my temper. "Commissioner Gork," he said, "we explained to you and Detective Finlay that I had agreed to tend to business matters in Mr. Hoff's office while Mrs. DeVere inspected chairs in opera Box Eighteen. My wife was accompanied by an elderly maid employed at the Opera."

The Commissioner sucked his gold tooth and sat back with a satisfied gaze through half-lidded eyes. "Your account, Mr. and Mrs. DeVere, is beefed up by the opera maid...Lilely."

"Sylvia...you interviewed her?" I said.

"Detective Finlay questioned her yesterday evening. She confirms she took you to the opera box, opened the door, and let Antony D.—as she called him—take charge because that box was his job."

"Since Leon Rankin rented the box," Roddy said. "This winter."

The Commissioner nodded. "Sylvia Lilely states that 'it didn't sit right' with her to walk away, so she stayed in the corridor and listened. She states that she helped Mrs. DeVere back downstairs."

"She did.... She took my hand, led me down...wiped blood from my face." I sounded shrill.

"...and also states that she "heard every word inside the box... 'Every word.' She would swear to it." The Commissioner raised his chin, spread his fingers on the desk, and faced Roddy and me. "And right there, we have a parting of the ways, so to speak."

"What parting?" I asked.

"The revenge," the Commissioner said, "matches up... the sharp glass, and the fact that Mr. Rankin refused to pay the young man's way to study singing in a foreign country." He glanced at the file. "Italy."

We nodded.

He scratched his whiskers. "But as for the rest of your story, Mrs. DeVere...the maid did not hear anything about Mr. Hoff. Nothing at all."

"But Antoine admitted it...he conspired with Maurice Hoff to commit the murder. Hoff promised to send him to Italy...."

The Commissioner smiled like an indulgent uncle. "Now, Mrs. DeVere, let us be patient. Could your ears be ringing...? Nearly knocked out cold, the ears will ring." He leaned toward the side of the desk. "Let us straighten things out here and now...take a few minutes. I'll just push this electrical button."

A moment passed as the window rattled, coal fumes perfumed the air, and a door opened behind us. The Commissioner rose as a familiar voice rolled a heavy, leonine, "Greetings."

"My thanks to you for waiting, Maestro Hoff," said Gork. "I need not introduce—"

"—Mr. and Mrs. Roderick Windham DeVere, dearest friends of the Opera? Certainly not!" Hoff had swept into the room, arms out, the lambskin cuffs of his greatcoat flaring wide. He gave a downcast glance at the floor. "And here we gather on this unhappy occasion...do stay seated, Mr. DeVere...Mrs. DeVere, you lighten this space."

He turned to Gork. "'Maestro' is an exalted title, Commissioner, but yours truly is merely the servant of the world's premier artistic vocal talent."

I dared not look at Roddy, lest I gag. Hoff's theatrics belonged on the stage, but the Commissioner looked impressed, even cowed.

A uniformed policeman carried a chair and seated the impresario at the side of Gork's desk, making a triangle arrangement.

"Commissioner Gork," said Hoff, "I yield to your further questions."

"Further questions?" asked Roddy. "Why 'further?'" His mild tone hid the steel.

"I was about to say," said Gork, "that I paid a visit to the opera house yesterday afternoon after church. Mr. Hoff was good enough to give up an hour for questions in the middle of opera practice."

"Rehearsal for *Faust*," Hoff said.

"Oh? And did Detective Finlay come too?"

"No, ma'am. The detective had other obligations."

"I see."

"So, we are are..." said the Commissioner, "to settle things...a meeting of the minds, we might say." He fingered the baseball on his desk, peered into the file, and turned a page. "We agree that Antoine D'Cee, known as Antony Dessey, was employed at the Metropolitan Opera as an usher and man of all work."

The Commissioner looked from Hoff to Roddy and me. We all nodded.

"...unknown to his employer," Gork continued, "this man was the natural son of the late Mr. Leon Rankin who rented an opera box for the 1898-1899 season and was himself the victim of homicide committed by Antoine D'Cee, alias Antony Dessey, on the night of January Second, 1899."

Gork clutched the baseball as he read from his file. "...the admission by himself, that D'Cee, known as Dessey, committed homicide against Leon Lee Rankin has been jointly reported by Lydia Lilely, employed at the opera house as a maid, and by Mrs. Roderick DeVere, opera boxholder and shareholder with Mr. DeVere."

Again, nods. Hoff opened his coat and crossed his legs.

The Commissioner looked at me. "Mrs. DeVere, I will spare you the suffering of retelling what happened in the opera box last Friday afternoon. Mr. Hoff has been informed."

"Informed, perhaps, during your visit to the opera house after church yesterday, Mr. Gork?" I asked. The Commissioner nodded and squeezed the baseball.

"I see." My voice sounded pinched.

Hoff leaned toward me. "...beyond shocking, dear Mrs. DeVere. How close you came ...the victim of an atrocious act by a deranged young man whose anger poisoned his mind."

The lambskin cuffs swung wide. "How can one possibly imagine such a thing when hiring employees among the swarms in New York City. Our opera patrons are devoted to performances, but we managers must strive to monitor the house...so many marginal yet essential workers, such as the maid."

Hoff gazed at the window and addressed the panes of glass. "...Sylvia Lilely has worked at the Metropolitan Opera since the grand opening of 1883...and before that, at the Academy of Music in its final years."

He swung his gaze to me...at me. "The touching life story that one could hear, if given the time. I have learned that Lilely has never once neglected her duties, not even in the historic blizzard of 'eighty-eight, when *Fidelio* was presented as a matinee."

His lips curled into a smile. "I also have learned that Lilely is the sole support of her ailing brother...a lifetime of care and sterling service...to continue under my supervision. How thankful she is for employment in her elder years when work is scarce."

He touched a thumb against his chin. "I assured Lilely that her position was secure under my watch. I believe she felt comforted."

My mouth opened. The elderly maid had been bribed and threatened. If she kept mum about Hoff, her job was safe. If she told everything she heard in Box 18, she would be out in the cold.

That sidewinder.... In the desert West, the rattler that whipped itself back and forth and sank its fangs deep—Sidewinder Hoff.

Roddy said, "So, you spoke with Lilely at some length, Mr. Hoff?"

"After what happened, Mr. DeVere, I would have been derelict in my duty not to speak with her, would I not?"

Roddy glared. "I suppose," he said, "that the newspaper notice of an 'unfortunate' fatal mishap in the auditorium was your doing?"

Bernard Gork broke in, "Now, Mr. DeVere, I shoulder some guilt on that score. I saw the piece in the *Tribune*, and I put it to the Maestro...to Mr. Hoff. 'Why the false account?'"

The Commissioner dug his thumb at the baseball stitching. "The same reason we asked you and Mrs. DeVere to look into the homicide…to keep it on the quiet side, what you call the 'q.t.' And what's the harm? The killer is dead, and Mrs. DeVere sits right here beside you…by the grace of God."

"—by the grace of my wife's quick thinking and acting," Roddy snapped back. A door slammed somewhere in the building.

Hoff pulled up his lambskin collar. "Let it be known," he said, "that efforts to find the young miscreant's friends or next of kin have not, as yet, succeeded."

He buttoned his coat. "If public notice of his death goes unanswered, he will be buried in the city's Hart Island cemetery. I have made arrangements." He stood. "Commissioner, we must not intrude further on your valuable time. If there is anything else…?"

Bernard Gork clawed his whiskers and gripped the baseball for dear life. He reached to press the button on the side of his desk and stood, which was our signal to stand too.

"What team do you like this next season, Commissioner?" Hoff asked.

"The Brooklyn Trolley Dodgers," trilled Bernard Gork.

The lilt in his voice signaled liberty. The uniformed officer appeared to escort us out. Down the steps, Roddy gripped my arm to keep me from whirling on Hoff. At the door, I thought, *You snake!* We started down the granite steps to the street. The saliva in my mouth tasted bitter from the coal vapors, from the charade in Mulberry Street.

On the sidewalk, Roddy guided me to our carriage, while Hoff stepped to a hansom cab waiting for him at the curbstone. *You snake!* The words hammered in my mind as we approached our honest coachman and horses at the curb. Roddy opened the carriage door for me, and I caught a glance at the silver smear of sun in a mass of cloudy gray. A second's pause, and cold, wet prickles against my face almost brought winter's smile. It had started to snow.

Chapter Thirty-two

THE SNOWFALL NEARLY SET a record. At breakfast, Roddy read, "'...large high-pressure system covering much of the eastern United States.'" He sipped his tea. "The *Herald* says it could be 120 centimeters."

To me, the metric system might as well be Swahili. "How many feet and inches, Roddy?"

"Nearly four feet...'A slow-moving cold front from the West.... Train service delayed at Grand Central.'"

"But *Faust* will go on tonight, won't it? January thirty-first?"

"Most likely...I'm sorry to say." The regret in Roddy's voice mixed pain and guilt—and rage. He swore he would never forgive himself for sending me upstairs in the opera house, never be so careless in our life together. "It's my blessing, Val, that you somehow wrested free—"

"—wrestled free, Roddy. I think an old memory from a wrestling demonstration at Piper's Opera House kicked in at the last second." I kept my eyes on my husband's stern face. "But Hoff failed, thanks to you," I said. "You saw it first…in Palm Beach, in our suite. You connected Maurice Hoff to Rankin's murder…but mastermind Maurice Hoff gets off Scot free."

Roddy reached for my hand across the table and spoke gently. "Val, don't…not again."

"He plotted to kill Leon Rankin, Roddy. I heard it. I heard the words. I could bring charges."

"Val…let's not put ourselves through it again. I'm furious. You understood…."

"…that it wouldn't stick, that the Wild West woman's case against the opera impresario would be thrown out." I knocked a spoon on the table. Our dog looked up from her bed. "The maid would not speak up, and others would not believe me, that's the point…not the Commissioner, not the Mayor…not J.P. Morgan…."

"I believe you, and that is what matters." Roddy's vexed eyes locked on mine. He folded his hands on the table. "Val, I am heartsick. You understand?"

I nodded.

"For the record, as an attorney…Maurice Hoff ought to be charged and prosecuted to the full extent of the law for conspiring to plot and execute two murders. The Police Commissioner let himself be played for a fool. Maurice Hoff sized him up and courted him. If the vile plan had succeeded, the usher would be on a liner to Italy, and I would be too consumed with grief to think clearly about your…."

My husband broke off and drained his tea. "It's time the Board exert proper oversight over the Police Department and hold every Commissioner accountable for his actions. My anger must have purpose. I will seek appointment to the Board of Commissioners of the New York City Police Department."

Roddy's cheeks flared red, and his glare warmed my heart. He glanced at a snowy windowpane. "I just hope the telephone lines don't come down in the storm, Val. I must speak to Taggart. The B&N rail stock will slide fast, and Star Coal will tumble next. If Taggart and I act quickly, a sale of Star stock will let us set up a trust fund up for Glenna May. She won't live in luxury, but she'll get by. You think she misses West Virginia?"

"I'm convinced she wants to go home, Roddy. And she needn't ever know her brother was murdered."

"And what about Lewis?" I asked.

Roddy scoffed. "Glenna May can invite her nephew to join her, or he can look for a rich widow in Florida and weep that the new Ocean Grande Hotel will not be a Rankin property. And he can deal with 'Alligator Joe' all by himself. Lewis Rankin, my dear, is no concern of ours."

Snowflakes ticked against the windowpane. "*Snow-Bound...*" I said. Roddy cocked his head. "It's a very long poem we studied in high school in Virginia City."

My husband smiled. "Every pupil in the country memorized lines from *Snow-Bound.*"

"... 'A universe of sky and snow!'" I recited. "And I remember, 'Dazzling crystal...Aladdin's wondrous cave'...."

"...our own cave at the moment, my dear," Roddy said. "So far today, we're snowed in, on the edge of a new month."

"So, let's just be snow-bound." what I'm seeing is...'And whirl-dance of the blinding storm.'" I pulled Velvet onto my lap and stroked her ears. The awful clock clanged the hour. Ten a.m., the day on the move. "It's been so wild, Roddy... an evening at the opera that caught us in...in the furies."

"Furies?" Roddy raised an eyebrow. "My mother fears that we're getting reputations as 'armchair detectives.' What do you think?"

"I think...give me 'furies.' And so, Mister Master Mixologist," I said, "if you were to pour a late morning cocktail for the 'whirl-dance,' what might it be?"

Roddy paused, drummed his fingers on the table, and beckoned the footman to request an orange, hot water, glasses, and two bottles, all of which replaced the breakfast things as Velvet and I watched the bartender set to work at the table.

Hot Brandy (for two)
Ingredients:
- Two ounces brandy
- One ounce Burgundy wine
- Eight ounces very hot water
- Four lumps sugar
- One orange

Directions:
1. In each 6-8 ounce glass, dissolve 1 sugar lump in four ounces hot water.
2. Add 1 ounce brandy and ½ ounce Burgundy to each glass.
3. Mix well.
4. Add orange slice to each glass and serve.

"Pungent," I said, as we raised our glasses "What shall we toast? The future…? The springtime?"

"As a matter fact…" Roddy said, "there's a letter on my desk. A good friend from school writes to say he could use help this spring."

"What 'help'? Where?

"…the return address is…the 'Windy City.'"

"Chicago? Then let's drink to Chicago." We touched glasses and sipped the sweet warmth. Roddy said, "You like sleighbells, Valentine DeVere, and the minute the snow stops, we'll go sleighing in Central Park. Noland will hitch Apollo and Atlas…."

"…with 'horse jewelry' bells on their harness," I said. "And we will sit side by side under a buffalo robe. As *Snow-Bound* says, 'Love can never lose its own!'"

"And I will take the reins," my husband said.

"We will both take the reins, Roddy. "The 'furies' demand that we both take the reins."

COMING SOON

A Gilded Freefall
By
Cecelia Tichi

Chicago and New York snarl the sleuthing couple in the upcoming Val and Roddy DeVere Mystery

Follow Cecelia on website
https://www.cecebooks.com

ABOUT THE AUTHOR

Cecelia Tichi is a native of Pittsburgh, the steel city of the Gilded Age, and is an award-winning teacher and author of numerous books focused on American culture and literature. Her most recent titles: *What Would Mrs. Astor Do? The Essential Guide to the Manners and Mores of the Gilded Age* was followed by *Cocktails of the Gilded Age: History, Lore, and Recipes of America's Golden Age* and the sequel, *Jazz Age Cocktails: History, Lore, and Recipes from the Roaring Twenties*. The "Val and Roddy DeVere" mystery series premiers with *A Gilded Death*.

CPSIA information can be obtained
at www.ICGtesting.com
Printed in the USA
LVHW091324160322
713610LV00007B/17

9 798985 121629